WISTERIA WONDERS

Wisteria Witches Mysteries

BOOK #3

ANGELA PEPPER

CHAPTER 1

ADULT FLAMINGOS ARE four feet tall, bright pink, and honk like they've just swallowed a kazoo. At least that was the sound made by the lone flamingo strutting around the staff lounge.

Moments earlier, it had been a quiet Monday afternoon at the library. My coworker, Frank Wonder, had been enjoying his afternoon snack of graham-flavored cookies. Then he'd opened the fake-snakes-in-a-can I'd set up for him. My prank worked a little too well. He'd abruptly turned into a flamingo. I suspected my witch powers were partly to blame for his man-to-bird transformation, but I didn't understand how.

Frank the Flamingo wobbled on one spindly leg and gave me a dirty look with his orange eyes.

I asked the bird, "Frank, are you a shifter?"

He opened his curved beak and let out a FZEEEBZZ-RAWWWK!

I didn't speak flamingo, but that sounded like a no.

Frank's orange eyes flitted around the room as he wobbled near the staff coffee maker. He took one step, crossed his stick-like legs, and tripped over his own webbed feet. Being a bird was apparently a new experience for him. I didn't even know any spells to turn people into birds, so how could I have done this to him? Either it was a freak accident, or Frank had dormant powers that I'd accidentally triggered.

What he needed was another shifter to teach him the ropes, like how my aunt was mentoring me on witchcraft. The only shifter I knew personally was my neighbor, Chet Moore. I'd already called him for help and was not so patiently awaiting his arrival.

Frank said RAWWWK-RAWWK!

"This must be very confusing for you," I said. "But I've called Chet to help us. Remember Chet? He's tall and handsome, and you're always referring to him as my beau, even though he's got me in the friend zone."

FAWZEEEE-KRRRRRK! The flamingo pointed his curved beak at me accusingly.

I held my hand to my chest. "You're right. This probably is my fault, but there are things you don't know about this town, and about me."

His long neck relaxed into an S-shape. He steadied himself, both legs locked straight. His kazoo squawking softened. WHUZEEEEeeee. ZEEEEee. ZZZEEERE. ZARRRAAA.

"Very good. Yes, I'm Zara, and you're Frank."

ZEEEEEKK!

I glanced across the staff lounge at the door that led to the parking lot. Where was Chet? The dispatcher had promised it would only be a few minutes. I wrung my hands and paced the staff lounge. I'd closed the interior door leading to rest of the building, but the head librarian was sure to notice soon. If Kathy popped her head in, how would I explain the presence of a flamingo? I knew a spell to improve the believability of my lies, but the spell could only do so much.

Frank made a soft cooing sound and walked toward me, his webbed feet making soft splat sounds on the floor. His walk was improving. He stopped in front of me, cocked his head, and stared up with one beseeching orange eye.

"You want an explanation," I said. "And you deserve one."

He bobbed his head and said ZEEEEEE. He walked toward the staff lounge's Grumpy Corner, a dimly lit corner with beanbag chairs and big pillows. He plopped on top of a beanbag chair and nodded for me to join him.

I went over and sat cross-legged on a pillow. Where to start? A stack of children's storybooks caught my eye. In a flash of inspiration, I had my opening line.

"Once upon a time, there was a town called Wisteria," I said.

Frank opened his curved beak in what looked like a silent laugh.

I continued in my story-time voice. "Wisteria was a special town, because it had more magic running through it than any other place in the world." That part was unsubstantiated, but you know what they say—*never let the truth stand in the way of a good story*.

Frank preened some pink wing feathers and nodded for me to continue.

"Magic is an elemental force, like water or electricity, and it acts a bit like both. Magic is wondrous, but also dangerous." I paused to let the story's tone settle in before moving on to the inciting incident. "One day, something strange happened, and the people in Wisteria started noticing unusual events. The magic was acting up." I paused for drama. "Luckily, there were some people whose job it was to protect the town. They drove around in vans marked Department of Water, but that was just their cover-up. They were secretly called the Department of Water *and Magic*. The DWM."

Frank opened his black, curved beak. KAAAAKAA! His long neck undulated, snakelike. He thrust his head forward, took my wrist in his beak, and gently shook my hand.

"Oh, I'm not part of the DWM," I said. "I only know about these things because I'm a witch."

He didn't react to that bombshell. He didn't even blink his orange eyes.

"Well, it was a big surprise for me," I said, chuckling. "I didn't find out I was a witch until a few months ago. Now I'm a baby witch, a novice, at the age of thirty-two."

He released my wrist and relaxed with his head on my knee.

There was a loud knock at the exterior door.

Frank flew up with a flap of feathers. FZEEEBZZ-RAWWWK!

I ran to the door and opened it to find three familiar faces: my neighbor Chet, plus the two DWM guys I'd seen with him once before.

I let them in, and we made hasty introductions.

The shorter guy was Rob, and the towering mountain of muscles was named Knox. "Just like Fort Knox," he said with a grin. "Because nothin' gets through me."

"Except bullets," I said.

Rob laughed and punched Knox on his enormous bicep. "She got you, big guy!"

Knox continued grinning, his teeth in bright contrast to his ebony-dark skin. "One little bullet can't keep me down," he said with a shrug.

Rob shook my hand. "It's nice to officially meet you, Zara, assuming you *are* you, and not an impostor."

"I swear I'm Zara Riddle," I said. "Which is exactly what an impostor would say."

We'd finished shaking, but Rob continued to hold my hand. "An impostor could never match the natural charm of a lovely witch such as yourself."

Chet, who was already walking over toward Frank, barked gruffly, "Rob, stop flirting with the witch and help me with the bird."

I turned and gave my tall, dark-haired neighbor a dirty look. *The witch* and *the bird*? What pooped in his cornflakes?

Rob and Knox joined Chet, and the three of them spoke softly to Frank. That was all they had? Talk therapy? I'd expected them to bring a few DWM gadgets at the very least.

Still talking softly, the three men cornered the flamingo. Frank responded by flapping up, feathers flying, and soaring over their heads. He crashed into the ceiling and landed in a pink heap on a table, feathers ruffling up like a crinoline. He looked like a fallen ballerina.

Knox wiped beads of sweat from his brow. He took off his jacket, revealing tight ebony skin over enormous, muscled arms.

While Rob and Knox continued to murmur softly to Frank, Chet came over to stand next to me.

"Your friend is worked up," he said.

I nodded. "And if your buddy Knox keeps stripping off clothes, Frank's never going to calm down. He adores big, strong men."

"I'm open to suggestions," Chet said coolly. "We need to get him calm, turn down his limbic system response."

"Frank is friendly and sociable, but he's an introvert," I said. "If all he needs is to calm down, you should get him somewhere quiet."

Chet quirked one eyebrow. "Somewhere quiet. Like a library?"

"Ha ha," I said flatly. "I was thinking his apartment."

A flash of pink feathers shot past us. Frank the Flamingo crossed the room and hit the door's push-handle with his body. The door didn't open. Frank let out a disappointed SKREEEAAWWWKK.

Chet said to Rob and Knox, "If he gets out, you two are on your own."

Rob swiped the air dismissively. "He knows better than to draw attention to himself."

I replied, "You don't know Frank Wonder."

Right on cue, the flamingo backed up and took another run at the door. This time, it flung open. In another flash, he was outside in the summer sunshine, his plumage a dazzling, surreal pink. He stretched out his wings, revealing a fringe of black flight feathers.

Rob waved his hand again. "At least he doesn't know how to fly. It takes ages to learn."

Again, I said, "You don't know Frank Wonder."

I ran to the door and stepped outside in time to see the flamingo shoot across the staff parking lot. His long neck stretched out straight while he flapped his wings. My breath caught in my throat. I didn't want him to fly away, and yet, deep down, I was also rooting for him. Who hasn't dreamed of flying? With a final squawk, he was up and away. I couldn't help but cheer for him.

Frank was airborne.

Sort of. He was up and down, a zigzagging streak of pink and black.

Behind me, I could hear Chet using his phone to call in a report to DWM dispatch.

I turned around to see Knox and Rob blurring as they exited the library. I blinked to clear my eyes.

The blurs coalesced into new forms. Instead of an Asian man and a black man, there were two birds—a crow and an eagle. Both of them were enormous, three times the size of a normal crow or eagle. As the sunlight flashed off their sharp beaks, I remembered the flashing of beak and talons in the woods. The day Chet and I were attacked.

My fingers tingled. Traces of blue lighting circled my hands like St. Elmo's fire. I clenched my hands together, palm to palm. The blue fire crackled but didn't hurt me.

The two dark birds jumped into the sky gracefully. The beating of their giant wings kicked up dust in the parking lot, sending grit into my eyes.

I blinked the grime away and watched as the giant, dark birds flew after the zigzagging pink flamingo.

Chet jogged past me, heading toward the Department of Water van parked on the street.

I called after him, "Now what?"

He looked back over his shoulder. "Go back to your job. Cover for your friend."

"What about Frank?"

"I'll come back for you," Chet said. "I'll pick you up at the end of your shift."

He climbed into the van without waiting for a response. He drove away in the direction the birds had been flying.

"Sounds like a solid plan," I said to the empty parking lot. "See you at five o'clock, assuming I don't succumb to spontaneous combustion."

I tentatively pulled my hands apart. The blue fire continued to crackle between my palms.

Once upon a time in Wisteria, things were strange. Again.

CHAPTER 2

I PRESSED MY lightning hands together and looked up at the sky. No sign of the three birds. Just blue sky with a picturesque smattering of fluffy white clouds.

I returned to the library's exterior door and tentatively touched the metal handle with the index finger of my right hand. The blue plasma at my fingertips discharged harmlessly. The crackling fire in my left hand continued to burn. I cupped my hand, and the plasma pooled on my palm, where it bubbled like the boiling contents of a cauldron.

I wondered if I should be concerned, if my flare-up of St. Elmo's fire was a warning sign.

Shortly after I moved to Wisteria, I was attacked in the woods by a winged beast. My witch defense system kicked in automatically, and I found myself shooting blue lightning balls from my fingertips. I didn't know I could do that, so I was nearly as shocked as the flying creature I blasted. Since that day, I've been trying to juggle being a single mother, working full-time as a librarian, and learning everything I can about my powers. Luckily, I work at a library, so I can do research on the job. I've become an expert in a few eclectic things, including sparky blue electrical discharge.

The name, St. Elmo's fire, was coined by sailors who witnessed the phenomenon sparking around the masts of their ships. They believed the blue "fire" was a sign of salvation from St. Erasmus, the patron saint of Mediterranean sailors, because it usually occurred toward the end of a bad storm. Chemically speaking, the light is from molecules tearing apart due to an imbalance in electrical charge. This results in plasma, or ionized air. St. Elmo's fire is blue because different gasses glow different colors when they become plasma. Nitrogen and oxygen, common in Earth's atmosphere, happen to glow blue.

If our planet's atmosphere were made of, say, neon, then St. Elmo's fire might glow orange instead of blue. Yes, I just said *neon*. As in the same gas they put into glass tubes to form those bright signs you probably see every day. A neon tube, whether it's advertising a brand of beer or a strip club, is St. Elmo's fire contained in glass. And the ubiquitous fluorescent tube produces a light unflattering to all skin tones because it contains mercury vapor that makes the phosphor coating glow white.

"Out you go," I murmured to my palmful of blue plasma. I clapped my hand closed, counted to three, and held my breath as I opened it. The fire was gone.

I shook both hands, snapped my fingers, and clapped three times. I made jazz hands. No blue lightning.

Once I was sure I wasn't going to zolt anyone by accident, I went inside and surveyed the damage to the staff lounge.

Frank the Flamingo had knocked over a few things, including a bucket of crayons. While I gathered the scattered crayons, I found three pink feathers, ranging in size from a downy bit of fluff to a quill longer than my hand. I picked up the feathers and examined them. They looked and felt real enough. Were these feathers pieces of

Frank, or magical objects? Would they change once Frank shifted back, turning into skin flakes, or hair, or maybe fingernails? Chet was so secretive about shifter physics, but this was my chance to find out on my own. I grabbed a clean sandwich bag from the drawer next to the fridge, bagged the pink feathers, and tucked the evidence into my voluminous skirt's pocket.

The lounge looked normal again, but my armpits were prickling with cold sweat. My face felt sticky, like I was coming down with the flu, but it was probably just a reaction to the stress, or my guilt, or both.

Frank will be back to his regular sassy self by Tuesday morning, I told myself. He probably wouldn't be ripped limb from limb by those two giant birds. Chet wouldn't allow it, plus Rob and Knox had seemed like good guys. They'd joked around and teased each other like good guys, anyway. Surely they wouldn't harm a feather or a pink hair on Frank's head.

But if they were the good guys, why had my defense system kicked in with the blue fire? Was it the triggered memory of the attack, or was one of them the same vicious beast who'd attacked me that day in the forest?

The more I thought about it, the more nervous I got. And I was hungry—famished—because the magical blue fire had eaten up calories. It didn't help my nerves at all when my stomach growled with such ferocity that I thought a tiger was sneaking up on me.

I gobbled down three of the eleven rainbow sprinkle donuts I'd brought in that morning, and then returned to my librarian duties.

The library, normally a cozy place to me, seemed very dark and eerily quiet after all the excitement outside. Almost like a tomb.

"Floral designs," said a pleasant, round-cheeked woman who was apparently talking to me. "Where you take cut flowers, and put them in a vase." She spoke slowly as she mimed a pair of scissors cutting. She made the hand gestures of putting cut flowers into a container.

She spoke to me as though I'd left my brain at home. I blinked at her and searched my short-term memory. She'd actually been talking to me for several minutes while I spaced out, pondering the magical wonders of Wisteria.

"Never mind," she said with a sigh, turning away from the counter.

I apologized and ran over to the opening in the counter, chasing after her. The sound of my lace-up boots on the floor got me an owlish look from the head librarian. I slowed to a speed walk and caught up with the round-cheeked woman.

"Flower arranging," I said with confident ease. "Sorry if I appeared dazed. I was just wondering if you meant 745.92, dried flowers and flower arranging, or 745.4, floral design in the decorative arts."

She gave me a delighted smile. "Aren't you clever. Those numbers come right off the top of your head?"

"Indeed." I gave my noggin a playful tap. "You never know what you might find up here."

* * *

I finished my shift without further incident, and punched out my time card as well as Frank's. Nobody had noticed him missing, so I hadn't needed to cast my bluffing spell after all. I grabbed my purse, said a quick good-bye, and left the library through the front door.

Chet was waiting for me in the Department of Water van as promised.

I approached the passenger-side door and paused. Recently, I'd gotten a little too close to another municipal services vehicle, and it had nearly killed me.

Well, technically it did kill me, but my aunt had kept my body going with some dark voodoo, keeping it on spiritual ice until I could hijack my way back in again.

I shook off the memory and opened the door. If whatever doesn't kill you makes you stronger, then getting over the fear of something that actually did kill you must make you practically impervious. I settled into the leather bucket seat and reached for the seat belt with a trembling hand.

Chet grunted something like a greeting and continued to train his green eyes on the screen of his phone. The two and a half wrinkles across his forehead deepened as he concentrated. Judging by the healthy glow of his skin, he'd completely recovered from the previous week's injuries. With the bright late-afternoon summer sunshine filtering into the van, lighting his long face and prominent cheekbones, his cheek hollows had no shadows. My neighbor, the wolf shifter, didn't look hungry for once. He had the strong, lean look of a professional athlete. Some of his scalp showed through his mahogany brown hair over his ears.

"You got a haircut," I commented and then I turned my attention back down to my seat belt. The tremor in my hand was making it difficult to get the belt fastened, but I clicked it on the third try.

"You must be rattled," Chet said, eyeing my hands. "I've never seen you like this."

"Then you've never seen me when the pizza delivery guy calls to say he can't find the house."

He snorted and started the engine. "There's the ballsy Zara I've grown to know and love." He coughed abruptly as he realized what he'd said. "And by love, I mean... Well, it's an expression."

"Love thy neighbor," I said. "That's also an expression."

He smiled and kept his gaze on the road ahead. "Good fences make good neighbors."

"And no beauty shines brighter than that of a good heart."

He whipped his head to face me. "What did you just say?"

I repeated the saying. "No beauty shines brighter than that of a good heart."

He nodded and returned his attention to the road. "True enough."

Our conversation felt familiar, as though we'd played the game of exchanging clichéd expressions countless times. I'd been living next door to Chet and the rest of the Moore family for only a few months, but our history went back at least sixteen years. He'd been a fan of my website during my Zara the Camgirl days. I was internet-famous for a while, part of the first wave of people broadcasting their lives over the Internet. I hesitate to call myself a "camgirl" because it means something different these days. Back then, being a camgirl hadn't involved stripping off clothes for strangers, except for the one or two times I'd forgotten the webcams were running in a room.

Chet had been a regular visitor to my Zara the Camgirl page, plus we'd talked in the chat room. It was a great little community of nerds and self-named oddballs. This was all right before YouTube took off and people started having their own channels, before the first YouTube star had been christened. Back in the "olden days," you had to be a computer nerd to handle the technical side of broadcasting your life.

Chet didn't seem like such a nerd now that I'd met him. He was quiet at times, but I wouldn't call him an oddball, either.

He glanced over at me. "How have you been feeling?"

"Discombobulated. Thanks for asking." I smoothed the folds of my skirt, touching the plastic bag in my pocket to make sure I still had the feathers. I could feel the large quill, so the feathers hadn't disappeared or shifted back yet. "How's Frank?"

"He's at the hospital getting checked out." He glanced my way. "What do you mean, you feel discombobulated?"

I rubbed my palms together. "When your buddies turned into giant birds, something happened to me. I got the blue lightning in my hands, just like that time we were attacked in the forest." I fidgeted with my fingers. "How well do you know those guys?"

He snorted. "Rob and Knox are like brothers to me. No, better than brothers, because I can always count on them." He paused, clenching his jaw hard enough to make the hollows in his cheeks catch a shadow. "Zara, I assure you, it wasn't either one of them who attacked us that day."

"Then who was it?"

"It could have been anyone. Or anything. Before we destroyed the Pressman house, we found plans for biomechanical creatures that would give you nightmares."

"Great," I said. "Because more nightmares are exactly what I need." I looked out the side window to catch a street name. Elm Street. "Where are you taking me? We're going to see Frank, right?"

"Not yet." He pressed some buttons on the control panel of the van. The radio came on, playing classic rock. Chet bobbed his head with the music—not in a fun, road trip way—more like he was giving the music his approval to continue.

I leaned forward and pushed another button at random. The station changed to modern pop.

He switched it back to the classic rock and held his hand above the buttons to block my access. Again, not in a fun, road trip way. More like a controlling, withholding jerk.

"Chet, have I done something to offend you? You haven't even talked to me since that night in the Pressman house, when I saved your bacon."

15

"You didn't save anyone's bacon. My backup arrived, as planned. If anything, you were in the way. My team knew exactly what we were doing."

My jaw dropped. "Are you telling me you went up there on purpose to engage in slimy tentacle action with that monstrosity? It was all part of your cunning plan to enjoy some quality time with a life-sucking, parasitic, googly-eyed, bug-infested, slurpy-noise-making Erasure Machine?"

"We got the situation under control," he said evenly. "And the Erasure Machine didn't have eyes, let alone googly ones. That's why it was using Perry Pressman."

"Right," I said with an edge. "Since you know everything, tell me, who was the impostor in my body? The big boss whose orders Dorothy Tibbits was following?"

"That was Perry Pressman," he said. "And now that he's dead, the case has been closed."

"No way," I said, shaking my head. "Perry was a decent man who got caught up in something. The person in my body was pure evil."

Chet sighed. "I don't know what to say to reassure you."

"I don't want reassurance. I want the truth. You guys should question Dorothy Tibbits. She's the link."

"Tibbits came out of her coma," he said.

"And?"

He glanced over at me. "We sent agents in to question her. She was exhibiting extreme memory loss. She didn't even know who she was, let alone why she was being tried for the murder of Winona Vander Zalm. She might not be fit to stand trial."

I groaned. "She's faking."

"The case is closed." His voice wavered.

Outside of the van, tires screeched and a horn sounded. I looked up to see the red light we'd sailed through without Chet noticing, let alone tapping the brakes.

Chet swore and checked the mirrors as we drove away from the intersection.

"It's fine," he reported. "Nobody got hit."

His near-accident at the red light told me more than his words or his body language. It takes more cognitive resources to lie than to tell the truth. He'd lost his focus on driving because he was telling me a story, a fictional one.

"You don't believe the case is closed," I said. "Deep down, you know something's up. Maybe it was an inside job, someone within your organization."

He shook his head vigorously. "No way. The intel about the Pressman operation came from investigators within the DWM. We started a file when Wick brought us the erased books. It wasn't one of our projects."

"Did the DWM put their top agent on the case?"

"It was a junior..." He trailed off. "What are you getting at?"

"Sounds to me like a cover-up. The junior investigator wasn't supposed to unravel the mystery until it was too late. Even so, you guys barely made it there in time. And you weren't prepared at all, because the Pressmans immediately disarmed the three of you and started feeding you to their machine. I hate to think what might have happened if I hadn't shown up there to save your bacon."

He was quiet, driving well under the speed limit and checking both directions at every intersection.

"Chet, they were working on a machine for erasing *people*. Can you imagine the damage another machine like that could do? Think about evil impostors snatching the bodies of everyone from regular citizens to top-level figures."

"No comment," he said.

"They could impersonate anyone." I thought about recent international news events. "Maybe they already have?"

He pursed his lips but said nothing.

I'd been fidgeting with my hands and the fabric of my skirt the whole drive. Now I found myself making the hand gestures for casting the bluffing spell. Would it work on Chet? He wouldn't appreciate being manipulated, but was already annoyed at me, so what harm was there in trying?

I cast the spell silently. The air between us sparkled with tiny points of light that only I could see.

"Chet, being a single parent is difficult," I said. "You don't want to burden your child with your problems, but you don't have a partner to confide in."

Softly, he said, "I don't."

My spell seemed to be working. "Chet, you can unburden yourself. You're not alone. You have me. I'm your friend, and your neighbor, and I'm here for you."

He sighed. "I want so badly to tell you about Chessa."

"Chessa?" The sparkling in the air between us brightened. Was this a person at the DWM who'd been acting suspiciously? It was a woman's name. Was she the impostor who'd been in my body? I sounded her name in my head. *Chessa.*

The name rang with familiarity, the way the Pressman name had resonated with me after I'd met the spirit of Perry Pressman.

My bluffing spell was still active, so I pressed on, sounding like a cheesy stage hypnotist. "Yes, you *want* to tell me about Chessa." Again, the ring of familiarity. "You're calm and relaxed, and once you tell me everything, you'll keep feeling calm and relaxed."

He slowed down the van, checked the mirrors, and did a U-turn. Now we were heading away from our homes, away from the center of town.

"Tell me everything," I cooed.

"I'd rather show you," he said. His voice sounded flat, unguarded.

I didn't want to break the spell, so I let him drive in silence.

CHAPTER 3

THE TWINKLING LIGHTS of my spell were fading when we turned onto a quiet residential street. Chet slowed the van and parked in front of a house the color of gingerbread. The front hedge was a row of cedars that had been trimmed into rounded shapes like green gumdrops. Flower beds along the front of the house were dotted with three shades of allium blossoms, looking very much like blue and purple lollipops.

Chet got out of the van without speaking. I did the same and then followed him along a walkway across the lawn. Bright-hued butterflies fluttered around our heads. I slowed and held up one hand. A butterfly flitted down and perched on my finger. It was a western tiger swallowtail, with scalloped wings of yellow and black tiger stripes, dotted near the tail with a sash of blue and a spot of orange.

In Mayan culture, butterflies were said to be ancestors returning for a visit to physicality. The winged visitors were said to bring wisdom, bringing order to the universe by balancing the old and the new. Many cultures associate

19

butterflies with souls and transformation, including the Irish, who say butterflies are the souls of the dead waiting to pass through purgatory.

The swallowtail took to the air and climbed the summer breezes. When my daughter was younger, she'd called butterflies "fancy caterpillars." It always made me laugh. Thinking about Zoey snapped me out of my butterfly daydream.

Chet was nearly out of sight, letting himself through a wooden gate at the side of the house. I ran to catch up with him.

Behind the brown house was a surprise—a smaller, cottage-sized version of the house in front. Unlike the big one, which was the color of baked gingerbread, this house was a pale green. The paint had a frosted appearance, like the pocked surface of beach sea glass.

The walkway leading to the house was bumpy, made of big, round river stones embedded in concrete. I stumbled over one particularly large rock. I loved the look of big river stones around a fireplace, but they were too whimsical for a walkway. I felt like I was tripping along a dried creek bed. And then, surprisingly, I had a sense of every stone in the path. I stepped on the smoothest spots, perfectly balanced all the way to the front door.

Chet turned toward me, his dark eyebrows drawing together in confusion. His green eyes looked at me then through me.

He spoke for the first time since we'd parked. "It makes me sad to be here," he said.

The twinkling of my bluffing spell was fading. I silently cast it again to refresh the effects.

"You'll feel better the more you talk about it," I said. "Does Chessa live here?"

He turned his head left and right, scanning the area robotically. The front of the green cottage was tidy, the lawn between it and the main house recently mowed and weed free. The cottage had no porch, but it did have a flagstone patio decorated with urns of red geraniums and three stone statues of wild animals—a three-point buck, a rabbit, and a raccoon—in lifelike poses. The stone animals were so lifelike, in fact, they appeared to have been turned to stone while fleeing some unseen predator.

Turned to stone.

Did Chet's friend at the DWM, Charlize, live here? During my brief time in the underground hospital's coma ward, I'd caught a glimpse of Charlize's golden curls writhing like snakes. Once you suspect someone of being a gorgon, it's hard to shake the thought. Was the name Chessa a nickname for Charlize? Were we about to knock on the door of a creature descended from Medusa?

Chet was in motion again, looking through the keys on his keychain, so I held my question lest I break the spell.

He used a key on his own keychain to open the cottage's front door. Nobody was home. I let him enter first and kept my gaze down on the scuffed hardwood floor until I was certain we were alone.

The interior of the cottage was as white as an erased book page. White walls, white denim sofas, whitewashed wooden furniture. The entryway and adjoining living room glinted with hints of silver accessories—silver door handles and silver picture frames. The centerpiece of the room was a fireplace framed with more of the rounded river rocks I'd seen on the entry path.

Whose house was this? It all felt incredibly familiar, as though I'd been there before. In a sense, I'd been there plenty of times—in my imagination. When I'd been raising an energetic child in a cramped, run-down apartment, I'd escape into glossy magazines filled with page after page of perfect living rooms—living rooms that weren't strewn with plastic kids' toys, unopened mail, and stained hand-me-down furniture. As I surveyed the ceiling of whitewashed beadboard, I imagined it overlaid with a text headline in a magazine. "Dream Cottage By The

Sea," the text would read, and it would be the color of green sea glass.

Chet walked over to the archway leading to the central hallway and kitchen, the soles of his combat boots making clunky footfalls that felt wrong in the pristine space. This was the kind of home where you took your shoes off at the door, and the hostess offered you white slippers. Chet stood in the doorway with a blank expression, like a robot on power-saver mode.

I asked him, "Why are we here?"

He didn't respond to my question. My question. My spell was for bluffing, not for questioning.

I took a different tactic and said, "You want to tell me why we are here."

He opened his mouth to speak, and at the same time, I cast the spell a third time for good measure.

"You want to tell me everything," I said.

The charge in the air changed with an audible crackle. He closed his mouth and blinked. He furrowed his brow, deepening his two and a half frown lines.

The sparkles of my spell changed color, from pastel to a rich violet. I'd known even before the sparkles changed color that I'd screwed up the spell in my eagerness. It was like hitting the wrong note in a simple piece of music. You might not know what you did wrong, but you know it was wrong.

Chet looked at me through the glittering violet sparkles. His eyes were focused now, and gleaming.

"Chessa? I've missed you so much."

"What?" I turned and looked over my shoulder. Was she standing behind me? No, there was only the open doorway leading to the lawn.

His boots scraped on the wood floor, and he was in front of me. He leaned in, and his hands were around my face, his eyes locked on mine.

I lost myself in those green eyes.

His face moved in, looming closer. He was going to kiss me. I froze, my desire for him to kiss me at war with my logical side—the one that knew I didn't want it like this, with him under some botched bluffing spell.

My logical side won, and I managed to push him away, both of my hands on his broad chest.

He took a step back but kept his large, warm hands on either side of my jaw.

Gruffly, he said, "Don't push me away."

"Chet, it's me, Zara. Look carefully, and you'll recognize me. Pale skin, freckles, bright-red hair."

He quirked one eyebrow and growled, "Your hair's not red at all. It's the color of honey wheat." Then he gave me a look I'd never seen on Chet's face, though I'd imagined it more than once. His gaze flicked over to the nearest soft furniture, a white sofa accessorized with satin pillows—pillows that were about to get knocked on the floor.

He tilted his head and gave me a questioning look. "Our life was so perfect. Why did you have to leave?"

I decided to play along for now, but if he tossed me on the sofa, I'd have to reconsider—*slowly and carefully* reconsider.

Breathily, I said, "I did leave. Yes. How long have I been gone?"

"Too long. A year now." He shifted his hands down my jaw and ran one fingertip over my mouth. My whole body trembled. I glanced over at the sofa, then back into his eyes. I lost myself in Chet's gaze, lost myself in the green of his eyes, glowing like backlit emeralds. I was at the bottom of the ocean, peering up at the sky through green, plankton-rich waters.

I gasped for air and took a step back.

Chet stood there with his hands in the air where my face had been. He murmured, "It's been so long."

I snapped my fingers, trying to "snap" him out of the spell. The violet sparkles remained, and he continued to make dreamy eyes at me.

I leaned forward from the waist and swatted his cheek. He caught me by the wrist and kissed my fingertips.

"You romantic beast," I said. "No wonder I wasn't getting anywhere with you. You're hopelessly in love with someone else. Some blonde named Chessa."

At the sound of her name, he wrapped his free arm around my back and yanked me toward him.

"Chessa," he said.

Thanks to the strength of his bicep, I was crushed against his chest like a cable-knit sweater. I ducked my face down against his neck so he couldn't kiss me. His throat smelled of aftershave and something else. Wolf.

With a playful tone, he said, "Stop your squirming."

The baritone rumbles of his voice passed through his chest and into mine.

"Chet, can you do me a favor?" I asked sweetly. "Pretty please?"

"Anything."

"Do you have that clicky pen on you? The one that pops spells?"

He pulled away from me, took the pen out of a jacket pocket, and gave me a quizzical look.

I asked him, "Do you know what's happening right now?"

He looked at me, then the pen, then me, then the pen again. "If I click this, you'll go away again."

I swallowed hard against the lump in my throat. I reached out and wrapped my hand around his hand and the pen. I poised my thumb over the button.

The device was a multi-pulse generator that sent out a shock of power to disrupt magical spells. I'd seen Chet use it at a restaurant to dispel my sound-dampening spell. If I clicked the button, it would shut down my botched bluffing spell abruptly. In theory. The truth was, I knew very little about the gadget and how it worked, other than it contained a limited number of charges.

He stared at me with hurt in his gleaming green eyes. And beneath the hurt, rage.

"I'm sorry," I said, and I clicked the button.

CHAPTER 4

THE PEN WENT CLICK, and my spell went POP. The twinkling lights floating around us guttered and faded away.

The light that had been shining in Chet's eyes also disappeared. The green of his irises turned dark, like wet pebbles on a desolate shore.

"You put a spell on me," Chet said coldly. He clutched the pen possessively as he shook off my hand.

I rubbed my hands together and glanced around the cottage's living room. The ceiling seemed lower than when we'd entered. My stomach hurt. I didn't like this new guilty feeling I was getting—the sensation of Chet being disappointed in me.

"We're even now," I said breezily. "Last week, you punched me in the jaw and gave me a wicked concussion." I tugged on one earlobe. "My ears are still ringing."

It wasn't true. My ears were fine, and I'd recovered completely, but he *had* punched me hard enough to knock my lights out.

The hollows in his cheeks darkened as he clenched his jaw.

"You cast a spell to deceive me," he said through gritted teeth.

"Sort of," I squeaked. "The spell was only supposed to enhance my believability. I cast it first when we were in the van, to make you feel comfortable talking to me about top-secret DWM stuff." I grimaced self-consciously. "That sounds bad now that I hear the words coming out of my mouth, but seeing as how I nearly died twice because of the whole Pressman thing, you could say I'm entitled to information about matters that concern me, personally, and my ability to, uh"—I tugged my ear—"remain alive."

He narrowed his eyes and continued to clench his jaw. He crossed his arms.

Was that ceiling even lower now? The tension in the room was unbearable. I ducked by him and passed through an arched doorway leading into a formal dining room. I circled the lacquered white table and went to the sideboard, which was a carved wood vintage piece, also painted a bright, glossy white to match the table. The long, low sideboard was topped with a slab of white marble and decorated with silver candlestick holders, white candles, and a bowl of ceramic fruit, also white. I picked up a glossy pear and felt its heft.

Chet followed me into the room. He'd removed his boots. He padded in on socked feet, as quiet as a stalking wolf.

His gaze went to the ceramic pear in my hand. "Zara, don't touch that. Put it down."

I hefted it to feel its weight. It was heavier than I expected.

"Is she dead?" I asked. "And by *she*, I mean the woman who lived in this immaculate white cottage. The woman with hair the color of honey wheat." I nestled the ceramic pear back into the bowl. "The woman you miss so much that when one of my spells backfired, you actually thought I was her. She's dead, right?"

He hesitated.

I ran my finger along the marble top of the sideboard. No dust. And the fiddle-leaf fig plant in the corner was green and thriving.

"She's been gone a year," he answered.

A year.

"You've been maintaining this place as some sort of shrine," I said. "She must have been a remarkable woman."

He didn't respond. With a clenched jaw and narrowed eyes, he watched me closely, as though he was waiting for something to happen. Something like... a ghost popping out of a closet and shooting up my nostril and into my head.

He wasn't crazy for expecting such a thing.

Because I am a Spirit Charmed witch, my specialty is —whether I like it or not—attracting spirits. So far, I'd been visited and possessed by three entities—or only two entities, if Chet's theory about what happened in the Pressman attic was correct.

There were a few benefits to a Spirit Charmed possession. I did retain some knowledge and skills from the spirits who passed through me, plus their antics kept life interesting. On the con side, I'd been electrocuted twice—once while *sleep toasting* in my own home.

Now I was wandering around inside the former home of a woman who'd been dead for a year. I was touching her treasured objects, basking in whatever energy of her remained. My heart fluttered in my chest. Her spirit could fly into me at any moment. I took a step back from the sideboard and clasped my hands together. Had I walked into a trap?

Chet continued to watch me vigilantly.

I shook my head at him as I crossed my arms. "Chet, you can drop the act that you're angry at me for the spell."

He quirked his eyebrow but said nothing.

"Stop pretending that bringing me here was something you did against your will," I said. "My bluffing spell isn't that strong. It simply adds a dash of charisma. It's like hypnotism. It doesn't make people do or believe something they don't want to." He didn't deny it, so I continued. "You brought me here because, deep down, you wanted me to be inside this house. You know that if her spirit's still around, it will be attracted to me. You *tell me* to stop touching her things, but underneath your words, your body speaks another language." Now I quirked my eyebrow at him. "Plus, *dude*, you took off your boots." We both looked down at his gray wool socks, and then back at each other's eyes. "You want to stay here a while, and you want me to touch her things."

He shrugged.

I took a breath and added gently, "You want me to say her name."

His nostrils flared.

"Chessa," I said softly.

He nodded.

I made my way around the dining room table, giving him a wide berth as I walked past him, and then down the short hallway, into her bedroom. Like the other rooms, the decorating theme was white and silver. The dresser was a deluxe design with mirrored surfaces. As I approached the mirrored dresser, I watched my many reflections for signs of a ghost sneaking up behind me.

No ghost yet.

I picked up her silver hairbrush and ran it through my hair with one long stroke. The room was so quiet, the bristles on my wavy red hair sounded like a roar. Chet stood in the doorway, watching.

I formed her name in my mind and in my mouth for the second time. "Chessa."

My body felt light, my head floating. Was I being pushed out of myself? Not yet. The lightness was probably anxiety response to Chet's intense staring, and not a ghost entering my consciousness. Not yet.

The cottage's stylish owner had an assortment of delicate, handmade jewelry on the mirrored dresser. The pieces were fashioned of silver wire, with beads of sea glass acting as gems. I picked up a bracelet and tried to fasten it around my wrist. The bracelet was loose, a bit too big for me. I couldn't get the tiny clasp shut with one hand.

Chet padded up silently, took the bracelet, and gently clicked it closed around my wrist.

I turned to him. His eyebrows rose expectantly. His expression was warm and open. His lips parted.

Together, we said her name. "Chessa."

And... nothing.

I said her name a fourth time. "Chessa?"

No ghost. I didn't see her or feel her.

Chet looked away, down at the hairbrush I'd left bristles-side-up on the dresser. He plucked one of my red hairs from the bristles and cast it aside. His shoulders shifted their shape, managing to look both slumped with exhaustion and tight with anxiety at the same time.

"So, saying her name three times didn't work," I said lightly. "Note to self. The *Beetlejuice* method of spirit summoning is not effective in the real world."

Still avoiding eye contact, he retrieved his multi-pulse click generator from his pocket and clicked it again. Nothing popped, because I hadn't cast any spells.

I gave him a dirty look. "Clearly, we have some trust issues," I said.

"You're the one who put a spell on me," he said icily.

"Oh, yeah? You're the one who manipulated me into resorting to that spell by being deliberately vague and clandestine."

He nearly smiled. "Clandestine?"

"I call it how I see it."

The trace of his smile disappeared. "But then you kept casting the spell repeatedly."

"Just to keep it going. Like throwing another log on a fire."

"You made me think you were her."

"Not on purpose. I screwed it up the third time, and something went wacky. I swear I wasn't trying to make you see me as anyone I'm not."

He blinked and looked across the room at something. I followed his gaze to the big white bed.

I put my hands on my hips. "You want to dig into these trust issues? Because I feel like I can't trust you, either. You brought me here hoping that I'd attract a specific spirit. And what if it had worked? What were you planning to do next? Were you going to throw me on that bed, rip off my clothes, and—"

He interrupted with a vehement "No!"

I had to finish my thought anyway, because that's just how I am. "And have sex with your dead girlfriend in my body."

His face drained of color. He lurched forward and caught himself on the dresser.

I took a few steps back. He seemed to be on the verge of something. It could be changing into a wolf, smashing things, or projectile vomiting. I backed up all the way to the doorframe, where I had a clear escape route.

He kept his hunched back to me as he spoke. "Your hair was blond, I swear. I thought she was here with us."

"Maybe she was," I said, my tone softening. "Sometimes a ghost takes full control and pushes me out, but other times I'm still present, going along for the ride. My aunt says I'll get better control over the spirits with practice." I looked over my shoulder, down the hallway at the bathroom. I hadn't seen that room yet, but the layout and decor were exactly how I expected, right down to the decorative seashells around the vanity mirror. Had I seen this woman's cottage featured in a magazine? Or was I experiencing the residual knowledge of her spirit?

"Chet, I can't say for certain that she is or isn't with us right now. Is there something you want to say to her?"

He still had his back to me. He was gripping the side edges of the dresser tightly, his knuckles white. "No."

"Nothing? You don't want to let her know how much you miss her?"

He was quiet.

"Chet, she might be in the room with us right now. I'm basically catnip for spirits, remember? Let's assume she's here. Watching us. Listening to this conversation." I was so convincing, I made myself shudder. "What do you want from her? A final good-bye? An answer to some burning question?"

"There's no point," he growled. "She's gone."

The room, despite being entirely white, seemed to get darker.

I sighed and leaned against the doorframe. "Work with me a little. Maybe I'll see her later tonight. It's been a hectic day, and my brain's probably full for now. If your girl Chessa shows up later, I could pass along a message."

He lifted up one fist and pounded on the dresser with it. The mirror didn't break, but the hairbrush and jewelry rattled from the impact.

"There's no use," he growled. "She's gone." He pounded the dresser again. "Chessa is gone." He hit the dresser a third time with his fist, and this time the mirrored surface did break, with a loud crack.

And then, in the silence that followed the sound of a mirror breaking, there was another voice. A woman's.

"Don't say that, Chet," the woman said. "She can't be completely gone."

I whipped around to find a woman standing in the hallway. She was blond, pretty, and dressed entirely in white.

CHAPTER 5

THE BLONDE IN WHITE gave me a cheery wave. "Hello, Zinnia."

"Zara," I corrected.

She shook her head, making her golden ringlets quiver. "Sorry, Zara. Gosh, you look so much like your aunt. And sometimes I mix up names that start with the same sound."

"That's fine, Chloe." I gave her a friendly smile. "I almost didn't recognize you without a glass display case full of cookies between us."

Chloe Taub was dressed in baker's whites because she must have come straight from her bakery, the Gingerbread House of Baking. The perky blonde was about thirty, with an oval-shaped face, big blue eyes, and loose blonde ringlets.

The first time I'd seen Chloe, she'd been in labor and climbing into a vehicle to go somewhere to give birth. She hadn't noticed me, but I'd caught a glimpse of something magical in her hair. Snakes.

35

Chet had refused to confirm that the blonde baker was a gorgon, yet he hadn't done much to deny it. Chloe also bore a striking resemblance to another supernatural blonde, the snake-haired nurse I'd encountered at the secret underground hospital.

Since the day she gave birth to her son, Jordan Junior, I'd seen Chloe a number of times at the bakery. She had always been friendly and professional. The snakes hadn't made any more appearances. I had to wonder, had the snakes been a product of my imagination, or was she really a gorgon? And if she was a gorgon, was she more powerful than me? I didn't *want to* fight her, but if it came down to it, could any witch, let alone a novice such as myself, survive an encounter with a gorgon?

Chloe walked over to where Chet stood. She leaned around him to view the mirrored dresser's shattered surface. She made a tsk-tsk sound.

"Look what you've done," she admonished. "She'll be coming back to us one day, and you're going to be in so much trouble for smashing up her dresser, you beast." She playfully punched him on the shoulder before turning toward me. "Chessa loved this piece. It cost a fortune to get it shipped here."

"It's a lovely piece," I said. "Or at least it was."

Chloe didn't seem surprised to see us there, let alone upset—other than chiding Chet about the broken mirror.

Chet put his hands in his pockets and looked recalcitrant. "I didn't hit it that hard," he grumbled. "And glass is a terrible surface material for furniture."

"Spoken like a true beast," Chloe said with an eye roll.

I chimed in, "Now he'll have seven years of bad luck."

Chloe's eyes widened. "Did you put a curse on him?"

"No, no, no," I said defensively. "He's just getting the standard seven years of bad luck for breaking a mirror."

"But you *are* a witch," Chloe said.

I crossed my arms and tried to look casual. "I've been called a lot of names over the years."

Chloe looked at Chet expectantly. "You haven't told her everything, have you?"

He frowned. "I was going to."

She playfully smacked him in the ribs.

He winced and growled in discomfort.

She went to poke him in the ribs again, but he jumped away, arms down to shield himself.

"I see you're still a busted-up wolf boy," she said. "You haven't healed from your late-night cuddle session with the tentacle wall monster."

He gave her a shut-up look and growled, "That's classified."

Chloe looked at me with raised eyebrows then back at Chet. "But Zara is one of us, and now you've finally brought her here, into our world. There's no need to keep secrets anymore. Plus now she can help with Chessa. I know she's not the person you expected, but it's still going to work." She turned to me, her eyebrows knitting together in a pleading expression. "We need to reach my sister, Chessa. Can you see her or feel her inside the house? Has she spoken through you yet?"

I looked at the smiling, angel-faced blonde and the surly, frowning wolf shifter. Sweet and sour. They both knew about my magic abilities, and they wanted my help. Even as I considered what it would feel like to tell them both to go to hell, I knew I could never say those words. The same stubborn streak of altruism that had drawn me to my profession of being a librarian also meant that I wanted to say yes to this request. Even though it was stranger and more personal than the average library request.

Plus I liked Chloe. How could you not like someone who offered you free samples of pfeffernüsse?

"I'm not sure," I said. "Nothing much has happened since we got here, but I feel *something*. Faintly. This cottage is very familiar."

Chloe pursed her lips and thumbed her chin as she studied me. "If you really are the Soul Catcher, maybe proximity to her body will help."

Soul Catcher? That was a new term for me. My aunt said I was *Spirit Charmed.* I hadn't gotten clarification on whether that meant I charmed the spirits or I was charmed by them. Recent events had led me to believe it was the latter.

Chloe asked plaintively, "Will you help us reach my sister?"

"I want to help," I said. "But I can't make any promises. I'm only a novice."

She made a disappointed tsk noise.

I explained, "So far, the spirits I've interacted with have come to me on their own." I tilted my head thoughtfully. "I suppose we could go visit Chessa's grave." My forearms prickled with goose bumps. "But it's dangerous for someone like me to walk through a cemetery. Hundreds of ghosts could rush at my face, treating my nostrils like the doorway to the hottest club in town. The polite ones would line up in an orderly fashion, but then the rude ghosts would line-jump, and when a few break the rules of social order, that always leads to chaos. I'm a lowly novice witch, so without the benefit of having a spiritual bouncer guarding the proverbial gates of my nostrils, the inside of my head would quickly become Grand Central Station with a live marching band and a disco ball."

Chloe poked Chet in the ribs again. "She hardly knows anything."

I couldn't argue with that.

Chet gave me a guilty look as he withdrew his phone from his pocket. "I've got to make some calls," he grumbled. His knuckles were red with blood from the broken mirror. He wiped them casually on his dark jacket. Underneath the blood, the cuts seemed to be sealing up already.

Chloe came over to where I stood—half in the room and half in the hallway—and took my hand. Her fingers were cool, and her palms were warm—ideal hands for a baker, because she could control how much her body heat warmed the butter in pastry by how she handled it. I looked down at her hand, wondering how I knew that, and then it came to me. Mrs. Dougherty, in my middle school home economics class. Probably. She was very methodical and precise.

Chloe tugged my hand. "Are you still with us? Are you...?"

She sounded hopeful that I was already channeling her sister. I forced a quick, apologetic smile. "Still Zara," I said gently.

Chet and Chloe exchanged a look. He nodded toward the door. Chloe blinked twice, as though acknowledging a silent order.

Grinning, she fixed her bright-blue eyes on me. Her mouth was smiling, but her eyes weren't. It occurred to me that her eyes ran on a different circuit from the rest of her.

She said, sweet as honey, "Zara, let's pop over to the main house for a while, just us girls. I was putting on a fresh pot of coffee when I noticed the door open back here." She tugged me toward the entryway. "You look like you could use a snack."

"I can't argue with that. Plus you know I'm addicted to your baking."

Behind us, Chet said, "I'll stay here and check on some things."

"Fine by me," Chloe called over her shoulder. "That will give us girls more *girl time*."

We walked out the open front door and started crossing the back yard on the diagonal, using a narrower version of the same bumpy river stone path that led to the front sidewalk.

We were halfway to the back entry of the larger brown house when I asked, "How did Chessa die?"

Chloe said, "Chessa's not dead."

It took me three more strides over the stone path to assimilate the new information.

Point one: Chessa had been gone for a year.

Point two: Chloe wanted me to visit her body.

Point three: She wasn't dead.

That left only one logical explanation.

"Chet's girlfriend is in a coma," I said.

Chloe opened the sliding patio door at the back of her house. "Fiancée," she said. "His *fiancée* is in a coma."

"Right. Chet's *fiancée* is in a coma." My mouth didn't like forming the phrase 'Chet's fiancée.' Even though he'd been acting like a moody burro all day, he'd previously laid the foundations for my crush with some kind gestures over the past few months. Now that I knew he was mourning a fiancée, his occasional hot-cold treatment of me made more sense. It would take time, but my heart would get the memo that Chet and I weren't meant to be.

I stood on the paving stones outside Chloe's house and wiped the corners of my eyes. There must have been a quick summer breeze that kicked pollen or dust into my eyes.

Chloe was already inside, apologizing for the mess.

I entered the main house, which was fragrant with the welcoming scent of freshly brewed coffee.

Girl time. Now I would have coffee and pastries with the blonde baker whose sister was in a coma. Presumably, the sister was equally blonde and beautiful.

Chessa was just like a real-life Snow White from the fairy tales, waiting for her prince to kiss her awake. Legend has it the kiss served to jostle her head enough for the chunk of poisoned apple to tumble from her sleeping mouth. But who had given the poisoned apple to Snow White in the first place? Hadn't it been a wicked witch?

CHAPTER 6

CHLOE'S HUSBAND, Jordan Taub, would be at the bakery for a few more hours, Chloe explained as she set platters of food before me on an enormous rustic wood table. She served all manner of pastries, from savory mini quiches to sweet tartlets filled with strawberry jam.

We made small talk about the food, and she explained that she had so much at home because the "imperfect" goods were unsalable at the bakery. A few of the dishes were experiments they conducted at home. And yet more of it was simply her favorites that she enjoyed making in her home kitchen to relax.

I checked the time and mentioned getting home soon to make sure my daughter ate dinner.

Chloe asked, "How old is she?"

"Sixteen."

"Of course she's sixteen," Chloe said with a chuckle, the laugh lines of which didn't extend to her bright-blue eyes. "I knew that."

"How did you know?" Zoey hadn't visited the bakery with me, as it was located past the point where our morning paths to school and work forked apart.

"Uh," Chloe stammered as she rearranged the serving platters on the table to make room for steaming cinnamon rolls, still hot from the oven. "Maybe Chet told me?"

"He might have," I said.

"In any case, you look way too young to have a teenaged daughter."

I gave her a practiced smile. I'd heard that phrase countless times. Sometimes it was a compliment, but more often it was a roundabout way for people to pry into my personal business. Other women always wanted to know how old I'd been when I'd gotten pregnant. With time, I'd gotten over being offended. People were simply curious, and I'd probably want to know the same thing if I were in their shoes.

"I had her at sixteen," I said.

"Smart," Chloe said warmly. "I'm not quite thirty, and my little guy runs me ragged."

As if on cue, a baby squeal filled the open-plan dining area. The cries came from a portable baby monitor sitting on the nearby kitchen counter.

"Be back in a minute," Chloe said. "I hope you don't mind serving yourself."

I was already reaching for the cannoli.

While Chloe tended to her little one, I sampled the cornucopia of goodies, starting with the supposedly "imperfect" quiches. I couldn't for the life of me guess what was wrong with them. If containing too much bacon and cheddar was a flaw, I didn't want quiches that were *right*. Next up was a cheese blintz, then a jam blintz, and, finally, one filled with both cheese and jam. I chased down the blintzes with a cup of coffee and cannoli. Technically, I started with a cannolo—the singular of cannoli—but the cream-filled pastry didn't want to visit my stomach without a friend or two.

As I succumbed to the gastric pleasures before me, I forgot all about my reason for being there.

It was Chloe's voice, coming through the baby monitor, that brought me back to my mission.

"Zara's going to help Mommy," she cooed. "What do you think about that?" The baby made a happy noise that caused the monitor to crackle. "That's right! She is a witch. But she's not a nasty, old, icky witch. Zara is a *good* witch."

Alone at the big table, I pushed my chair back and rubbed my belly. I said to myself, "Zara tries to be a good witch, but Zara has a weakness for buttery pastry."

A few minutes later, Chloe returned to find me munching a gingersnap. She cradled a rosy-cheeked baby boy who was grabbing for her golden curls with both pudgy hands.

"Zara, meet Jordan Junior, our little gingerbread boy. Would you like to hold him?"

I wiped the crumbs from my hands and reached out eagerly. "All the better to nom-nom his tasty little arms." I knew from chatting with Jordan at the bakery that they called him their gingerbread boy because his skin tone was halfway between Chloe's pale skin and Jordan's dark coloring. I took the baby and hummed a melody I used to sing for Zoey. The humming, combined with the lovely baby smell coming off the crown of his head, brought back all sorts of memories—some good, some bad, all of them surprisingly crisp and clear.

"Thanks for holding Junior," Chloe said. "He has a knack for waking up right when I'm about to eat, and I'm famished."

"Eat," I told her, and then I confessed how much food I'd already put away in her absence. "You can put it on my bakery tab," I joked.

She laughed. "At least we're in Wisteria now, so there's no need to count calories."

"What's that all about, anyway? How does the magic keep people from gaining weight?"

She shrugged. "Why look a gift horse in the mouth?" She loaded up a plate and started eating. "My sisters and I were born here, so I didn't know the rest of the world was different. When Jordan and I moved away, our lives became more *challenging*, which can be fun, but also a real pain in the butt. Everything out there costs more, and you get less." She washed down a snickerdoodle with creamy coffee. "Eventually, we admitted there was something missing in our lives. I hate to say it, because I don't like to sound lazy, but we were both tired of struggling so hard. We had an honest talk and decided that we'd had our adventures in the outside world, and now it was time to come *home* and start a family."

"And is your life better here in Wisteria?"

She blinked at me, her blue eyes as bright as a sunny sky. "Isn't yours better here?"

"Sure, but that's because I own a gorgeous house, have a great-paying job, the people here are so nice, and there's a bakery on every downtown block."

"Exactly," she said.

I nodded slowly before resting my chin on Junior's warm head. Chet hadn't come over to check on us, and I wondered how much time we had for "girl talk." I wanted to hear more about Chloe's sister, such as what kind of mishap had put her into a coma. Was it related to the coma that Dorothy Tibbits had been in before she lost her memory? Was Wisteria plagued by some wicked witch with a basket full of poisoned apples?

The baby squealed and wriggled on my lap.

"How old is he?" I asked, smoothing his swirl of dark hair.

"Almost three months."

"If your sister's been asleep for a year, she wouldn't have known you were pregnant. This nephew will be a big surprise if she comes back."

The baby squealed again in what seemed to be a protest.

I kissed the top of his head and corrected myself. "You'll be a big surprise *when* she comes back. *When*."

Jordan Junior bounced happily on my lap, plump arms waving wildly. He was strong for three months, no wobbling with his head, plus he had to weigh a good fifteen pounds.

"Chessa knows," Chloe said. "I mean, she knew we'd been trying." She coughed and looked away, at a collection of souvenir spoons decorating the wall. "Jordan and I had some stork-summoning problems."

"And by stork, you mean the fairy tale version—the bird who delivers babies?" Silently I added, *And not that one or both of you is a stork shifter?* I would have asked about her magical abilities, but I wasn't sure of the etiquette. Never mind that Chet had already blabbed to her about my witch status.

"Fertility problems," Chloe said heavily. "We went through the whole roller coaster ride. Vitamins and lifestyle changes. Jordan switched to boxers and baggy pants. We blew through our savings on treatments. Then, finally, a year after we'd all but given up, we moved back here to Wisteria, to this house. My sister was already living in the cottage at the back, so she and I became even closer." She took a deep breath. "And then we got our little miracle." She looked pointedly at Junior on my lap.

Junior twisted his torso, cocked his head, and looked up at me with an eerily intelligent stare.

I looked into the baby's eyes. They were a dark gray, halfway between his mother's baby blues and his father's dark-brown eyes. I silently asked, *Are you in there, Chessa? Did you already give up on your body and reincarnate into this adorable baby boy?*

Junior blinked and then crammed his whole fist into his mouth with a joyful squeal.

"Wow," Chloe said. "He's as comfortable with you as he is with his auntie, Charlize."

A cold tingle went down my spine.

"Charlize? As in the..." *Don't say gorgon!* "The blonde who works with Chet?"

"She's our sister."

I stiffened to keep from trembling. *Don't show weakness!* I'd been fairly certain Chloe was a gorgon, but having it confirmed caused an unexpectedly strong fear response deep within me.

My voice high and squeaky, I asked, "How many of you are there?" My brain yelled its own more direct question: *EXACTLY HOW MANY GORGONS ARE IN THIS TOWN?*

"Just three of us sisters," Chloe said breezily. "We're triplets." She reached out to take Junior back from me. He went over with a happy squeal. She bobbed him on her lap while he batted his eyelashes at me.

"Triplets are rare," I said. *Except with gorgons,* I screamed in my head.

"Multiples run in the family, so I'm lucky I only got this one." She kissed the swirl of fluffy brown baby hair at the top of his head. "Really lucky."

"And he's lucky to have you," I said. *Who wouldn't want a gorgon mother? Except maybe, oh, everyone?*

She gave me a funny look, eyes squinting. Her *gorgon* eyes squinting. I cleared my throat and looked down at a stack of peanut butter cookies between us.

Chloe said, "We don't know yet if he has any abilities. I'm the least powerful of my sisters. And Jordan, well, that's another issue entirely." She chuckled knowingly, as though I were in on the joke. I had no idea what kind of powers her husband had. Maybe it was better that I didn't know.

"I see," I said, my gaze firmly fixed on the cookies.

"Still hungry? Help yourself, *Zara*." She said my name like she was tasting it.

"Totally full," I said.

She made a hissing sound, along with a rattle. The baby hadn't been holding a rattle. It had to be the snakes in her hair. I hadn't glimpsed any snakes coming out of Chloe's head, but that didn't mean they weren't there, hiding under a glamour.

I kept staring at the cookies. I was curious about the hissing and rattling, but I didn't dare look up at her hair, because I might get caught and frozen by her eyes. My knowledge of Greek mythology was neither wide nor deep, but I knew the basics about Medusa, the snake-haired gorgon who turned people to stone with a glance.

"Zsssarra," she said, tasting my name again, and hissing.

At the edge of my vision was her shadow on the wall. The shadow revealed unnatural movement around Chloe's head.

"Zssssarrrrrrra, are you afraid to look at me?"

I reached for a butter knife and angled it so I could see her in the reflection. Her golden curls were twirling, snake-like, alternately hissing and rattling their tails. My breath caught in my throat, and I held still. Very still. Was I already frozen, turned to stone? No. I could feel my heart pounding.

Her voice thick with anger, formerly sweet Chloe said, "Zara, I'm not a monster. My sisters and I are descendants of the gods. Unlike you *witches*." She said the word *witches* like she had tasted it, found it repugnant, and was now spitting it out. Her terrible hair snakes continued to writhe.

A male voice said, "I can't leave you alone for a minute."

I whirled around on my chair to see Chet, standing just inside the sliding glass patio door, shaking his head.

"Me?" I pointed to my chest.

In the dim reflection on the glass door, I saw Chloe make a similar gesture and also ask, "Me?"

Which one of us was he chiding?

"Time to go," Chet said to me. "Let's be on our way, Zara." His suggestion had the weight of a pack leader's command.

He didn't have to bark his order twice. I was up from the chair and out of the house in two shakes of a lamb's tail.

As we made our way out of the back yard, I glanced back at the stone lawn ornaments in front of the cottage— the frightened-looking buck, rabbit, and raccoon.

In light of the whole Chessa-being-a-gorgon thing, the expressions on the stone animals' faces were even more chilling.

CHAPTER 7

"THANKS A LOT for the warning," I said with heavy sarcasm. "Things could have gotten awkward back there if Chloe's supernatural powers had been a complete surprise to me." I paused. "Oh, wait. It *was* a complete surprise. Because now that I think about it, you didn't give me any warning, whatsoever. I suppose you've been too busy lately. Then again, you did find time in your hectic schedule to tell Chloe all about me being a witch."

Chet kept his eyes focused on the road ahead. We'd been driving for ten minutes in silence. Well, he'd been silent. I'd been talking non-stop. He kept stonewalling me, pretending to be deaf.

"Last month, I specifically asked you about Chloe being a gorgon, and you wouldn't tell me," I said. "Are we friends or not? Friends tell friends about gorgons."

Still no response.

"What's next on your agenda?" I asked. "Do you pull out one of your DWM gadgets—maybe a normal-looking tin of breath mints—and use it to shock me into paralysis before you toss me into a pit of angry scorpions?"

He clenched his jaw.

"Chet, I know you heard me, because I saw you clench your jaw. You should try talking about your feelings sometime. If you keep bottling stuff up, you're bound to crack a molar." I turned and looked out the side window at the passing scenery of shrubs and houses. "Of course, given your wolf-boy healing powers, you'd probably spit the cracked molar out and grow a new one in five minutes."

"It would take more than five minutes," he said gruffly.

I clapped my hands. "It's a miracle! The wolf boy's hearing has been reinstated! And now I shall brace myself for the flurry of answers that are surely coming my way."

"I don't like being called wolf boy."

"Fair enough." I gave my head a sassy shake. "I don't like being left alone with an easily offended gorgon."

Chet sighed. "She wasn't going to turn you to stone, Zara." He glanced over at me. His eyes had settled to a shade between emerald and black, their regular moss green. "What did you say to upset Chloe, anyway?"

"Nothing. Which is ironic, because, as you may have noticed, I can be rather colorful and outspoken at times. I set her off when she noticed I was avoiding eye contact, which I naturally did once I realized *what she was*." I rubbed my forearms. "Gorgons are real." I studied Chet's stony profile. "And your own fiancée is a gorgon. Wow. I bet you guys never fought, not even once. Or if you did, you always let her win."

He didn't respond. We were back to the stonewalling silence.

I kept the rest of my thoughts to myself until we arrived at the front of my house, where Chet pulled the van up to the sidewalk. He shifted into park but didn't shut off the engine.

"Just dropping me off?" My voice sounded high and squeaky, betraying my emotions. Now that we were going

50

our separate ways, I felt bad about leaving things on a sour note.

He said, "I'll let you know when I can get you in to visit Chessa in the coma ward."

"Oh, goody. I can't wait to go back *there*, to the spooky underground hospital."

He growled, "If you don't want to help, say so."

"You don't know what you're asking me to do."

He shifted in his seat, making the leather squeak, but didn't say anything.

"The other spirits never gave me a choice in the matter." I reached for my seat belt but didn't unfasten it yet. "Chet, you don't know what it's like to have your body taken over by powerful forces."

He turned to face me, one eyebrow quirked. "I don't? What do you think happens when I turn into a wolf? Do you think I'm still me, with all my human thoughts and emotions?" His expression was part amusement and part fury. I was used to Chet's mood falling on the spectrum between warm and awkward. This belligerent side was more upsetting than when he'd questioned my parenting skills.

He said, "You're not the only one who struggles. Why do you think we keep our powers secret from the world?"

"I wouldn't know, *Chet*." I said his name like I was spitting on it. "My handbook for *How to Make Friends and Influence Shifters, Gorgons, and Other Scary Monsters* must have gotten lost in the mail." I released my seat belt with a mighty click.

"You can do it," he said gently. "If you're worried that you can't find Chessa, don't be. You've caught the spirit of someone who wasn't dead once already."

"At least once," I said. "Twice, if you count the boss spirit who you knocked out."

His upper lip curled. "I told you already, that was still Pressman. We'll both be better off if you accept answers for things and move on. If you keep expecting to see monsters in the shadows, you'll find them. Witches have a way of manifesting things they expect." He paused. "Like what happened to your friend, the flamingo."

"His name is Frank, and I don't appreciate you implying his flamingo makeover was my fault."

He shrugged one shoulder. "If the shoe fits..."

I pushed open the passenger side door with a vengeance. "If the shoe fits, I'm going to put it on my foot, and then kick you so hard—" I jumped out and slammed the door before I finished the threat, which went on for nearly a minute and became extremely colorful toward the end.

By the look on Chet's face, he heard me perfectly well, even through the closed door.

* * *

Inside my house, my sixteen-year-old daughter greeted me by looking at my hands and frowning. "No sushi?"

I held my hands out, palms up. "Invisible sushi," I joked. There was nothing on my palms except for dirt. After Chet drove away, I'd spent fifteen minutes in the front yard taking out my frustrations on the weeds as well as a few plants that probably weren't weeds.

Zoey was reclining on the living room's sofa, reading an art book about the history of cartooning. She was not amused by my invisible sushi joke. "Mom, you said that since we weren't seeing Auntie Z tonight, you'd pick up sushi." She closed the book and sat up. "It's not like you to forget about something as important as dinner. Something's wrong."

I walked over to the main floor's powder room and started washing the dirt from my hands. I left the door open, and called out, "Your mother had a very *interesting*day, and she hopes the rest of the week is boring in comparison."

"Are you going to tell me what's going on, or are you going to feed me a made-up story about bumping your head while looking for recipes in someone's attic?"

I dried my hands slowly and smiled grimly at myself in the mirror. My redheaded, hazel-eyed offspring looked like me, talked like me, and even thought like me—at least enough to know when I was lying. She hadn't bought my cover story about the night I tangled with the Erasure Machine. Fair enough. I couldn't complain about having a smart kid.

I came out to find the living room empty. I found Zoey in the kitchen, rummaging through the fridge. Her favorite broken-in blue jeans had loosened since the move, and slid down to show an inch of her underwear at the back.

"You need a belt," I said. "We should go shopping."

Her head still in the fridge, she said, "We have some of the cashew-chicken chow mein, but not enough for two people."

"All yours," I said. "I've already eaten. I had bacon mini quiches, cheese blintzes, and cannoli."

She turned around and gave me a hurt look. "You had cannoli without me? You're the worst." She dumped the chow mein on a plate and put it in the microwave.

I waved my hands excitedly. "The plastic thing! I'm going to tell Aunt Zinnia you haven't been using it!"

She gave me a dirty look, placed the plastic lid over her food with a thunk, and restarted the microwave. We'd recently switched from having the inside of our microwave look like a crime scene to having the inside of the plastic thing looking like a crime scene. In fact, we were excited to see how much exploded food we could get coating the plastic thing before Zinnia's next visit.

I took a seat at the kitchen's island, where we ate most of our meals, and rested my elbows on the counter. Using my telekinetic witch magic, I filled two water glasses, and set out napkins and utensils for Zoey. My telekinesis was limited to what I could lift or move with my body, and required the same amount of effort as doing it the regular way. Using it didn't save me energy when I was tired, but Zinnia felt it was good for my fine motor skills to practice in the kitchen with simple things. We'd affixed a frosted coating to the lower half of the kitchen window so that casual passersby on the sidewalk wouldn't catch sight of me juggling carrots and chopping them in midair.

The microwave beeped, and Zoey joined me with her steaming food.

I asked in a robotic voice, "How was your day at school?"

"My principal is a demon, and the cheerleaders are all zombies."

"For real?"

She grinned. "Just teasing you, Mom. I had a boring Monday. What happened to you?"

"I accidentally frightened Frank Wonder so bad that he turned into a flamingo. Pink feathers and all."

"He's a shifter?"

"That's what Chet thinks. I called the organization he works for, and he showed up with two other guys, who turned into huge birds themselves and flew after Frank."

"More birds?" Zoey paused with her fork midway to her mouth. "Is Frank going to be okay?"

"That depends. Do you want the reassuring answer, or the truth?"

She frowned at the chunk of chicken on her fork. "Suddenly, I feel weird about eating bird meat."

"We could try being vegetarian again. I'll make that baked eggplant thing from the vegan cookbook. With extra flakes of nutritional yeast."

Zoey jammed the forkful of chicken and noodles into her mouth, followed quickly by another. "Over it," she said. "No need to take drastic measures." She dug into the chow mein with a vengeance.

"You're a good egg," I said.

She paused and gave me a confused look. "What are you talking about?"

"I don't know. It just seemed like a motherly thing to say."

"Maybe in the nineteen-hundreds," she said, smirking.

she took few more bites of chow mein. "How are they going to get Frank to change back?"

"Treat him to a day at the bird spa." I smirked at her. "Actually, I don't know. They're working on calming him down. Once he settles, as long as he's not injured, he should just snap back. In theory."

"He'll be fine," Zoey said confidently. "I think Frank is one of those resilient people who knows exactly who he is, even when he's a flamingo." She paused and flicked her eyes up thoughtfully. "Fun fact: A group of flamingos can be called a *stand*, or a *flamboyance*."

"I'll be sure to tell him that," I said, smiling.

"What else happened?" She narrowed her eyes, as though peering into my soul. "You don't usually threaten to perform internal exams on people unless they've really ticked you off."

I grimaced. "You heard me yelling at Chet."

"I think the whole neighborhood heard you yelling at Mr. Moore."

I sighed and floated over a second fork so I could steal a bite of her chow mein. "Did Corvin ever mention anything to you about his dad having a fiancée who's been in a coma for the last year?"

Zoey wrinkled her nose. "Corvin is more interested in making fart sounds with his armpits than talking about icky grownup relationships."

"Did you know he can see ghosts?"

She nodded slowly. "No, but that explains a lot." She gave me another X-ray look. "But you and Mr. Moore weren't fighting about Corvin. So it must have been about this fiancée, the one in the coma."

"Her name is Chessa." I tasted the chow mein, surprised to be hungry considering how much pastry I'd put away at Chloe's house. "Chet wants me to intentionally attract her spirit."

"And then what?" Her nose wrinkled as she presumably reached the same sordid conclusion I had earlier.

"Not *that*," I said. "He swears it's not a sex thing. He didn't map it out for me, but I'm guessing he wants to wake her out of her coma, Sleeping Beauty style. He needs to knock the chunk of poisoned apple from her mouth."

Zoey chewed her food thoughtfully. "Sleeping Beauty was cursed by a disgruntled evil fairy. She was a princess who pricked her finger on a spinning wheel, and went into sleep for a hundred years, along with everyone in the castle. You're thinking of Snow White."

"I always mix those two up."

"Snow White has the seven dwarves who sing *Hi Ho*."

"Right. But Snow White was just a regular common girl, not even a princess. Chessa is a *gorgon*."

Zoey's face froze, mid-chew. She blinked and gestured for me to continue.

I started over from the beginning, with the bluffing spell I cast on Chet in the van, and the subsequent visit to Chessa's lily-white cottage. I showed my daughter the sea-glass bracelet, which I was still wearing, and told her about my visit with Chloe, as well as the bombshell about the three sisters.

Zoey took it all in without comment.

When I was done, she said, "And when did you meet the other gorgon? Charlize?"

"Last week, at the hospital. After I, um, bumped my head while looking for recipes."

She narrowed her eyes. "Funny how that happened the same night that house in town exploded from a gas leak and burned to the ground."

"Funny," I agreed.

She reached across the table and took my hand. I gave her fingers a reassuring squeeze. She pulled my hand closer and examined the loose-fitting sea-glass bracelet on my wrist. "This is pretty."

"It's Chessa's. She loved the beach, apparently." I fidgeted with the clasp. "I put this on to try to strengthen our connection when I was in her house."

"Is it working?"

"Not yet. Maybe. I don't know."

"If she loved the beach so much, then we should go to the beach tonight," she said. "We can watch the sunset."

"I'd love to." My phone started buzzing inside my purse. I excused myself and pulled it out.

The call was coming from the Department of Water. On the Caller ID, they'd left off the secret part of their name.

Zoey peered over at the screen. "Don't tell me you forgot to pay the water bill, too."

I laughed, though it stung from being a little close to home. "I've got to take this," I said. "Can you give me some privacy?"

She pushed back from the counter. "Gladly. Along with the dirty dishes." Smirking, she headed for the door.

"Zoey, hold up," I said. "If your principal really was a demon, and the cheerleaders were zombies, you'd tell me, wouldn't you?"

In a singsong voice, she said, "Eventually," and left the kitchen.

My phone continued to buzz so hard it nearly vibrated out of my hand. The Department of Water and Magic must have boosted the signal to my phone to make it turbo buzz.

I answered the call with an authoritative, "Go for Zara."

CHAPTER 8

"YOU'RE A WITCH," said the male voice on the phone.

"I've been called a lot of things," I said, for the second time that day.

"Zara, this is wonderful news," he gushed. "Just wonderful. I love that you're a witch. I mean, *of course* you're a witch. Tell me, what kind of creature is your beau? Is he a shifter, like his two macho friends?"

"Frank!" I nearly cried from relief at hearing his voice. "How are you feeling?"

"I was *flying*. How do you think I'm feeling?"

His words were clear, but his voice was faint. I switched the phone to my other ear.

"Frank? Can you speak up?"

He chuckled. "Not really. Listen, I'm probably breaking all sorts of rules by using this phone in the first place. They didn't want me to have contact with anyone until I'd been debriefed, whatever that means."

"I hope they don't wipe your memory again."

There was a pause. "What do you mean, *again*?"

"We had another... *incident* at the library last week. You didn't turn into a flamingo that time, but you did get knocked unconscious after becoming acquainted with a magical creature—a bookwyrm."

His voice pitched up high. "Is that what that critter was? A bookwyrm?" He chuckled on the other end of the call. "I thought that wormy dude was a particularly vivid and specific fever dream from when I had the twenty-four-hour flu." I heard the breeze of him sucking in a breath of realization. "Which wasn't the flu, after all," he said. "Everything's falling into place. I wonder, did you and your aunt drug me and turn me into a helium balloon?"

I cleared my throat. "So, they didn't permanently wipe your memory."

He made a tsk-tsk sound. "You've been keeping secrets from me, but now—" There was a muffled rustling, like a hand being put over a phone receiver.

"Frank? What's going on there?"

He returned, his voice softer. "We're going to talk, you and I, but not now. Dr. Bob stepped out for a minute to get my booster shots and a cup of chai tea to calm my nerves, so I grabbed this official-looking phone and dialed nine. I got an outside line, and you were the first person I called."

"I'm touched," I said, and I meant it. "Frank, did you know you were a shifter?"

His voice got even quieter. "He's coming back. How about we meet at my place tomorrow, an hour before work? I'm in the Candy Factory, third floor."

There was a clatter over the phone line, and then the call ended.

* * *

After the phone call from Frank, I circled the kitchen, wringing my hands while I used my magic to dust the tops of the cabinets. As far as nervous habits went, at least it made the house cleaner.

I wondered, what were they doing to Frank at the DWM? Why would they be giving him booster shots? And what kind of doctor called himself Dr. Bob? It sounded like the name you'd give a puppet on a children's TV show.

I hoped that Zoey was right about Frank's ability to adapt. He truly was a person who knew exactly who he was, so maybe he'd be fine. And I'd see him in the morning. I could do myself a favor and not worry about Frank until I saw the whites of his eyes.

I absently played with the wire-and-sea-glass bracelet on my wrist. I had other things to worry about, such as locating Chet's fiancée.

And what if I did reach her spirit? Chloe hadn't shared with me the details of what had happened to Chessa, or her specific state. Was it really a coma, or a vegetative state, or a minimally conscious state? If the DWM was as well equipped as I suspected it was, had they run CT scans, MRI, and EEG? Or, given her supernatural genetics, did any of the traditional medical tests even matter?

She'd been gone for a year now. You hear stories about people waking up after a dozen years, but it's exceedingly rare. I didn't need a medical degree to know the chances of her coming back were slim.

If I did start communicating with her spirit, wouldn't I just be delivering bad news? She could ask them to pull the plug. Let her go. And then Chet would be free to move on. Just... move right on with his life. Chet would be free to date other people, such as a certain redheaded neighbor.

I hung my head forward guiltily. It was rude of me to think about the woman's fiancé that way while her body was still warm—assuming gorgon bodies were warm blooded. And not just rude, but dangerous. Spirits could harm me. The ghost of Winona Vander Zalm had nearly electrocuted me, and she wasn't even angry with me. If Chessa's spirit did suddenly turn up inside my head, I didn't want it to be while I was thinking about her man.

I pushed Chet from my mind, cleaned up the dinner dishes, and settled on the couch to do some reading.

My book of choice was about myth-based fairy tales. The title came from a set of ancient-looking books I'd picked up secondhand. My aunt had seen them and noted that they were good titles, "more accurate and not as sanitized as most books about mythical creatures." They certainly were gloriously uncensored, right down to the woodcut illustrations depicting gruesome torture. After I saw how many people were killed by being rolled down hills in barrels lined with spikes, I'd never thought of fairy tales the same way again. Or barrels.

I leafed through to the section on gorgons. The book included several variations on the tales surrounding the monsters. Most legends agreed that the gorgons were descendants of a sea monster. Chloe had claimed a lineage to gods, not monsters, but in mythology these were often one and the same. I continued reading. While the women might have started life as regular humans, they were transformed by an act of violence suffered by one of the sisters. That part certainly sounded familiar. In the stories, the three women had different powers, and were sometimes described as having hands of brass, or as being giant, scaled beasts with wings.

Were they dragons? I scanned the pages. A giant, scaled beast with wings certainly sounded like a dragon to me, but there was no mention of the D-word in relation to the gorgons. I scanned the gory illustrations, trying to find a reference point for their size when in winged form. This flying thing was certainly noteworthy, considering my history. I rubbed my temples as memories of the attack in the wood came back to me. The monster who'd ripped Chet's wolf hide to shreds had beaten the air with powerful wings. Dragon wings? I could feel the wind on my face. Unfortunately, I couldn't step into the memory long enough to see if our attacker's wings were made of feathers or dragon scales.

I shut the book, set it aside, and rubbed my temples some more.

What was I forgetting? The sun's fading rays lit up the dust motes floating in the air. I had forgotten to wax my wooden furniture, but that wasn't it, as I'd forgotten to wax furniture for at least a decade. I got a sudden urge to write in a diary, of all things. Was that the thing I was trying to remember? I hadn't kept a journal since my exhibitionist days back when I was Zara the Camgirl, broadcasting my home life for all of the Internet, including Chet Moore.

Chet.

My mind cleared.

The beach.

The ocean.

Blue water sparkled in my mind, melting away my weariness and bringing clarity. I remembered my promise to my daughter.

I called up to Zoey, "If we want to catch the sunset, we should be going soon!"

She came running down the stairs, ready to go.

I stretched as I rose from the couch, and spontaneously struck a yoga pose, followed by a ballet pose. I was feeling whimsical and free.

Zoey looked at the mythic fairy tales book on the coffee table and then at me. "Should I be keeping an eye on you, for signs that a gorgon in a coma has taken over your body?"

"You should definitely watch my hair for snakes." I broke from the pose and patted my sometimes-unruly red locks.

"Sure," she said, and she led me to the door.

We went outside, where the temperature was mild, and the sky was already turning lavender. I wasn't sure which direction was the best way to get to the beach, because I hadn't yet walked there directly from the house, so I let her continue leading the way.

"Corvin showed me a shortcut," she said, pulling out her phone. "I just need to check something." She angled her body so I couldn't see her screen.

I stopped and waited, admiring the purplish colors of the sky as she looked up her secret map, or whatever it was.

"This way," she said brightly, leading me past the Moore residence. I glanced over at the blue house. It was a lovely old Gothic Victorian building, similar to mine, but with a circle window in the attic. I admired their funky, goat-topped weather vane, as I usually did.

A few blocks later, Zoey said, "People don't get engaged unless they're in love, right?"

"These days, in this country, that's usually the case. But you're a clever girl and you knew that, so you must be driving at some point. Spill it."

"Have you ever noticed that whenever we walk by the Moore house, you sigh like a lovesick teenager?"

I let out a low laugh. "I do not."

She stopped walking and blocked my path on the sidewalk, facing me.

"Proof," she said, holding up her phone so I could see the screen.

It was a video from a few minutes earlier—a shaky video—of me, walking. On the bumpy video, my face tilted up. It showed me looking at something, and my whole expression changed from a pleasant one to a look of pure sadness. My lips parted, and I sighed. Audibly.

Busted.

I pushed the screen away. "Zoey, this is just proof that you're a ding-dong."

She huffed, "You're the ding-dong. Look at yourself." She started the video playing again and waved it in front of my face.

I looked into Zoey's eyes. "What's this supposed to prove? I'm envious of their weather vane, because it's got a cute little goat, and I've half a mind to get one for our house." I shoved my hands in my skirt pockets. She played it for a third time, and there was no denying what the video showed.

"Fine," I said, exasperated. "You got me, Director McDing-Dong. Great filming. I do sigh whenever we walk by Chet's house, but only because I have a crush on him."

"You're *in love* with him."

"Zoey, you're still young, but if some boy manages to pry your adorable, freckled nose out of your textbooks, you'll soon discover that love is a very complicated emotion. There are many varieties of romantic feelings, like that soft serve ice cream place with the fifty different flavors, only with an infinite number of flavors."

"If love is like soft serve ice cream with an infinite number of flavors, then Mr. Moore is strawberry swirled with coconut, which are two out of three of your favorite flavors, and the ones you always ask for, even though you believe you're mildly allergic to both."

"You're right," I said lightly. "I'm mildly allergic to Chet. Just talking about him like this is causing my chin to itch."

I rubbed my chin as I circled around her on the sidewalk, and continued walking along the street. "Let's talk about something else. I'm your parent, not your girlfriend. Remember the lectures about boundaries? The ones you regularly give me about how normal mothers should be?"

She caught up with me and linked her arm with mine. As we walked, she leaned her head against my shoulder.

"Mom, I'm just trying to look out for you."

I reached up with my free hand and patted her head. "I know."

"It's just that—" She made her adorable worked-up noise and cut herself off with her own emotions before spitting it out. "It's just that Chessa was Mr. Moore's fiancée, which means she was in love with him, so if her spirit gets into you, wouldn't that make you feel like you're in love with him?"

I stumbled over a tree root in the sidewalk. Zoey's linked arm steadied me.

"You make a good point," I admitted. "The spirits affect me in ways I can't predict." I turned to her and forced a grin. "You're worried my crush is going to get even stronger after she visits me. I'll become unbearable to everyone around me. I'll be looking out our windows at his house and sighing tragically, all hours of the day."

Zoey's cheeks reddened. She tugged my arm to turn left, and we walked diagonally through a park, past well-maintained slides and swing sets. I knew she had more to say, so I waited.

Finally, it came out in a single outburst.

"Mom, maybe Chessa has already been inside you, but she's weak, so you didn't notice. You've been different since we decided to move. And don't say that everyone's different after a move and how that's the whole point of moving. You pitched coming to Wisteria as being purely for economic and career reasons, but what if there was something else going on and you didn't see it? Remember, you didn't even know you were a witch, let alone Spirit Charmed, so you wouldn't have been expecting to get possessed. Meanwhile, this Chessa lady has been floating around without her body for a year now. What if she found you back in February, got into your head, and convinced you to find a reason to move here, all so she could use you for her own agenda?" Zoey paused long enough to inhale. "And furthermore, I'm not worried about her spirit *increasing* your crush on Mr. Moore. I'm worried that you never had a crush of your own in the first place. What if everything you feel about him, all your emotions and reactions, from the sighing to the joking around to today's yelling session in the front yard, has always come to you from *her*?"

CHAPTER 9

AFTER MY DAUGHTER'S bombshell of a theory, we walked in uneasy silence.

Chet Moore belonged to another woman, a woman whose love might have infected me like a spiritual virus.

What if everything I felt about Chet—my girlish crush, my sensual daydreams, and even my outrage at his secrecy—also belonged to her?

Even more alarming, my decision to abandon my old life and move to Wisteria might have been guided by this woman's invisible hand.

I tried to recall the exact point in time I made the choice to move, but I couldn't remember any details about where I'd been or what I'd thought. Entire weeks of my life now felt distant and dream-like.

At the time of the decision, whenever friends and coworkers asked about the move, I'd given them all the same answer. "It's just something I have to do at least once in my life, and why not now?" I'd explained that it wasn't so much a strong desire *to* move as it was a certainty that if I *didn't* move, I'd always wonder about that other life not lived. Most people understood about the special type of regret for roads not taken. My words, once spoken, felt reassuring, but underneath my practiced speech there was a lingering fear I'd made a terrible mistake.

During the weeks before the move, I'd been disturbed by anxious thoughts about accidents and illnesses. Every single bad thing that happened in the future would happen due to my move. If I stayed where I was, I'd never be crossing a street at the exact moment a truck driver in Wisteria lost control of his brakes. But as soon as I moved, I'd be setting in motion a chain of events that would eventually come back around, correcting the wrongness of me being somewhere I wasn't meant to be.

These thoughts were intrusive and constant. They wore me down. I knew it was just anxiety, but knowing the name of the beast wasn't enough to banish it.

The day the movers loaded all our earthly possessions into a big, white truck, my fear turned sharp, like the point of a pin, threatening to burst my bubble of hope. I was practically vibrating that evening, pacing the apartment of our kindly neighbor, Mrs. Hutchins. She'd invited us over for one last tuna-noodle casserole. Zoey and I would spend the night on her pull-out sofa, since our beds and sheets were already on their way to our new home.

At dinnertime, Mrs. Hutchins ordered me to stop pacing and wearing out her rug, and sit at the kitchen table. Then she opened her copy of the Bible to a dog-eared page and read, "Trust in the Lord with all thine heart; and lean not unto thine own understanding. In all thy ways acknowledge him, and he shall direct thy paths." She set the book on the table between us and gave me a meaningful look.

In response, I'd said something sassy. I couldn't remember what, exactly, but Zoey had kicked my shin under the table. I apologized for my sass, thanked Mrs.

Hutchins for her wisdom, picked up the Good Book, and read the passage myself. Over and over.

Later that evening, before bed, Mrs. Hutchins had sat with me and prayed. With her kind words and the touch of her wrinkled hand on mine, her small, sparse apartment became the most wonderful, welcoming place. I couldn't imagine leaving the comfort of her home, let alone the city in which I'd raised my daughter.

Once the lights went out, I cried silently into my pillow, careful not to disturb Zoey, who lay on the squeaky pull-out bed beside me.

I reached for the bible Mrs. Hutchins had left on the side table, and clutched it to my chest. The tears stopped flowing. I slept deeply, and in the morning, I trusted that something bigger and wiser than me was directing my path.

I had no idea it might be a gorgon.

* * *

"This way," Zoey said. "The beach is right on the other side of the path." She pointed to a gap in an old wooden fence and sniffed the air. "We're so close, you can already smell the ionization of the waves."

I hesitated and looked around. I hadn't been paying attention to my surroundings. We were in the middle of an alley—an alley belonging to wealthy people, judging by the size of the estates and height of the mansions.

"As your parent, I can't condone trespassing," I said, my brain switching into parenting mode. Compared to being manipulated by the wandering spirit of a gorgon, trespassing was the least of my worries, but sixteen years of being a single mother had created its own set of instincts.

"Mom, this is an *official* path to the beach," Zoey said, a note of contempt in her voice as she looked up at the nearest mansion. "We're still technically on city land. This is a public access point that these"—she waved at the two mansions that stood like gates on either side of the trail —"greedy private owners have tried to imply is theirs. They put up this fence without permission, and they're hoping people will just go around and forget about this way."

"They're trying to take over public access to resources?" I was already feeling worked up, but now my ire had a scapegoat. The wooden fence made me as angry as people who try to shut down library funding. I gave it a kick, knocking loose another plank. These selfish mansion owners deserved much worse. Manipulating others for their own gain? You can tell a lot about people when they try to hoard communal resources for themselves.

"Hold onto that outrage," Zoey said, leading the way through the gap in the fence. "One day when I run for mayor, you can vote for me."

"Already planning for a career in politics?" I let out a low whistle. "Your mother had better keep her reputation clean."

She chuckled. It was way too late for that.

We passed through a woodsy trail and emerged at the ocean. The sea at sunset lay before us, pretty as a postcard.

"Look at that view," Zoey said proudly. "What do you think?"

"You're talking to me like I've never seen the ocean before, but I've been to this beach thousands of times." I pointed at a small island in the distance. "That's the rocky island where the black oystercatchers—the birds with the long red beaks—hang out."

She looked at me, her eyebrows rumpled with concern. "Mom, are you trying to freak me out? You've only been to the beach two or three times since the move, and it was always cloudy or rainy. I don't think you've seen that island before."

I kicked some pebbles by my feet. She was right about my lack of beach visits. I'd been busy since the move, and while proximity to the ocean had been a deciding factor in the move, I hadn't exactly made the most of it. Yet I had the feeling I'd been to this specific beach countless times already. And now, standing at the wet edge of the gentle blue waves lapping at the shore, I felt a powerful urge to shed my clothes and dive into the water.

I caught myself unbuttoning my blouse and slowed myself. Something was happening. The invisible hands were guiding me again, leading me to the water. Was this Chessa? I heard nothing inside my head, nothing but the soft lapping of the waves. The sound of the water grew stronger as I listened. The ocean called to me, inviting me to bury my secrets within its dark waters.

I could resist the urge if I wanted to, but I didn't want to. Why not go with the flow and see where it took me?

"Something's happening," I said to Zoey calmly. "Keep an eye on me."

"As always," she joked, and then, when she realized I wasn't playing around, "What's happening? Is it the spirit?" She tilted her head and watched me unbutton my blouse. "You're acting weird. I think we should call Auntie Z."

"Not now," I said. "There's no time."

"No time for what? Are you going to take off your clothes and dance around a bonfire?" She snorted. "So much for my future career in politics. Nothing says witchcraft quite like dancing naked around a bonfire."

"No bonfire," I said, looking around. We were alone on the beach, within a cozy, protected cove. Nobody was there to see us, and the water was so lovely and light beneath the darkening sky. I finished unfastening my buttons and shrugged off my blouse. "Just keep an eye on me and see what happens."

And something was happening already. The center of my chest fluttered, and the sides of my neck tingled. The tension in my neck muscles melted away, and then melted some more. I hadn't realized how much tightness had been in my body until it was gone, and my body felt limber and pliable. Deep within my mind, the pilot light for my worry furnace blinked out. I should have been concerned, but I wasn't. Serenity washed over me like a sweet candy coating made of rainbows. Everything was as it should be.

"Mom, are you still you?" Her voice was distant, and I sensed it with more than my ears. I could taste her worry inside my own mouth, as a metallic tang.

"Zoey, you should relax and enjoy the beautiful sunset. Come into the ocean with me."

"You and who else?"

"Just me," I said. "But I could be changing shape, shifting into a dragon, or a serpent, or a monster. Does my hair look snaky?"

She took a lock of my hair and examined it closely. "It looks normal. What are you doing now? Are you seriously going to take off all your clothes? Mom!"

I was already kicking off my boots and skirt. I stripped down to my underwear, and held out my arms to feel the ocean breeze on my bare skin. My skin tightened, and not just from goose bumps. Every inch of my skin felt tougher, like a neoprene suit. The sand beneath the soles of my feet turned as soft as talcum powder.

I looked down at myself, expecting to see scales all over my body, but I was still human, still flesh. Just a redhead on the beach in her underwear. My typical underwear was pink or white, to match my pale skin, but as luck would have it, I'd put on a set of black bra and panties that morning. To any casual observer passing by in a sailboat, I would appear to be a normal woman going for a sunset dip in her bikini.

And that was exactly what I wanted to do.

But I didn't walk toward the water yet. I stood still and wondered, why was I in Wisteria? Who or what guided my decisions? Did my feelings belong to me? Did Chet...

Oh, shush. Just shush, a cool voice in my head said. *No more worries. Shhhh.*

And then all I heard was the water before me and the breeze in the trees behind me.

My thoughts about the past and the future were silent, as though someone had clicked the mute button on my worries. There was only now, this purple and blue and aquamarine sky, and the ocean, and me, merging into the blue. I walked forward, toward the waiting waters.

My daughter cried out in embarrassment, "Skinny dipping? Really, Mom?"

She wouldn't have to worry much longer about being seen with me. I would disappear soon.

I waded into the crisp, cool water. The sand here was dotted with rocks, but I knew they wouldn't cut my feet. The water lapped up my toes, my ankles, my shins. It was cold at first, then nothing. The blue ocean welcomed me like a long-lost friend. When I reached waist-high water, I tilted forward and dove under.

I opened my eyes. The water didn't sting. I saw through it as easily as air. Below me, bright-orange starfish were doing their wiggly starfish maneuvers on the craggy rocks. Seaweed floated by, tickling my legs and arms. I kicked my way along, five feet below the surface and then twenty feet. The pressure increased with depth, yet it was no problem. I could go down, down, down, as deep as I wanted.

A tiger rockfish, banded brown over a pink body, peeked out from a crevice to say hello in its fishy manner. I waved hello, catching sight of my own hand, which was not a hand, and yet I could not say what it was. Only that it was not a hand. I glanced over at my shoulder, which was no longer a shoulder, but something else. Something as soft and green as seaweed, yet hard to focus on. I was smoke. Ink. Closer to plasma than solid matter.

The tiger rockfish seemed to see something behind me, then swished away in a hurry.

I rolled in the water to see what had scared the fish. I caught a glimpse of a long, undulating arm, like that of a squid or octopus, and then it was gone. There was nothing chasing me, only me, and I was Zara, yet I was also something else. My heart might have pounded in terror, if I'd had a heart. Or arteries.

Brightness flicked around me. A Starry Flounder flashed his diamond-shaped body at me. *Tag, you're it,* he seemed to say. He flicked his tail and fled. I gave chase, my body like a flaming underwater comet.

This is fun. What's around that rock?

* * *

I eventually turned toward the surface for fresh air, even though my lungs hadn't been burning at all. As I neared the boundary between sea and sky, my body took form once more, no longer plasma or smoke or inky seaweed or whatever indescribable thing it had been.

I was me again, Queen of the Ocean, Ruler of the Sea.

I was... *what?*

The sky was purple, and the setting sun was a smoldering ball of orange. I kicked steadily, treading water, and wrapped my arms around myself to check that I was human. I was Zara again. Perhaps I'd been the Ruler of the Sea for a few minutes, but now I was a Very Wet Witch in Her Underwear.

The shoreline was much farther away than I'd expected. Zoey, barely recognizable, waved at me and shouted something. I couldn't hear the words over the distance and the slurpy sounds of the water lapping. Judging by her body language, one arm waving wildly, she wanted me to come back in. I acknowledged with a wide wave of my own, and began swimming back toward her, this time sticking to a breaststroke at the surface so she could see me. Traveling this way was much slower, and way less fun.

I was human again, but my skin was still as strong and resilient as neoprene, and my legs were not tiring.

Halfway back, I noticed a rowboat coming my way. The boat was hard to miss, being as bright and yellow as a ripe banana. I tilted upright, treading water, and waved at the boat's occupants. The rower was a man from my neighborhood, Arden, accompanied by his friendly brown labradoodle, Doodles. Arden and I had spoken a few times, usually while he was walking the dog and I was setting the garbage can out on the curb.

Arden returned my wave, and paddled nearer. The sky was darkening, night closing in around us. He frowned, straining to see me in the water, the effort making his expression seem angry. Whenever we'd chatted on Beacon Street, Arden had been pleasant. He had friendly gray eyes, receding hair, and fluffy white-gray eyebrows. The dog had equally fluffy eyebrows, though his were brown.

"Oh, it's you," he said. "Zara Riddle." He stopped paddling and sat upright with the paddle resting across the boat. "I thought you were someone else. There was another young lady who used to swim in this area, but... I should have known better."

"Hi, Arden. Hello, Doodles." I bobbed over to the edge of his yellow boat and steadied myself with my hands on the edge. The sun's rays were fading quickly, the night turning the yellow boat gray.

Doodles, who wore a red life preserver perfectly made for a dog his size, greeted me with a face lick. I leaned back and waved to Zoey on shore to let her know I was fine. She gave me an impatient wave. I held up two fingers. She crossed her arms and paced the shoreline.

Doodles had licked most of the seawater from my face. I thanked him and gently pushed him away. Dog saliva was no improvement over seawater, but I could wait to wash it off.

"I hope you're heading back to shore now," Arden said.

"Pretty much," I said. "This other young lady who used to swim around here, did she have blonde hair?"

"Uh..." Arden's fluffy eyebrows raised and lowered. The dog turned away from me and watched his master, resting his brown, curly-furred chin on Arden's knee.

I didn't have the dog's patience. I prodded the man with another question. "Was her name Chessa?"

Arden nodded slowly. He looked down at me in the water, the angle making his fluffy eyebrows completely shadow his eyes. "So, you've heard," he said gravely. "Such a sad story."

"I hear she's been in a coma for a year now."

"Has it been that long?" He gave the dog a pat on the head. "Time sure flies. Hey, that reminds me of a joke. Time flies like an arrow. Fruit flies like a banana."

"Good one," I said, laughing softly.

He played with the dog's long ears. "Whenever we bumped into Chessa out here, I'd tell her a joke. She had the strangest laugh, like a sea lion barking. Doodles here must have thought she was a sea lion, because he stopped barking at them after the first time he met her."

I looked right at the brown dog and asked, "Is it true, Doodles? Was she a sea lion, or some other sea creature?"

The dog's gaze darted between me and its master.

"She was such a cheerful young lady," Arden said. "That's why it was so shocking when she... you know."

"Arden, I don't know. What happened to her? What put her into a coma?"

He glanced around the open water. "I hate to say it, but from what I heard, she cut herself up real bad and threw herself into the water, not far from here. I heard she washed up on the shore, right over there." He glanced over at Zoey and gave her a wave.

"She cut her wrists and then tried to drown herself?"

"I heard it was more than just her wrists." His face wrinkled and contorted as he seemed to struggle, processing the idea. "The papers didn't report so much as

78

a peep about it, but that's because they tend not to publicize suicides. Talking about it has a way of pushing other people over the edge."

I gripped the edge of the yellow boat.

Suicide.

Now, that was a key point that Chet or Chloe could have kindly mentioned.

If I were to offer myself up as a medium for a wandering ghost, I'd appreciate a heads-up that the spirit in question might be suicidal. Shifting into a sea creature was a pleasant-enough surprise, but getting the urge to harm myself would not be good at all. Not at all.

CHAPTER 10

TUESDAY MORNING, I jumped out of bed and did ten jumping jacks to start my day. No way was I going to let Chessa's roaming spirit make me sad or suicidal. No way! I was going to be ten times happier than usual, if that was what it took to keep the black dog of depression at bay.

The old wood floorboards under my bare feet squeaked like applause. So I did ten more jumping jacks as an encore.

Zoey came stumbling into my bedroom, wide eyed. "I thought we were having an earthquake," she said. "I came to rescue you."

"My hero! Your jeans are on backward."

She looked down at her backward jeans, the butt of which was puffed out from the bottom of her nightshirt. "This is the style now," she said. "The front butt balances out the back butt."

I touched my toes and shifted gracefully into a plank pose. "Join me," I said. "Get both of your butts over here. There's no happier way to start your day than with joyful movement to get the blood pumping."

"Mom, that's what coffee is for." She left my room, ~~mumbling about my sanity.~~

I called after her, "Pour my coffee in a to-go mug, because I'm going to see Frank this morning."

She grunted to acknowledge my request.

It was my fault she was tired and sleepy. Whether it's magic or not, there's a finite amount of Morning Person energy available in our two-person family. Whenever one of us wakes up extra perky, the other compensates by taking the extra-grumpy end of the teeter-totter.

While she corrected her number of butts and then clattered around in the kitchen downstairs, I started getting dressed for my breakfast with Frank Wonder.

I stared at my closet for two full minutes of indecision. Why was choosing the right outfit for the day so tricky? I hadn't looked inside Chessa's closet, but based on the decor of her house, I had a feeling it was full of tasteful shades of pastel, white, and sandy brown. She almost certainly had an impeccable wardrobe, full of high-quality textiles and flattering cuts.

My wardrobe, on the other hand, could be described as eclectic, or eccentric, or a very good start for someone attending Clown College.

But now was not the time to feel regret. No. I was going to be bright and colorful and happy all day, even if it meant closing my eyes and grabbing something at random.

And what I grabbed was a pink blouse. Normally, I stay away from the color pink, as it attracts too many well-meaning comments from older ladies advising me that redheads should never wear that shade. But I do love pink just as much as any other color, plus it seemed like a fun way to honor Frank's new beginning as a flamingo shifter. And I had the perfect skirt to pair it with. If my outfit didn't scream Ten Times the Fun, I didn't know what would.

I pranced down the stairs to greet my daughter.

When Zoey saw me enter the kitchen, she dropped her spoon with a clatter.

"You must be possessed," she said.

"You think?"

I twirled, spinning out my vintage black skirt with the pink poodle embroidery. The poodle skirt was one I'd purchased from a props department sale run by a community theater group in our former hometown. The skirt had been worn during a performance of *Grease*, and it was the perfect pairing for my bright-pink blouse.

"Definitely possessed," Zoey said.

"I'm not possessed by anything but the joy of theater and dance!" I twirled again.

"We need a stun gun," she said. "Or those darts they shoot at zoo animals."

"Zoey, I'm still me." I opened my eyes wide and stared at her. "And that's our new code for when I'm not possessed—*I'm still me*—because it's something a spirit wouldn't think to say. Plus I'll stare at you, like this." I made my eyes so wide, they began to water.

She watched me closely as she poured steaming coffee into a travel mug for me. "Are you planning to go swimming again later today?"

"If I do, I'll give you some warning." I gathered my hair into a high ponytail to complete my vintage 1950s look. "I'm sorry I gave you a scare last night."

She sniffed and looked away. She would deny it, but she'd been frightened when I'd waded into the ocean and disappeared under the water. She'd called my aunt on her cell phone before I'd even resurfaced.

By the time I finished my chat with Arden in his yellow boat and got back to shore, Zinnia had been brought up to speed on the whole Chessa-gorgon situation. Zoey told me as much as she patted the side of my head dry with the sleeve of her sweatshirt before handing me her phone.

My aunt's voice came from the tiny speaker. "Zara, did ~~you shift into another creature? Zoey said you were~~ underwater for a long time. Longer than five minutes."

"Something happened, but I couldn't have shifted." I looked down at my wet body. "I'm still wearing my underwear." I was also wearing Chessa's bracelet, the sea glass glinting in the disappearing light.

"Your underwear?"

Zoey hadn't told her *everything* after all. "I mean I'm still wearing my bathing suit," I lied. "It would have fallen off if I'd turned into, say, a sea lion."

"Zara, shifting is not an organic change, like a caterpillar turning into a butterfly. It's magic, and magic has a mind of its own. The clothes can shift with you, and then back again."

"Are you sure about that?" The one time I'd seen Chet shift, he'd been naked when he changed back. That was an image I couldn't shake from my memory. His clothes hadn't shifted. But then again, when Frank had changed into his flamingo form in the staff lounge, he didn't leave any clothes behind. There was still so much I had to learn about magic and shifters.

"The only thing we can be certain of with magic is that it's uncertain."

"Maybe I did shift," I said. "Do you think it's permanent? Like, I'm a shifter now? Witch plus shifter. I'd be a double threat."

"We ought to conduct some controlled experiments," Zinnia said.

"It's not totally dark yet. I could go dive back in."

"No! Don't!"

"Okay. I'll wait."

"Zara, you must resist your impulsive urges to dash madly into the face of danger. Safety should be your top priority."

"Absolutely," I said while giving Zoey a slight eye roll and stuck out my tongue to let her know I was getting a lecture.

"Stop making fun of me," Zinnia said.

"Can you see me?" I looked around the protected beach cove. Zoey and I were still alone.

Zinnia sighed. "Were you even listening?"

"Yes. You were saying it would be a disaster if I accidentally cast two conflicting spells on myself and got killed, like that time you killed me."

She paused before finally saying, "I know you're attempting to give me a hard time, but I'm afraid that particular incident only underscores my point about safety."

"Safety first," I agreed. "Hey, thanks for comforting Zoey today when I went underwater, and thanks for being our mentor. Let's meet up soon, okay?"

"What's that sound? Are your teeth chattering?"

"No," I said, but my teeth chattered even louder. "Yes," I admitted. "It gets chilly after the sun goes down and your skin turns back to regular human skin."

She told me to go and get myself warm at home, and ended the call abruptly.

Zoey helped me get my clothes back on, both of us mystified by how difficult it is to get clothes over damp skin.

"You're so sticky," Zoey said. "Are you sweating glue?"

"I don't think so. This is just a taste of how difficult life would be if nobody had invented towels."

"Towels are pretty magical," Zoey said with reverence.

"They truly are." I wrestled the sleeve of my blouse over my damp arm then paused to appreciate the everyday magic of towels.

Zoey took one last look out at the dark sky and ocean. "What was it like?"

"Beautiful," I said. "Like being inside one of those underwater documentaries shot by scuba divers."

"Maybe I should take up scuba diving," Zoey said. "That way I can keep up with you whenever you turn into a mermaid."

I squealed. "You saw me turn into a mermaid?"

"Maybe I saw something green glinting, just under the water, but I can't be sure."

"We should watch *The Little Mermaid* tonight, for research."

She laughed. "And we have to sing all the songs, too. For research."

We walked home by the same route, the shortcut feeling sinister in the dark.

Back at the house, we huddled on the couch together, watching the Disney movie. We hadn't seen it in years, and while we didn't learn anything new about being a mermaid, we did laugh as we sang along with the songs.

After the movie, Zoey went to her room to read, and I took a hot bath in the claw-foot tub. I kept having to add more hot water. There was a chill in my bones that couldn't be banished. After my underwater swim, I couldn't deny that I was changing, under the influence of something or someone.

If I had Chessa's abilities, I might also have her emotions. And not just her tender feelings toward Chet, but all of her emotions.

Had she really tried to kill herself? Whatever drove her to cut her arms and throw herself into the ocean could become my fate as well. In trying to save Chessa, I could lose myself.

Despite my efforts to exercise and be cheerful the next morning, the weight of dread pooled inside me, dark and inky.

No, I told myself. *No inky pools of dread.* Not today.

I forced a smile, kissed my daughter on the cheek, and got ready to leave the house, snapping the lid on my travel mug of coffee.

"Have fun at school," I told Zoey.

"Have fun at work," she said. "Say hello to Frank for me."

"I will." At the mention of Frank, I checked on the three pink feathers in my purse. They were still solid and pink, unchanged. There was so much for me to learn about magic and shifting, and I was excited. Not depressed or suicidal at all. Just excited, with a side dish of anxious.

I called a taxi to take me to Frank's place.

CHAPTER 11

THE TAXI DRIVER knew the address for the Candy Factory. He dropped me off at a tall redbrick building that evidently was a former factory turned into modern lofts.

Frank was getting his mail from the communal brass boxes when I walked up to the glass doors. He looked rested and ready to vault off a springboard into a triple twist. He'd been an Olympic hopeful in his youth, and even at fifty-five, he moved with a flexible ease on his skinny legs, which were currently clad in a pair of orange paisley trousers.

Frank saw me approaching the door, and flashed me a bright smile of teeth so white, they were blue. He opened the door and greeted me with a hug. His dyed-pink hair seemed eerily prophetic, now that I knew about his flamingo side.

"Good morning to you, foxy redhead," he said.

"You've been underselling your apartment building," I said, gesturing up to the avant-garde chandelier at the peak of the lofty entry. "The way you talk about your low-maintenance place, I pictured something more modest. This place isn't ostentatious, but you have to admit it's fabulous." I ran my hands over the exposed bricks of the interior wall. "And it was a candy factory?" I licked my lips. "Just imagine all the delicious caramel and sugar treats that were made inside here. If these walls could talk, they would say, 'Here, have a candied apple.'"

Frank snickered and nodded for me to follow him into the stairwell.

"I'm glad that's what you hear the walls saying," he said. "Because 'Have a candied apple' is much better than 'Die, die, die!'" He gave me a knowing look and paused for drama before continuing up the stairwell. "This old building did house a business that made candy, at some point, but it was also the base of operations for a pest control company for nearly two decades. You could say the poison of choice was *actual poison*. It was owned by the Wick family during that time. And before that, well, let's just say the developer who converted it into lofts was smart to downplay that particular period of Wisteria history."

I stopped caressing the exposed brick walls. "Was it a leper colony?" I shook my head. "No, it's too grand a building, and there are plenty of small islands off the coast that would have served better for a leprosarium."

"You're getting warmer."

"And you're really going to make me guess, aren't you?" I touched the wall again, and experienced a sensation of loneliness and gloom, along with a feeling of claustrophobia. I suddenly wanted out, and feared I'd never escape. Underneath that, I feared what I would do if I did escape. "It was a prison," I said coldly. "A prison for the criminally insane."

"Correct." We'd reached the door of Frank's place, on the third floor. He gave me a look of admiration as he ushered me in.

Once he'd closed the dark wooden door behind us, he said, "That was wonderful, Zara. It must be so exciting to be a witch, and such a powerful one. I don't throw many parties, but I've had a few visitors over the years, and not one of them has inferred the building's original purpose without a plethora of hints."

"It was a lucky guess." I rubbed the chill off my forearms as I looked up at the exposed wood beams, half expecting to see a ghostly noose and semi-transparent skeletons hanging from the rafters.

But there were no ghouls on the ceiling, or anything upsetting about the inside of the lofted apartment. Frank's decor was thoughtful and minimal, a mix of country-style antiques and clean-lined modern pieces. The foreboding I'd experienced in the stairwell was gone. Frank Wonder's personal living space was downright cozy, a reflection of his warm personality.

Frank was at the stove, standing over a sizzling pan. "Omelet?"

"If that's what I'm smelling, yes, please." I took a seat at the bar-style counter where I could watch him cook. As he offered me a coffee, I realized I'd forgotten my half-full takeout mug in the taxi. This forgetfulness was cause for concern. Was Chessa a tea drinker? Had she been possessing me during the taxi ride over? It wasn't like me to lose coffee.

Frank served me a lovely breakfast that was only diminished slightly by his joke about producing the eggs for the omelet himself. I pretended to gag, we both laughed, and we got down to discussing the proverbial elephant in the room.

I held back telling him about my underwater swim and possible shifting ability. This morning's social call was all about Frank, and his new shifter powers. I wouldn't be rude and overshadow his excitement with the idea that I could be a real-life Ariel the Mermaid.

Frank was eager to talk about his newly discovered flamingo shifter abilities. He told me it hadn't hurt at all to shift back and forth, and once he'd calmed down and gotten back to human form, he'd changed back one more time under the supervision of Dr. Bob at the DWM. He'd been discharged with a clean bill of health, and now, after a good night's sleep, he'd never felt better. I told him I was so happy for him.

"Before this, I dreamed about flying every night of my life," Frank said. "And yesterday, after I actually did fly, I dreamed I was bowling."

"Uh. Congratulations?"

"I bowled a perfect game," he said proudly. "And I had other dreams, too, which is new for me, because it's usually just flying."

"Your subconscious is moving on to new things."

"I'll say. Who knows what I'll do next?" He took a break from eating toast to fidget with his dyed-pink hair. "The creature inside me has been dormant for so long, dreaming about getting free, but it took a good shock from a witch to break me out of my shell." He gave me an earnest look. "I can't thank you enough, Zara."

I retrieved the feathers from my purse and placed them on the counter. "I found these on the floor at the library," I explained. "Since then, they haven't shifted back or disappeared. I kept them out of curiosity, to see what would happen." I felt myself blush. "Nothing happened, and now I feel creepy about bagging parts of your body as evidence."

Frank snorted a laugh and picked up the plastic bag. "Nonsense. These are wonderful souvenirs of my first time shifting. I might get them framed." He held the bag up to the light streaming in through an overhead skylight. "Yes. I *will* have these feathers framed, and I will *proudly* hang them on my wall." He looked at me. "Do you have any souvenirs of your own, from when you first turned into a witch?"

"Nothing you could frame," I said. "There was the Murder Toaster, but I turned that over to the police."

"Murder Toaster?" Frank sucked in a breath excitedly. "We don't have long before work, so talk fast, Zara. Talk fast!"

I rose to the challenge, and—after the reassurance of secrecy—filled him in on all spirit-related shenanigans from recent months. I felt bad about hogging the conversation when I wanted to hear more about his time at the DWM, but he insisted nothing interesting had happened beyond a physical examination and a few hours of talk therapy with the staff doctor.

We agreed that we were both glad to have someone to talk to about our secrets.

As he tidied up the kitchen, Frank said, "Since we're being completely honest here, I want to know how you got the librarian job. Did you cast a spell?"

I swore to him that I hadn't, and couldn't have, because my witch powers hadn't activated until my daughter's birthday. I'd gotten the job the regular way. There weren't any librarian postings at my local libraries, so I'd done a national search online and seen the listing for Wisteria. I'd never even heard of the town before, but I applied anyway.

"Impossible," Frank said. "We have a huge waiting list of applicants, so we don't advertise at all, let alone in national databases."

"Weird," I said, and then I thought of my first "accidental" meeting with Zinnia, and her insistence that she'd had nothing to do with my move, other than writing the reference letter when asked about me by the head librarian.

I looked down at the silver-wire-and-sea-glass bracelet on my wrist. *Magic has a mind of its own.*

Frank leaned over his kitchen counter and examined the bracelet. "This bracelet belongs to the other woman? The tragically moribund Chessa?"

"She's not dead yet. But yes, it's hers. And it's possible she was the invisible hand guiding me here, to Wisteria."

"You think a ghost made a national job posting on the Internet just for you?"

I pursed my lips and swished them back and forth, processing. "It sounds crazy when you say it out loud. But then again, so does pretty much everything that's been happening to me lately."

"Well, however or whatever or whomever it was leading you here to Wisteria, you need to be careful." He glanced up at the skylight, smiled at the blue sky, and then slowly lowered his chin. He gazed at me with a peaceful expression. "Be careful of this sea devil, this snake-haired seductress." His words of warning didn't match his relaxed expression, which made it all the more disturbing.

I swallowed hard. Frank was gullible enough to open a can of spring-coiled fake snakes, but he also had one of the sharpest minds of anyone I'd known. If he also suspected Chessa was behind my cross-country move, it wasn't such a crazy stretch.

"You really think she's a sea devil? Did you meet her sister, Charlize, when you were at the DWM?"

"Briefly," he said. "She didn't show me her shifter form, though."

"Consider yourself lucky." I fidgeted with the loose bracelet. "Did you learn much about how the shifter trait runs in families?"

"No, but I was only there for a few hours. Dr. Bob said he'd be in touch soon. Why?"

"On the taxi ride over here, I noticed an interesting graphic on the driver's shirt. He'd been to Singapore recently, and was wearing a souvenir T-shirt with a *merlion* on it—that's a mythical creature with a lion's head and the body of a fish."

"You think Chessa might turn you into a merlion?" He picked up a bag of coffee and pointed to the familiar Starbucks logo. "What about a mermaid? As far as sea witches go, at least mermaids are beautiful and alluring." He paused and narrowed his eyes at me. "There's something you're not telling me. Come on, Zara. No more secrets."

I grinned and nodded. I was lucky to have such a sharp-minded friend. I hurriedly told him about my adventure at the beach the night before, how I'd been drawn to the ocean, disappearing from Zoey's sight for several minutes.

Frank squinted at me. "Why didn't you look at yourself and see what you were? As soon as I turned into a flamingo, I knew what I was."

"I don't know." I shrugged. "My arm looked like smoke, and I think I saw some tentacles behind me, but it might have been a passing squid."

"Weird. You need to get the skinny on Chessa's abilities, either from her fiancé or her sisters."

"They're so secretive," I said. "But I'm going to demand some answers before I help any more."

"Good. You need to know if you're going to suddenly turn into a merlion."

"Or something worse," I said. "There are so many sea-based creatures. There's Charybdis from *The Odyssey*, who causes massive whirlpools. Or, the Inuit Myths talk about Qalupalik, a humanoid creature with green skin who lives in the sea. This baddie makes a creepy humming sound before showing up to steal children. Then there's the Dobhar-chú, a primitive beaver, or a dog-otter combo thing from Irish Folklore. Sounds cute, but you won't like the Dobhar-chú when it's hungry... for your meaty flesh."

Frank clutched his hands to his chest with a theatrical gasp. "You wouldn't devour your friend!"

I shrugged playfully.

His eyes widened. "But I'm so old and sinewy. Yuck. You'd have to cook me for two days in a pot of wine, like *coq au vin*."

I nodded at the mermaid logo on the Starbucks coffee. "Don't worry. If Chessa's not a gorgon after all, she's probably something sweet and alluring. A woman with a house so lovely wouldn't be an icky monster."

"Don't be so sure of that. She could be overcompensating."

"Or she could be a beautiful, kind mermaid."

Frank raised his eyebrows. "Or she could be the evil seductress type of siren who sings, calling sailors to their deaths."

"I'm hoping for more of a clumsy redheaded princess who sings happy songs about life under the sea."

"I'd pay good money to see that," Frank said.

He and I discussed sea creatures of lore and legend while we finished tidying the kitchen.

I did my share of the dishes the traditional way, using my hands. I'd showed Frank my levitation skills, but I could see he wasn't entirely comfortable being around flying utensils. Not yet.

We were about to leave for work when Frank stopped me at the door.

Hesitantly, he said, "Do you trust me to try something?"

I took a step back. "Go ahead. Shift away."

"Not that." He smiled sheepishly. "I was thinking about trying something for your problem." He shuffled his feet. "Growing up, I had an uncle who called himself a shaman."

"You come from a supernatural family? That explains a lot."

He scrunched one side of his face. "Not exactly. Uncle Felix usually announced he was a shaman somewhere between drink five and drink seven. He would gather the family around, get everyone worked up, and then put on a show, summoning spirits. The thing is, a few times, it seemed to work. Silverware would rise up into the air, chandeliers would swing, and doorbells would ring on their own."

"Spooky," I said, rubbing my forearms. That explained why my floating spoon demonstration had made him uneasy. Even being a witch and having the ability to do all those things myself didn't take away the tingle I got from hearing ghost stories.

Frank reached for the door handle. "Never mind," he said. "My uncle's been dead for years, and while I do a hilarious impression of him that cracks up everyone in the family, it's a stupid idea for me to try to talk directly to this sea-witch spirit that may or may not be haunting you."

I stopped him with a hand on his arm. "No, Frank. It's not a stupid idea. And even if it doesn't work, I'd enjoy this supposedly hilarious impression of your uncle."

"Okay, then. Brace yourself for Uncle Felix." Frank rubbed his hands, and then mimed tossing back a drink, followed by four more. I had to admire his commitment to the impression.

He took my hands, closed his eyes, and let out a low, guttural moan.

"Spirits of the deep," he intoned. "I call upon you to visit the living, here in the mortal realm."

The hairs on the back of my neck stood up.

He continued. "Spirits of the deep, I call upon the one named Chessa, the one who walks between the living and the dead, the one who has been missed by her beloved sisters and beloved beau for twelve long months." He trembled. His eyelashes fluttered, but his eyes remained closed. "Spirits of the deep, I ask you for an audience. If Chessa is the reason why Zara Riddle was drawn to Wisteria, show us a sign."

The floorboards around us squeaked. Neither of us had moved an inch from where we stood, just inside Frank's door. Something at the edge of my vision moved. Was it the door handle, turning? If it had been, it stopped.

Frank moaned again.

The hairs on the back of my neck, as well as on my forearms, could not be more upright.

"Chessa," he hissed. "Chessa, show yourself!"

The fierceness of his command startled me, but not as much as the icy sensation on my wrist. Something cold gripped me tightly, to the point of pain. My bracelet unclasped itself and fell to the floor with a clatter.

"Don't trust him," Frank whispered, his voice hoarse and otherworldly. "Be afraid."

Frank's eyes flew open, and he yanked his hands from mine.

CHAPTER 12

THE ICY CHILL on my wrist spread throughout my body.

I repeated Frank's words as a question. "Don't trust him? Be afraid?"

His wide-open eyes were blank. "What? Did I say that?"

"Don't joke around," I said.

"I swear I wasn't joking around," Frank said. "That must have been our *sign* from the Spirits of the Deep. Unfortunately, I have no idea what I meant by it."

The chill in my body was already dissipating. I cleared my throat self-consciously. What were we doing?

I looked down at the bracelet on the floor. "That might have been a sign, I guess. Or a loose clasp."

"Do you feel anything?"

I put my hands on my waist and adjusted the waistband of my puffy black skirt with the pink poodle embroidery. "I feel overdressed."

"Besides that," he said patiently.

I rubbed my wrist, recalling the chilly sensation I'd felt. "I did feel something where the bracelet was, like an icy cold hand, or a metal handcuff."

"A sign." Frank nodded gravely. "Uncle Felix would take anything, even the smallest draft that flickered a candle, as a sign from the other realm. Or as a sign that his drink needed a refill."

"It's too early for drinking, right?" I gave him a sidelong look.

"Sadly, yes."

"We should be getting to our jobs at the library. I'll keep wearing the bracelet, unless you think this was a sign she doesn't want me to borrow her stuff?"

He knelt and picked up the silver-and-sea-glass bracelet. "It might have been a coincidence. This clasp is loose, and you were fussing with it for a while before I called upon the Spirits of the Deep."

"Speaking of Spirits of the Deep, isn't that a song?"

Frank stood and helped me fasten the bracelet back onto my wrist. "You're thinking of 'Rolling in the Deep,' by Adele."

"I love that song."

"Me, too. We can listen in my car on the way to work."

* * *

We left the apartment, took the elevator down to the underground parkade, and started out for work in Frank's car.

It was another beautiful summer day in Wisteria.

Frank asked, "Shall we roll back the convertible top and crank the Adele tunes?"

"Actually, if you don't mind, I'd love to phone Chet and see if I can get more information about his fiancée."

"Good idea. We can research gorgons and sea monsters at work today."

"Assuming she is one. Just because her other triplet sisters have snakes for hair doesn't mean she does, too."

"What makes you so sure?" Frank stopped the car and checked both ways before making a left turn toward the library. "Oh! This must be intuition from your psychic connection with coma girl."

"Hold that thought," I said, turning to show him the phone at my ear. "It's ringing."

Three rings later, Chet answered his phone with a gruff sound that passed for *hello*.

"Did I catch you in the middle of something, Mr. Moore?" I didn't know why I was calling him Mr. Moore, but it made me smile.

He hesitated before answering. "I've got some time." He added, seemingly as an afterthought, "For you."

I put him on speakerphone so Frank could listen.

"Mr. Moore, I've decided to help you communicate with your fiancée, but I do have some concerns. If I'm going to do this for you, I'll be putting myself at risk. It's only fair that you start being more forthcoming with me."

"I can't exactly go around telling everyone classified information," he said, his tone defensive.

I looked over at Frank, in the driver's seat. He widened his eyes in a *yeah-right* expression that probably matched my own.

Chet continued, in a more even tone, "Zara, I've kept some details close to my chest—"

"Your hairy werewolf chest!"

He growled with displeasure at being called a werewolf, just as I knew he would.

"Go on," I said, happy with myself for tipping him off balance.

"Zara, you may discover I haven't always been completely honest with you, but I have my reasons. Go ahead and ask me whatever you want to know, and I'll do my best."

"What kind of shifter creature is Chessa?"

"That's classified."

"But her triplet sisters are gorgons, right?"

"Also classified."

"Chet, I saw their hair snakes! With my own eyes!"

He paused. "This is not a secure phone line."

"Fine." I adjusted the bracelet, which had felt chilly ever since dropping to the floor. "I guess this whole thing can wait until we have a secure connection. If any spirits show up today, I'll tell them to take a number and come back later. I'm installing one of those deli number systems inside my head."

"That's funny," he said.

"If it's so funny, why aren't you laughing, Mr. Moore?"

"I don't know. And stop calling me that. It's weird."

I swallowed hard and spat out my most pressing question. "Was Chessa suicidal?"

"No!" He sounded flustered, like a man discovering he'd walked into a trap. "No, she wasn't suicidal. She had her problems, but she was full of life."

"Then how did she wind up with her arms slashed, washed up on shore?"

He paused again, and when he spoke, the phone connection was so eerily clear, it was as though he sat in the front seat between us. "You've made contact." He let out an audible breath, crystal clear over the phone's speaker.

I flicked my bracelet again. I'd learned of her reported suicide from my neighbor, not from direct contact. But between the underwater swimming and this morning's bracelet sign, I'd apparently made some sort of connection. Enough to justify fudging the truth. "Sure. You could say that."

There was the sound of fingers typing on a keyboard. "We're bringing you in tonight. I've cleared you for access to the ward, so you can see her. You can sit with her. And I'll be there the whole time."

"Can Frank come along?"

"Who?" Chet sounded genuinely confused. "The flamingo? No way. If he knows what's good for him, he'll stay clear of DWM business. Tell him to stick to the library, and his human form, where he doesn't put our entire operation at risk like a wild pink bird on the loose."

Flatly, I said, "I'll be sure and let Mr. Wonder know that you send your warmest regards."

"Keep your schedule clear tonight," Chet said. "I'll be in touch as soon as I can." He made a grunt that sounded like good-bye, and ended the call.

I put the phone in my purse and turned to watch Frank for a reaction.

We were already at the library, pulling the car into the staff parking lot.

"Your beau has a mean side," Frank said.

"I'm sorry he was so rude about you," I said.

Frank shrugged it off, but I'd seen the hurt on his face. "In my fifty-five years on the planet, I've heard far worse."

"He would never have said that if he knew you were listening."

"Well, you can't blame him for being sore about a big pink bird flying around the city." He tilted his head to the side. "Do you suppose that's why Wisteria has such a well-stocked zoo despite being a relatively small town? Could the zoo be a handy cover story for various shifter operations? I can think of at least two times in the past year alone that there was a story on the news about escaped zoo animals wreaking havoc."

"Well done, Sherlock Holmes. I do believe you've uncovered one of Wisteria's many mysteries."

Frank beamed with pride as we got out of the car and walked toward the library in the morning sunshine.

I didn't dare burst Frank's bubble by suggesting that the zoo might be more than just a cover story. The tourist attraction could very well be stocked with certain supernatural residents of Wisteria, trapped in their animal states. Locked up in cages, forced to live as zoo animals.

No, Frank didn't need to hear about that.

CHAPTER 13

THE FIRST PART of Tuesday morning went by quietly. At half past ten, Kathy, the head librarian, went for her coffee break, leaving me alone at the circulation desk.

The minute I was on my own, in walked a serious-looking man in a dark suit. He was average height, around forty, with dark hair turning steely gray at the temples. He didn't come wandering in, nor did he stroll. He marched with a purposeful stride, straight toward me.

"Zara Riddle," he said coolly. "Right where I expected you to be. How reassuring."

I fluttered my eyelashes. "Detective Bentley! What a surprise to see you here, in the big building where we keep all the books. Would you like a tour?" More eyelash fluttering. "Or do you have to get back to... *detecting* things, or handing out parking tickets, or whatever it is you do when you're not checking up on your fellow municipal employees?"

"If that's how you treat a man bringing you a gift, I'd hate to imagine the abuse I'd receive if I showed up unprepared."

He placed a white bakery box on the counter between us. A sweet vanilla aroma rose from the box, and a pleasant cologne scent came from the detective. He was much cuter than I'd given him credit for. Had his jaw always been so chiseled and strong? Maybe it was just his proximity to fresh baked goods.

"Detective Bentley, I'm sure you've never been unprepared a day in your life."

He almost smiled.

We both looked down at the white box.

I pulled a letter opener from a drawer, and ripped through the Gingerbread House sticker affixing the lid. Inside were eleven rainbow sprinkle donuts and one chocolate éclair.

"How thoughtful," I said. "It's a shame someone got to the bakery before you and snapped up the twelfth rainbow sprinkle donut." I closed the box and gave him a smile of my own, warm enough to melt the éclair. "Is this a bribe? What can I do for you in return? Have any pernicious perps you'd like me to shake down with my cheap, fake-magic tricks?"

"Pernicious perps," he said, evidently amused by my turn of phrase. "Perhaps you can be of help to me another time."

"Thanks for the donuts, anyway."

"I must be honest, Ms. Riddle. This is a gift from Chloe Taub. She assured me you'd understand the gesture. You do know whom I'm referring to, don't you? Chloe and her husband are the owners of the Gingerbread House."

"I know who she is." But did *he* know who she was, I wondered. Or *what* she was? "Thank you for the delivery." I reached into my pocket, grabbed a loose bill and handed it over. "Keep the change."

His mouth tightened, yet he took the money and slipped it into his tailored gray suit jacket without breaking eye contact. The bill had been a twenty. *Totally worth it.*

Detective Bentley started to turn away, then stopped. With a casual air, he said, "Since I'm here anyway, might you direct me to the section about amnesia?"

"Fiction or nonfiction?"

His upper lip twitched. "It's regarding Dorothy Tibbits, so you tell me."

"I hear she's suffered some kind of terrible illness," I said. "Rumor is, she's as blank as a water-damaged hard drive. Is it true?"

He turned back toward the counter, put his elbows on the surface and, moving slowly, leaned over to look down at my puffy, fifties-style skirt. Then my legs. My ankles and shoes. Then back up again, slowly, his steely gray eyes in no hurry.

"You're wearing a poodle skirt," he said.

"Ten points for the detective. You certainly know your fancy dog breeds."

"This attempt you're making to modernize is to be commended. The last time I saw you, you looked like you'd just stepped off a pioneer wagon train. Now you're all the way up to the 1950s." He nodded. "Very interesting."

I felt my cheeks getting warm from the compliment. Technically, Detective Bentley had made an *observation*, not an actual compliment. But the look in his steely gray eyes was *very* complimentary. Especially when he leaned over the counter to take a second look at my legs.

"Amnesia," I said with a professional brightness. "That will be under call number 612.82, where you'll find a few books about the hippocampus and memory." I plucked a note card from the stack we kept at the counter. "Shall I jot down the call number for you?"

He tapped his temple. "No need. I have a memory like a steel trap."

After a third peek over the counter at my exposed calves, he turned and headed off in the direction of the Human Physiology range of shelves.

The instant Detective Bentley had disappeared around a corner, Frank appeared at my side. He had an uncanny ability to detect both donuts and handsome male patrons. Frank grabbed the bakery box, peered inside, and squealed with happiness.

"I'll take these into the break room for Kathy," he said. "As soon as she's done with her break, I'd like a meeting with you to discuss recent developments." He gave me a serious look.

* * *

Ten minutes later, Frank and I were digging into the rainbow sprinkle donuts.

"You've been holding out on me," Frank said.

"Now what?"

"You never told me about the volcanic heat that's been building between you and Mr. Gray Suit."

"Volcanic heat? Between me and Bentley?" I rolled my eyes. "When you were at the DWM, did this Dr. Bob fellow check your eyesight?"

"My eyesight is perfect in both forms. I'm telling you, Zara, I saw the way Mr. Gray Suit was looking at you, and I nearly caught on fire."

I snorted. "Detective Bentley? Please. I've been trying to set him up with my aunt."

"Why?"

"Because he's close to her age, and... I don't know." *Because I thought Chet and I were a done deal.*

"That detective has got your number, girl." He licked his fingers and grabbed a second donut. "Forget about Chet Moore. That beau is a no-beau. But anyone who brings pastries has my seal of approval."

"These are a peace offering from Chloe," I said, and I relayed my conversation with Bentley.

That led to us going over everything I knew about Dorothy Tibbits and her recent bout of amnesia. Frank was confused by my recent body-swapping adventures, so I mapped it all out on a napkin.

After a few questions, he clarified, "Dorothy Tibbits left her body in police custody, and possessed this Josephine girl, whose father was building a doomsday device."

"It was an Erasure Machine, but close enough. It would be a doomsday device for anyone who got their mind wiped by it."

"And, at the same time, some other unknown bad guy or girl took over your body after your aunt killed you."

"After she *accidentally* transferred my soul out of my body, yes."

"I have a theory." Frank took the pen from my hand, rotated the napkin, and began adding to the stick figure that represented my body. The lines he added were curly and snake-like, coming from my head. "What do you think?"

My mouth turned sour. Before I could respond to Frank's shocking new theory, one of our pages came in for her shift and greeted us cheerfully. I snatched the napkin from the table and shoved it into the pocket of my poodle skirt.

I waited for the page to leave, but she didn't. Her shift didn't start for half an hour, and she was settling in to do some reading.

Frank was waiting patiently for my response to his theory. I pulled out the crumpled napkin and looked at the drawing of myself, in the Pressmans' attic, with snake hair.

On that horrible night, someone had taken control of my body, and I didn't believe it was simply the ghost of the senior Pressman. It was someone much more powerful, someone evil. Someone working on bigger schemes.

Frank nodded for me to meet him in the alcove where we kept the cleaning supplies.

I followed him into the alcove, where I whispered, "I think you're onto something."

He raised his pink eyebrows. "You agree that coma-girl Chessa has already taken your body for a full test-drive. The picture certainly fits."

I crossed my arms over myself protectively. "She might want a new body, but I'm not done with this one yet."

"You need to be very careful," Frank warned. "Don't go to the DWM tonight with Chet. I have a bad feeling about this."

"Listen, if she could take over my body any time, she'd have done so already. The test-drive last week could have been a crime of opportunity, made possible by my zany aunt's spell."

Frank snapped his fingers. "Your aunt! You need to get some lotions or potions from her. Something that will act like a barrier." He gestured at my pink-bloused, poodle-skirted body. "We need something to keep Zara on the inside and spirits on the outside."

"Don't think I haven't asked. My aunt is looking into a few things, but for now, all I have is my impeccable fashion sense."

He handed me a jar of petroleum jelly. "Here."

I gave him a skeptical look. "Vaseline? You want me to grease myself up for protection? Is this Holy Vaseline?"

He gave me a patient smile. "It's for the stack of leather-bound reference volumes that need some softening up." He winked. "That's why you and I met here in this alcove, remember? We certainly didn't meet here to have an affair. I'm not dreamy Detective Bentley."

I rolled my eyes and left the alcove.

The page who was reading barely glanced up from her book.

I glanced through the door leading to the circulation desk. Detective Bentley was currently checking out a stack of books, including a few about brain injuries.

I lingered in the staff room to kill a few more minutes. After a while, I asked the page, "What are you reading?"

"It's a book about Werner Herzog," she said dreamily. "He played a bad guy in the first Jack Reacher movie, but he's also a German movie director. He makes films about heroes with impossible dreams, or people with unique talents."

"Impossible dreams and unique talents? That sounds like... some people I know."

She replied, "His quotes are so funny and so *illuminating*." She closed the book and jumped off her chair. "Smoke break," she said apologetically. "I know, I should quit. I only started smoking to annoy my mom, and now I'm hooked."

After she left, I opened the book and riffled the pages. My aunt had taught me her spell for finding things in books. I performed the spell, and jokingly asked the book to show me something *illuminating*.

The book parted to reveal a quote:

"What would an ocean be without a monster lurking in the dark? It would be like sleep without dreams." - Werner Herzog

"Very cheeky," I whispered to the book. "That sounds an awful lot like something you borrowed from Steinbeck. Let me guess. The ocean is a metaphor for consciousness, and Chessa is the monster within ourselves?" I smiled at my private joke. It sounded exactly like something a German director might say to explain an art film.

The book wasn't finished. The pages began flipping again. I tried to clear my mind, to erase my previous instruction, but the pages flipped with a fury. One page suddenly ripped itself free of the book and shot into the air. The torn page swayed through the air, tacking from side to side before settling on the table like a fallen autumn leaf.

On the page was another quote by Werner Herzog: "*I believe the common denominator of the universe is not harmony, but chaos, hostility, and murder.*"

"Thanks," I said dryly to the book. "Good job illuminating for me." I gently closed the cover.

I slowly backed away, leaving the book on the table.

Later in the day, I was still pondering the book's ominous warnings when I got a text message from my neighbor.

Chet Moore wrote: *Cleared for access tonight. I'll pick you up at the end of your shift and we'll go straight down to hell.*

I wrote back: *Straight down to hell? No way. Count me out.*

He replied: *Damn autocorrect. I meant *straight down to say hello.**

Sure, you did. Because who would willingly go straight down to hell?

CHAPTER 14

"INTERESTING THEORY, BUT it wasn't Chessa in your body that night," Chet said, his eyes on the road ahead.

He'd picked me up from the library at the end of my shift, and we were now in a Department of Water and Magic van, heading toward the secret DWM headquarters. I wanted more answers than I'd squeezed out of him on the phone that morning, but I didn't dare cast my bluffing spell again. I had to rely on my regular human powers of persuasion, appealing to his logical side. Flattery wouldn't hurt, either.

"But why not?" I asked calmly. "It's only logical. You're a smart guy, so I'm sure it's crossed your mind before now. She's a powerful entity in need of a working body, and my body was available that night. Think about it."

He took his eyes off the road and glanced over at me, his expression bordering on playful, much to my surprise. "*You* think about it," he said.

"I've been thinking about it all day. I can't stop thinking about it. In fact, if that light up ahead turns red and you stop the van, I might jump out, grab a ~~broomstick, fly to my house on that broomstick, never~~ mind that I don't know how to fly, then pack my things, and get on the next bus leaving this town. Or if there's no bus, I'll jump on yet another broomstick."

The light turned yellow, and he sped through the intersection. "Zara, I know it wasn't Chessa in your body, because whoever it was tried to kill me."

"Did it, really? Everything happened so fast. She might have miscommunicated."

"Your theory is preposterous. Whoever was controlling your body, they had one goal, and that was to feed me to the machine for fuel." He turned his full attention back to the road and shuddered. "You know, sometimes my clothes will wrinkle against my skin a certain way, and for an instant, I can feel those tentacles sliding over me, finding the perfect places to pierce my skin."

"That's awful," I said. "Does the DWM have a staff therapist you can talk to, or some kind of PTSD treatment?"

"Forget I said anything," he growled abruptly. "I'm fine."

"Well, if not for you, since you're such a big, strong man who doesn't need help, then how about for me?"

He gave me a questioning glance. "Do you think you need a therapist?"

"Of course not," I snapped. "I'm sure being possessed by the spirit of a woman who tried to kill herself should have no potential negative side effects. None whatsoever."

He paused before answering. "I'm right next door. You can always talk to me."

"Like how Chessa talked to you? Some help you were. Was it after one of your helpful chats that she cut herself up and dove into the ocean?"

He winced, and I saw the pain wash over him. I immediately regretted my hurtful words.

"Chet, I'm so sorry. I didn't mean that."

"Of course you did." He kept his eyes on the road. His hollow cheeks grew more shadowed. "No need to apologize. I deserve all that, and more. I mean, if you only knew..." He trailed off and shook his head. "Never mind. What's done is done."

We drove in silence.

I thought of what I'd overheard at Chloe's house, when she was talking to the baby. "Zara is a *good* witch," Chloe had said.

Was I? Was I a good witch? *Zara tries to be a good witch, but Zara has a weakness for buttery pastry... and for losing her temper at the people she loves.*

"Chet, I do want to help you and Chessa," I said with a sigh. "I was just asking about therapy out of concern for you, because I'm a good witch who thinks of others." *Zara is a good witch.*

"I'm serious," I said. "I was called to being a librarian because of my innate desire to help people." I shifted in my seat, rearranging my fluffy skirt. "I need to help others even when it's not necessarily appreciated."

"And you're okay with putting yourself in danger to help people?"

"My aunt has advised that I make safety more of a priority. I'm trying to be more careful, but most times you don't realize how much danger you're in until it's all over and you're looking back."

"That's true," he said. "And you do seem to be dealing well, all things considered."

I thought of the prophetic book, and its quotes about chaos and murder. "Oh, I do get the heebie jeebies now and then, but even with everything that's happened lately, I'm surprisingly well adjusted. It must be a side effect of being a witch." I patted the embroidered pink poodle on my skirt then crossed my hands in my lap. "And I can't ever complain about being bored, that's for sure."

Chet sniffed in agreement, and gave me the first smile I'd seen on his face in a long time. "Never a dull moment in Wisteria."

We left the outskirts of town and turned onto a side road, narrow but paved.

We approached an iron gate, guarded by a tall watchtower. I leaned forward to look up at the tower's window. Someone was manning the post, but I couldn't see their face.

The gate opened, and we drove through.

"So, *this* is the secret access point for the DWM headquarters," I said. "Very clever. It looks exactly like the access for a drinking-water reservoir."

Chet nodded. "Which it also is. The department manages the clean-water supply for the regional district."

"Hence the name," I said. "You guys must work hard to keep things running smoothly."

"We do," he said.

I smiled inwardly. If you want to win points with someone without the use of magic, tell them their job sounds difficult.

"You probably don't get nearly enough credit for keeping our town safe," I said.

He tilted his head left and right, stretching his neck with an audible crack. "We don't do it for fame or glory," he said.

I was tempted to compare his vocation to mine, at the library, but bit my tongue. Helping patrons find books about flower arranging wasn't the same as taking the hit from bullets and tentacles.

He gestured at the terrain before us with his chin. "Keep your eyes on that rock wall up ahead. This is the best part."

I did, and as I watched, the rock wall split in half, slid apart, and offered access to a tunnel. Chet cranked the wheel hard and spun the back tires with a hot squeal on the pavement before shooting us into the tunnel.

"Fancy driving," I said. "The DWM must have an excellent training program."

"Basic evasive maneuvers," he said. "It's good to stay sharp."

We passed another checkpoint, where a mechanical arm shone a green bar of light through the van's windows, scanning us both.

After that, we reached an underground parking lot that resembled a normal parking lot for a big-city mall. Chet pulled into a parking spot with a practiced ease. There were at least twenty empty spots between the one he chose and the door to the elevator. If the spots were assigned, as I suspected they were, Chet was at least twenty people from the top of the organization.

We got out of the van and proceeded to the elevator's security panel, where he used a key fob on his keychain. He also held still for a retina scan. The screen above the panel flashed to life with a familiar female face. It was Charlize, the gorgon triplet sister of both Chloe and Chessa. Her blonde hair framed her round face with soft ringlets. There was no sign of the snakes, but I saw them in my mind's eye, overlaid across her normal human appearance.

"You're early," Charlize said. "Why didn't you take Zara to get a bite to eat, like we planned?"

Chet looked away from her to give me a guilty look.

I stepped closer to the screen and answered for him. "Because we're not dating, sweetheart. I'm here strictly on business. Buzz us in now so we can get on with it."

Charlize widened her eyes. "Folks, we've got a live one here." She shook her curls. "It must be true, what they say about redheaded witches. You're all... straight to business, like a struck match. I hear your type is all fire and brimstone in the bedroom, too." She leaned back in her chair, covered her microphone, and spoke to someone off camera.

Exasperated, Chet said, "Just hit the button. *Please.*"

The screen went black, and the elevator dinged as the doors opened.

Once we were in the elevator, I said to Chet, "For the record, it's true about the fire and brimstone. The only reason I'm a single mother is because, back home, I kept incinerating my dates with the power of my kisses. But at least those poor guys went out with smiles on their faces."

Chet held his hand to his mouth and whispered, "There are cameras everywhere."

I held up my hand to my mouth and replied, "I know."

The elevator seemed regular enough, except it went down instead of up.

Down, down, down.

CHAPTER 15

THE DIGITAL FLOOR display listed alphanumeric codes, nonsequential, but I did count twenty changes in the code, and my ears popped with the change in elevation.

The doors opened to what appeared to be a typical office-building hallway.

"We're taking a quick detour before the coma ward," Chet said as he led the way down the hall. "Stay close, and don't make eye contact with anyone or anything."

I did stay close, but when a man walked by accompanied by a creature that was the size of a child's pony but with the head of an iguana and the body of a lion, I had difficulty keeping my eyes to myself.

The iguana-lion flicked its pink, forked tongue in the air between us. "Hey, Chet," the beast said with a surfer-dude casual air. "How's that new office chair working out for you?"

"Very ergonomic," Chet replied. "Thanks for eating my other one."

The iguana-lion chuckled as it continued on its way.

As soon as we were alone, I asked Chet, "What was that?"

"His name is Steve, and he's one of our in-house lawyers."

"But what is he?"

"I told you, he's a lawyer," Chet said. "They're a special breed."

We'd stopped at a closed door. Chet tried the handle, but it was locked. He muttered under his breath with frustration.

"Allow me," I said.

I held my hands over the door handle. I imagined the mechanism inside the lock, and the driver pins pushing up to align the tops of the key pins—or at least I tried to. Without a visual of the shape of the ridges on the matching key, I couldn't get it right. And if I'd had the key for a visual reference—well, I wouldn't need to use magic.

When Chet saw that I couldn't get the door open, he said, "Never mind," and turned away. "We shouldn't be here, anyway." He took my elbow and nudged for me to come with him.

"I'm no quitter," I said, staying where I stood. "Remember what Charlize said about redheaded witches? I'm like a struck match."

"You shine brightly?"

"That's right." I grinned and looked down at his hand, which was still on my elbow. "And if you try to hold onto me, you're going to get your fingers burned."

He let go and gave me some space. I tried the door again, this time picturing myself on the other side, giving the door handle a simple twist to unlatch.

The handle gave a satisfying pop and turned. The door creaked open.

I didn't have long to bask in the glory because more people—or creatures—were approaching. Chet pushed me into the unlit office and closed the door behind us.

The dark, windowless, underground room felt black and dangerous in the way that only an office in a secret organization's lair, twenty stories below ground level, could feel. I could see nothing, but I heard a soft hum—probably the HVAC system—as well as Chet's breathing, and the rustle of the crinoline under my poodle skirt.

In the darkness, Chet asked, "Did something follow us in here, or is that your skirt I'm hearing?"

"Yes and no. It's the crinoline underneath my skirt. It's got boning, like a corset."

"Boning," he said with a chuckle, and then he pawed at my breast.

I gasped. "Found something you like?"

He made a strangled sound and whipped his hand away from my chest. "I was trying to flick the light switch."

"You could try flicking what you were grabbing, but you didn't even buy me dinner tonight, so I'm not—" The lights came on with a blinding flash, and I stopped talking. Chet had found the light switch, and he looked horrified enough without me having to finish my sentence.

I looked around the ten-foot-by-ten-foot room. The walls were painted a soft teal, decorated with framed prints of sand dollars and seascapes. That part of the room was as pleasant as the waiting room for a fancy dermatologist. The desk, chair, filing cabinet, and other accessories were all white. A pair of silver-wire-and-seaglass earrings lay on the desk next to a white pencil and a half-finished crossword puzzle. It looked as though the office's occupant might be back any minute, except for the year's worth of dust on the computer monitor.

Under the bright overhead lights, the ease between us froze back into a block of ice. Chet paced the room, looking over everything with stiff, robotic gestures.

"This is Chessa's office," he said. As if I hadn't figured it out already.

I surveyed the contents of the room. Other than being prettier than the typical office, with all its pale decorations, it was a standard office. An oval mirror on a pewter frame stood to the left of the computer monitor. On the metal frame, a tiny pewter woman in a long dress leaned over to peer at her reflection.

"That mirror was a gift," Chet said.

I traced the curls of the pewter girl's hair with my finger. Her ringlets seemed to have a life of their own. "I can see why someone saw this and thought of her."

He cleared his throat.

I picked up an ivory box, the size of a necklace gift box, and peered inside. It was empty, except for a plastic insert with a hollow space for a pen.

"What was this?" I showed Chet the box. "Is this how your fancy spell-busting pens come packaged?"

"No, they come in a kit with other weapons."

I sniffed. "Who do I need to sleep with to get one of those weapons kits?"

Chet gave me a horrified look.

"It's an expression," I said.

"You don't need a weapons kit. You already have too much power."

I gave my nose a twitch. "Power is like chocolate. You can never have too much."

"Let's see if you can control the powers you do have. Are you getting any feelings, being in this room?"

I took an audible breath and waited. "Mild claustrophobia."

"Anything else?" He looked at the empty pen box, which was still in my hands.

"This was an AG7," I said, closing the ivory box. "It just popped into my head. That must be knowledge put in my head by Chessa."

He didn't seem impressed with my naming of the pen model.

I opened a desk drawer and examined the orderly contents: colored markers, Post-It notes, assorted paperclips, three different mirrored compacts, a ball of elastic bands, and an unopened box of granola bars—the gross, healthy kind with no chocolate. I took out the elastic ball and gave it a bounce on the floor. It took a funny angle and shot away from me, but I used my powers to nab it midair before it marked up the pale teal-painted walls.

Chet pulled open a file drawer and thumbed over the tabbed contents. "She kept meticulous records of everything," he said. "I wish I could find her journal. She mentioned that she kept one, but I've searched every inch of this room, and the cottage, and I can't find it." He stared unfocusedly at a seascape print on the wall.

I took a seat in the dusty white chair and gestured to the computer monitor. "Maybe she went digital."

"The network admin already checked," he said.

"Ah, but maybe the network admin didn't know where to look. A girl's gotta keep her secrets, and one way to hide a diary is to call it something else, like TPS Reports." I pressed the button to switch on the monitor. A username and password prompt popped up. Without thinking, I typed both in and hit the Return key.

The system gave me access.

Chet looked at me in astonishment. "Chessa?"

I replied, "Why don't you try sticking your tongue down my throat and find out?"

He jumped back like I was made of blue lightning. "Sorry."

"You're not wrong to make that assumption," I said. "Something or someone clearly guided my fingers to type in her password. Plus I'm not usually so forward with you." Not that I didn't want to invite him to stick his tongue down my throat regularly, but I'd controlled myself until today.

"Chessa can be very direct," he said. "Flirtatious."

"Did she have other boyfriends besides you?"

~~"Of course not," he snapped. "Why would you say~~
such a thing?"

I held my hands up. "Easy, wolf boy. No need to chomp my head off. We'll get you a bowl of Puppy Chow right after this."

He tilted his head. His lips moved wordlessly before he spat out a response. "Chessa used to joke about feeding me Puppy Chow."

"Maybe we're getting warmer. That's what you want, isn't it? For me to strengthen my connection with Chessa so that she can get inside me and then you can—"

"Zara!"

I laughed flirtatiously, thrusting my chest forward so it was straining against the buttons of the pink blouse. "We're getting warmer and warmer," I teased.

He glanced around the tiny room guiltily.

My fingers were moving again on their own, typing commands even though I wasn't even facing the screen. I whispered to Chet, "Don't look now, but something's happening."

He took a seat on the edge of the desk and watched over my shoulder. I slowly turned my head and watched the screen as well.

My fingers were flying, punching in a series of passwords and access codes. The tapping on the keys sounded like a rainstorm.

And then I stopped; my hands flew up, folded together, and landed in my lap.

It was time for me to look at what the spirit had found. "She wants us to read what's on the screen," I said.

"That's classified," he said, reaching to turn off the monitor.

I swatted his hand away, and jabbed him in the ribs, right where I'd seen Chloe poke him the day before. He whimpered and gave me a dirty look but let me continue viewing the screen.

I asked, "What am I looking at?"

On the computer screen were scans of ancient-looking text. The lettering of the text—if it was text—was similar to hieroglyphics, with its alphabet of shapes using straight edges so it could be pressed into clay tablets with simple tools. But this wasn't a scan of a tablet.

"These pages were hand-written," I said. "On paper that looks like it turned to dust seconds after these scans."

"You're right about the paper," Chet said, still rubbing his ribs where I'd jabbed him. "The document was stored in a sealed container, underwater. Once the Department opened the box, oxygen got in, and the paper started rapidly deteriorating."

"How old is this? Was the paper material silk, or bamboo? Hemp?"

"Mulched tree bark, we think. It turned to dust almost immediately."

"But you got copies of it, right?" The librarian part of my brain got excited about adding the relic to our Local History Collection.

Chet shook his head. "The crew scanned as much as they could, but much of it was lost to dust and time."

"What kind of container? Where was it found? This artifact should be preserved and displayed for the public, not buried down here in the bowels of your weird bureaucratic whatever-this-is."

Chet glanced at the door, frowning. "I shouldn't have brought you here."

He was getting jumpy, regretting giving me what I wanted. I had to cool it with the demands and keep him calm.

I held one finger up. "Hang on." I took a deep breath and mimed removing a hat.

He whipped out his pen-shaped multi-pulse click generator. "No more spells," he warned.

"I'm just taking off my librarian hat," I said. "It's a metaphor. See?" I did it again, swooshing the imaginary hat from my head. "Now that my librarian hat is off, I can stop advocating for public access to your secret ancient knowledge."

"Put your witch hat on," he said, the smallest twinkle of amusement in his eyes.

"Good idea." I mimed finding a pointed hat on the desk and putting it on. The whole pretend-hat operation felt silly, but I committed fully, and moving my arms around helped break up the tension in my shoulder muscles.

I turned back to the computer screen and hit a series of keystrokes, presumably guided again by Chessa's spirit, because I didn't know what I was typing.

A new layer of information appeared on the screen. English text floated above the ancient lettering—a decoded partial translation.

"Chessa was working on this before her accident," I said, more statement than question.

"She's been working on it most of her life. She's the one who found it, in a shipwreck, when she was a child."

I could almost see the shipwreck, feel it around me as I floated through, moving easily in the water. I felt the joy of discovery at finding the sealed box within a pile of debris. Chessa was sharing her memory with me, so that I would know Chet was speaking the truth.

"And it inspired her to become a code breaker," I said. "A cryptographer. Or, specifically, a cryptanalyst." I felt the knowledge in my gut before it bubbled from my mouth. "With a specialty in ancient languages."

Chet didn't respond, except to suck air in between his clenched teeth. Once again, we were getting warmer. He was still sitting on the white desk, right next to me. His body language was contradictory, slumped yet tense. I sensed he was excited about my connection with Chessa's spirit, yet worried about the same.

I caught a memory of him, grabbing my arm, demanding to know where I was going. "What's wrong with you?" I was sobbing, running out the door, needing some space, somewhere quiet to think. I had to put the puzzle together. I had to prove—

The memory popped, like a soap bubble bursting. It was gone.

"What's happening?" Chet grabbed my arm. "What's wrong?"

I gasped and yanked my arm from his grip.

He stared at me, dumbfounded. "Chessa?"

"Still me." I rubbed my temples. "Ouch. I think a bunch of knowledge about matrix algebra just obliterated some pop music lyrics."

He reached for the computer monitor's power switch again. "Let's not get overloaded. We still have to go down —"

I swatted his hand away again, this time with a forceful karate chop.

A force was guiding me back to the text on the monitor. My gaze was riveted to the screen. He'd have to fight me to get the monitor shut off now because I'd just spotted, in the midst of the partially translated text, something that made my whole body pulse with energy.

Written in English over the chunky letters was my daughter's full name: Zolanda Daizy Cazzaundra Riddle.

"That's Zoey," I said, pointing. "Chet, you'd better start talking right now, or I'll hit you with so many of my witch spells, that clicky pen of yours is going to explode."

He held up both hands in a don't-shoot gesture. "It's complicated, and it's classified, but you could try reading the text next to her name."

I leaned in and read the text. "It says... Soul Catcher. What does this mean? Is this supposed to be Zoey's witchcraft specialty?" I turned toward Chet and pointed a finger at his ribs. "And don't tell me it's classified, or I'll poke you. This is my daughter we're talking about. I want the truth."

He let out a resigned sigh. "The truth is we don't know everything. We've had this for almost seventeen years, and we've barely decoded ten percent of what we scanned before the paper disintegrated. The truth is..." He slid off the desk and paced the area between the desk and the door. "The truth is this document isn't a top priority for the DWM. Chessa was working on it in her free time, and only because she had a personal interest in it." He paused and looked pointedly at the office's closed door. "People around here are more concerned with present-day politics and power, not ancient forecasts about the movement of souls."

The movement of souls? But what could possibly be more important than that? I shook my head, unsure if the scorn I felt was my own or Chessa's.

"Chet, what does Soul Catcher mean?"

He leaned back against the door. His gaze flitted around the room, his dark-green eyes like those of a wild dog trapped in a kennel.

"Chessa had a theory about souls, how there were a finite number of Original Souls, that moved from person to person over multiple lifetimes. There are divine powers that move along with the soul." He glanced at the computer screen and hunched his shoulders in a defensive gesture. "We don't know what it means to be a Soul Catcher. Hell, we're not even sure if that's the right translation. In that ancient language, the word Catcher is very similar to the word Destroyer. And with the way that line is smudged, it could be either one."

I snorted. "You've met Zoey. She's a straight-A student and a terrific kid. She's no Destroyer."

He straightened up and cracked his neck left and right. "You're her mother. You'd defend her to the end of days."

He was right about that. I read the name on the screen again. This was my daughter, all right, because there was no other person on the planet named Zolanda Daizy Cazzaundra Riddle.

"What if I'd named her something else? Or what if, as soon as we get out of here, I apply to change the spelling of her middle names to Daisy Cassandra? She wouldn't even notice."

"We don't know how it works." He flipped a hand helplessly in the direction of the screen. "It's possible that when we opened up the vessel all those years ago, the simple act of looking at the prophecy altered it."

"The *prophecy*?" I rolled the white chair away from the monitor. "Now, that's a word with a lot of weight to it."

"Chessa was the one who started calling it a prophecy."

I pointed my thumb at the screen without looking. "Is there anything in here with my name? Am I in here? Or you?"

"Not on any of the pages we scanned." He opened the door a crack and peered down the hallway. He closed the door softly and looked me straight in the eyes. "Zara, the artifact holding this information was discovered by Chessa not quite seventeen years ago. Have a look at the date in the header and tell me if it means anything to you."

I turned back to the screen, hit a few keystrokes, and examined the document's header.

The tension in my shoulder muscles turned sharp, like a knife in my spine.

Yes, the date meant something. I knew that date very well. It was kind of a big deal.

"There was a big storm that day," I said.

"Anything else?"

Damn him. He already knew, but he wanted me to say it. "That's the day I conceived Zoey."

He didn't look at all surprised. "When she was born, how did you decide on her name?"

"It just came to me." I looked at the screen again. "Obviously this can't be a coincidence. Did the prophecy make me give her that name?"

"I wish I could tell you more, but—"

"It's classified."

"No," he said slowly. "The truth is, now you know as much as we do. Chessa felt she was close to a discovery, and she was putting in long hours before her accident, but she must have been working on it in her head, or on notes we can't find."

I put the puzzle pieces together. "So, if this prophecy has something to do with my daughter, I need to get Chessa back and find out what this means."

"Sure," he said. "I just want her back because..."

"Because you love her."

He clenched his jaw and turned the door handle. "Shall we?"

CHAPTER 16

CHET LED THE WAY, and we stepped into the elevator. My thoughts were still back in Chessa's office with the ancient prophecy, and I stumbled briefly over my own foot.

He caught me by the elbow. "Zara, we can take a few minutes if you're not feeling up to it. We have a cafeteria on the premises, and the food is surprisingly good."

"Cherry cheesecake?"

His green eyes brightened. "That was Chessa's favorite," he said.

"Warmer and warmer." I touched the bracelet on my wrist. "Our connection is getting stronger."

Chet stared at me, his pupils getting bigger and bigger. "Much stronger," he said softly.

"My connection with Chessa," I said. "Not with you."

"Right." He jerked his head back and straightened up. He reached for the elevator's buttons. "We could stop at the cafeteria, and you could eat some cheesecake, if you think it will help. She's been like this for a year now. Another twenty minutes won't matter."

I grinned. "You think I need a full twenty minutes? You haven't seen me destroy cheesecake."

His hand hovered over the control keypad for the elevator. "Cafeteria?" His words were saying we could delay, but his eyes said otherwise. His eyes begged me to help him connect with his lost love, as soon as possible.

"Straight to the coma ward," I said. "Once we bring Chessa back, we can all celebrate with a round of cheesecake."

He nodded and punched in an access code, then leaned forward and held still for another retina scan.

As the elevator progressed down, I asked, "Why didn't we do this yesterday?"

"The doctor wouldn't sign off to give you access. I had to throw my weight around." He smirked. "He must have gotten the strange idea that you're a trouble maker." He looked down my body. "A trouble maker straight out of a musical production of Grease."

"Good eye for musicals," I said. "How many doctors do you have around here? Was this the same one I saw with Charlize when I was getting patched up?"

Chet shook his head. "You weren't supposed to see anyone. Were you conscious for long?"

"All of about three minutes, but it was memorable. Your buddy Charlize tried to give me a heart attack. She told me I'd been out for twenty-five years, and people had flying cars now."

Chet grinned. "Charlize is funny. You two should hang out sometime, if you don't mind the competition."

I gave him a sidelong look. "Competition?"

"Yeah. For being the funny girl."

"Right. Because she's *soooooo* funny."

The elevator dinged and opened, and two guys joined us, one a towering mountain and the other short by comparison.

It was Rob and Knox. Fear shot through me, and my reflexes kicked in with a vengeance.

I jumped back, raised my hands, and jolted both of them with blue lightning.

They went down.

The air around me went murky, as though the elevator were filling with smoke. Nobody else seemed to notice the smoke, and on some level I knew it wasn't real. Just a memory. Chessa's memory, of cold water and darkness and death.

My eyes refused to focus. I could hear the two men on the floor groaning. The elevator doors were trying to close, making a loud dinging noise, and then a more aggressive alarm. Chet was pushing me, shoving me backward, putting me in the elevator's corner. He blocked me into the corner with his body.

The world was slow motion and loud, then quiet.

My head got hazy, and I felt someone else pushing into my mind. I was still there, just behind a smoky curtain.

I heard myself speak, but the voice was not my own. "Chet, I was attacked. By a bird."

My vision was still a black haze, but I felt his body rotate. He turned toward me, grabbed my wrists, and pressed my palms together. His face was a blur of light in the darkness, in the deep waters.

"I know, Zara. I was there with you in the forest that day," he said. "But you've got to believe me, it wasn't Knox or Rob. They would never hurt you."

"Chet, it's me," the spirit whispered with my voice.

I knew who it was before she said her name.

"I'm Chessa."

"Zara, this is no time for your jokes."

"Chet, the cuts on my wrists are from talons. From a bird. I didn't try to kill myself. I was attacked."

"By who?"

"A bird. I told you. You can't trust them."

"But you were depressed. Are you sure you didn't hurt yourself?" He was shaking me by the shoulders, his face still blurry. "Chessa, you were erratic, paranoid. I should have noticed something was wrong."

The veil inside my mind shifted, like a gauzy curtain in the breeze. My voice raspy, the spirit said, "Talk to my sister. Talk to Chloe. She knows why."

The elevator's door-open alarm stopped. With a cheery ding, the doors closed, and the elevator began to move.

Inside my mind, the curtain fell away. The elevator interior came into crisp focus.

Chet still had me boxed into the corner. Behind him, both Knox and Rob were conscious, seated on the floor and watching me warily.

Chessa was gone, outside of my body, but Chet didn't know. He pulled me in close and kissed me. His mouth was exactly as tender and strong as I expected. It was as though I'd kissed him a thousand times. The rasp of stubble on his upper lip stung in a familiar way. I leaned into the kiss.

He pulled away with a sudden jerk, wiping his mouth.

He eyed me with suspicion.

I waved one hand guiltily. "Me again. Just Zara."

"She was here," he said, scrubbing his lips with the back of his hand.

"Not anymore. And would you stop wiping your mouth like that? I'm starting to take it personally."

He stared at me, his green eyes bright with fury and pain.

I put my hands on my hips. My confusion quickly turned to rage. That look on his face, that accusing expression, always set me off. Or her. I couldn't tell, and it didn't matter. She and I were one, commingled, and we wanted to yell at him.

I spat out, "Why are you so upset about making contact? You got to talk to her. What exactly did you think was going to happen when she possessed me?"

He wiped his mouth again. "This was a bad idea."

I clenched my fists. "You think? How about you stop kissing people you shouldn't be kissing?"

"Chessa?"

I couldn't say yes, and I couldn't say no. I was so mixed up. I wanted to kiss him again, and I also wanted to pick him up and throw him against the wall of the elevator. Was it love, or hate? Was it Chessa, or me? I couldn't tell.

All I could do was glare at him and hope to get control of myself. He glared back. Oh, how I wanted to slap him. Or kiss him. And dig my nails into his muscles.

In the silence, there were two clicks—clicks that spoke of danger.

I leaned around Chet's body to find Rob pointing a gun-like weapon at me. Knox was doing the same.

In his deep, baritone voice, Knox spoke calmly. "Don't be scared of us. We would never hurt you."

Rob chimed in, his tone strident and offended. "Why would you blast an unarmed man like that?"

I stammered before explaining, "I'm sorry, but it was pure instinct. Something programmed into my body. And since you guys are both big shifter birds, can you blame me? My defenses got triggered, probably because of that time Chet and I were attacked by the vicious bird thing." Not to mention Chessa's claim just now that she'd also been attacked by a bird. But she'd said so after I'd already blasted the guys, so I couldn't pin the blame on her.

Rob and Knox slowly lowered their weapons and exchanged a look.

Rob said to Chet, "Hey, man. You were attacked by a winged creature? You never told us about that."

Chet shrugged it off. "It's Wisteria. Things happen. I'm not going to report every minor skirmish."

The guys exchanged another knowing look.

I pointed at them. "Chet, these two know something. They know what attacked you. And maybe what attacked Chessa." I swallowed. "Unless it was one of them."

Chet said, "Guys?" He let out a low chuckle. "Would you put Zara's mind at ease by pinkie swearing that you didn't try to kill us, or Chessa?"

Rob shook his head. "Chet, man. That's not funny."

Knox grabbed the silver railing inside the elevator and raised himself to his full, mountainous height. "You never told us you got attacked."

Rob grabbed Knox's trunk-like forearm and used it to get himself upright and standing. "You should have told us," he said. "You should have filed a report, man."

Chet shrugged. "It's just one of those things. And besides, I was busy making sure Zara was okay. As you can see, she's excitable and unpredictable."

All three of them looked at me.

My cheeks grew hot. I fidgeted with my skirt. *Great.* Now I was feeling guilty. I was ashamed about zapping the guys, and stealing a kiss from Chet, even though both had been instinctive. How could I make this uncomfortable feeling go away? I had to say something to defuse the tension.

I pointed in Chet's direction. "He was naked," I said. "A big bird swooped down on us in the forest, and then suddenly Chet stripped himself naked. He turned into a wolf, too. And he saved my life." My cheeks felt hotter and hotter. *Talk faster,* I ordered myself. "But I have a question for you, Knox and Rob. Is it true you guys can shift with your clothes on or off, and it's just a personal choice?"

Rob and Knox exchanged a look and started to chuckle.

Knox asked me, "What did Moore tell you?"

"What he always says when I ask him stuff." I did my best impression of Chet's uncomfortable face. "*It's classified,*" I said in a deep, irritated voice. "*Now I'm just going to be all broody and then rip my clothes off with no explanation at all because I'm Chet, and that's what I do.*"

The guys chuckled harder, enjoying my impersonation.

"Typical Moore," Rob said. "Always taking his clothes off, rather than taking an extra second to shift with them on. If I had a dollar for every time I had to loan him the jacket off my back, I'd be a rich man."

Knox said to his shorter buddy, "We could both be rich."

Rob grinned. "I'd buy myself a memory wipe, to erase the sight of Moore, completely nude, slaying those bone-crawlers with his bare hands."

They both shuddered.

Chet didn't join in the joking around. He leaned in between them and pressed a button to restart the elevator.

Rob gave me a quizzical look, eye to eye. He and I were the same height. "What are you doing here, anyway?"

"It's classified," I said with an eyebrow waggle.

Knox said, "Coma ward. For Chessa."

Rob swallowed audibly and backed up to the doors of the elevator as though I had girl cooties. "Good luck with that."

CHAPTER 17

AFTER THE LONGEST and strangest elevator ride of my life, we arrived on the floor with the coma ward.

Rob paused in the open doorway and gave me a playful look, his dark, heavy-lidded eyes mischievous. "Try not to zap anyone else with your blue lightning, okay? Most of us meat units down here are so expendable, we should be wearing red shirts. But the DWM has a lot of sensitive electronics down here, and they don't take kindly to equipment destruction." He shot a meaningful glance up at Knox. "Which is a lesson this big guy learned the hard way at our staff Christmas party."

Knox furrowed his large brow. "What? Everybody had fun. Even Moore."

Rob shook his head. "But they'll never let you play Santa Claus again, man."

"We'll see," Knox said. "Nobody else can go ho-ho-ho like me."

"Your ho-ho-hos are unmatched," Rob agreed. "As are those tree trunks you call arms. Have you been hitting the gym without me?"

Knox gave him a puzzled look. "Yes."

Rob pretended to be hurt. "Without me?"

Knox frowned. "I don't understand. You don't even know what floor the gym is on. You say you will meet me there, then you never come, and you tell me you got lost."

"I'll be there next time," Rob said, laughing. "I'll write the directions on my hand."

Knox grunted.

The two exited the elevator and turned left down a brightly lit gray hallway.

After I watched them walk away, I turned to Chet. "Your coworkers seem nice," I said. "I'll try not to electrocute them anymore."

"You should have more control over your powers," he said coolly.

"And you should have more control over who you kiss when you think you're kissing someone else with borrowed lips." I tilted my head and gave him a studious look. "Speaking of which, how did you know it switched back to me? I'm not asking because I want to trick you into smooching me, honestly. Do I shimmer, or give off a weird smell when I'm possessed? I need to know so I can teach my daughter how to tell when I'm being a puppet for a spirit versus being a puppet for my regular wacky self."

He led the way out of the elevator and turned to the right. "I knew it was you because Chessa would have pushed me away rather than kiss me back. She was extremely flirtatious, but only with words. She would never show physical affection in front of our coworkers."

"Why not?"

"Because of her powers of attraction. If she became activated, it had unpredictable side effects."

An image flashed through my mind. Rob and Knox fighting each other while Chet pulled them apart. An instant later, the two of them were acting dazed and apologizing to each other. Another memory from Chessa's vault.

"Men would fight over her," I said. The pieces were falling into place. That sort of effect sounded like the powers of either a siren or a mermaid, for sure.

Chet stopped at a door and pressed his hand to a panel next to it. He turned to me, his green eyes burning brighter than ever.

With a deep, serious tone, Chet said, "Men would die for her."

"Including you?"

The door clicked, and he pushed it open.

"First things first," he said, nodding for me to stick close to him.

We entered a clean, bright room with lighting so pleasant, I almost forgot I was twenty-some stories beneath the sunny surface. The room had equipment on the walls for six beds, but five of the spots were vacant, the beds wheeled away elsewhere. In the corner was a fabric curtain drawn across one lonely bed, its wheels visible at the bottom of the pale-green divider.

The seriousness of the situation struck me mute. As much as I wanted to tease Chet about kissing me or ask what Knox did at the Christmas party, no words came to my lips. I was about to see Chessa's dormant body for the first time, to gaze upon the face of the woman who'd been gently possessing me, revealing to me the wonders at the bottom of the ocean, as well as the taste of her fiancé's lips.

My stomach clenched. Anger coursed through me without warning. Oh, how I hated her, this woman I'd never known. I suddenly despised her for showing me everything she had, and all the powers I didn't have, and the love I didn't deserve. Who did I think I was? I hadn't earned my gifts. What right did I have to receive so much power through no self-sacrifice? I was still alive, breathing, walking around. The nerve. I could move objects with my will alone. I could...

Someone was waving a hand in front of my face.

I straightened up and breathed out my tension. Where had that sudden flare of self-hatred come from? I could be hard on myself, but never like that. Those were the emotions of someone who'd lost everything, and thought I had been the benefactor. Chessa? I'm trying to help you. Please don't hate me.

"Ms. Riddle," a man said. It wasn't Chet.

"Hello," I said with forced lightness. The self-hatred was still lingering, and it was hard to be polite through clenched teeth.

The man, who had a musical lilt to his voice, an Indian accent, said, "It didn't take you long to find your way back here, did it, Ms. Riddle?" I knew him. He was the doctor who I'd last seen drugging me back to sleep after my head injury. Anger flared up again, this time at a target other than myself.

I reached out to shake the man's hand, and accidentally discharged a blast of blue lightning. The light flared as it struck the man right in the solar plexus.

He flinched and took two stumbling steps back but recovered quickly.

"She's quite the handful," the man said to Chet. He rubbed his chest where I'd jolted him.

"Oops," I said. "Maybe I should invest in some gloves for these things?" I wiggled my fingers apologetically.

The man gave my hands a solemn look and introduced himself as Dr. Bhamidipati. "Don't even try to pronounce that," he said. "Everyone calls me Dr. Bob." He kept looking down at my hands. "I'd offer you my hand, but my sense of self-preservation tells me you might eat it, or turn me into a frog."

"Sorry about my hair-trigger reflexes," I said, checking my hand for blue lightning before offering it to him.

He shook my hand carefully yet firmly.

"Delighted to meet you, Ms. Riddle."

"We've met before," I said, waggling a finger at him. "The last time I saw you, I was down here with a concussion, and you were putting a sedative in my IV line. You knocked me out before I could get answers."

"I do hope you'll forgive my lack of bedside manner," Dr. Bob said with a kindly smile. He was roughly sixty years of age, and a very short man—so small-boned that my own hand had engulfed his when we shook. He'd looked a lot more menacing when I'd been dazed and confused in a hospital bed. Dr. Bob had black hair, brown skin, and a dark birthmark on his right cheek. His upper lip was asymmetrical, with a vertical scar that turned from pink to white as his kindly smile widened. He looked like a doctor who'd sell a line of vitamin supplements on television—the perfect mix of east and west, wisdom and modernity.

He exchanged pleasantries with Chet, then turned back to me. "Ms. Riddle, I was just writing up a glowing report of your friend Frank. I was very impressed by his resilience."

"He's a tough old bird," I agreed.

The doctor chuckled. "Ms. Riddle, you're very fortunate to have such a fun coworker to keep things lively at our town's library. And he's lucky to have you in his corner as well." Dr. Bob flicked his gaze to Chet, frowning briefly before looking back at me. "The DWM could use a few more gems like yourself and Mr. Frank Wonder. Some of the people around here take themselves way too seriously." He reached up and took hold of the ends of the stethoscope slung around his neck, striking a casual pose. "How is Frank feeling today?"

Chet shifted restlessly from one foot to the other, but Dr. Bob held still, waiting for an answer from me. He seemed genuinely interested in my friend, which made me like the man, despite my first instinct to electrocute him.

"Frank Wonder is feeling terrific," I reported. "He told me that for the first time last night, he didn't dream about flying."

Dr. Bob's dark-brown eyes twinkled, and the birthmark on his cheek creased with lines emanating from his eyes. "How exciting it is to discover your own abilities." He released the stethoscope and turned toward the curtained bed. "Speaking of abilities, let's observe how powerful your connection is with our Chessa." He cleared his throat. "We all miss her so much."

The three of us walked around the curtain and gathered around the hospital bed. Nobody said anything. Machines were whirring steadily, but the woman in the bed was breathing without the use of a ventilator.

Chessa lay on her back, the very picture of a beautiful yet cursed princess in a fairy tale. Her light hair wasn't gold like her triplet sisters', but platinum, and wavy rather than curly. Like Chloe and Charlize, she had a round face and delicate features, with a small mouth and large, wide-set eyes that were softly closed. A few flaws marred her perfection. Her lips were chapped and cracked despite a glossy application of salve, and her eyes were sunk in too deep. She was gaunt, and her soft-pink cheeks were crisscrossed by thin white scars.

Chet shifted closer to her head as he made a strangled, pained noise. It obviously hurt him to look at her, yet he wouldn't look away.

When I looked at her, I got an eerily familiar feeling, mixed with the sensation I was floating around outside of my body again. In my mind's eye, I could see the group of us as though I were a fly on the wall—the doctor in his white lab coat, me in my ridiculous musical theater costume with the pink poodle on my skirt, Chet twitching on the edge of shifting into a wolf, and Chessa playing the role of Sleeping Beauty. What a curious assortment of humanity we were. How strange that fate had brought us all together this way. Fate, and a partially translated prophecy.

After a few minutes, Chet said to Dr. Bob, "Someone's been putting makeup on her. Was it Charlize? She's usually more pale."

Dr. Bob leaned over and examined the comatose woman's face. "It could be a trick of the new lighting down here," he answered with his lilting Indian accent. "And she looks positively tanned next to Zara, on account of her milky pale skin."

I held up my left arm, showing the whitest part on the underside of my forearm. "In the Riddle family, we call this shade 'marshmallow.' By midwinter, it's dangerously close to 'skim milk,' though."

"Ms. Riddle, your type of genetic mutation is very rare," Dr. Bob said. "In Denmark, it is very much an honor to give birth to a redheaded baby."

"Sure, but in some parts of France, if you pass a redhead on the street you've got to spit and turn around or you'll be cursed." I grinned. "Growing up this way, I've heard about all the redhead superstitions from around the world."

He leaned his small head back in a relaxed, conversational gesture. "In Greek mythology, they say certain redheads don't ever die. They become vampires."

I shrugged one shoulder. "Then I must be one of those, since I've already been killed once."

"You were killed?" He seemed about as surprised as any person would be.

"I was shocked and then lightened right out of my body. I floated around for a while."

"How very interesting." He rubbed his clean-shaven brown chin. "Did you see anything on the other side, when you were a spirit?" The doctor kept his eyes trained on me. It seemed we were both avoiding looking at Chessa, both avoiding dealing with the business at hand. Chet, meanwhile, had already taken a seat next to her bed.

"I saw a few scary things," I said lightly. "Such as Grampa Don Moore in his underwear."

"You poor thing," Dr. Bob said warmly. He raised his dark eyebrows. "Did you know that redheads are more difficult to sedate? They require twenty percent more anesthesia. That's why some wake up during surgical procedures." He glanced over at Chessa's inanimate face, as though hoping the words 'wake up' would have some effect.

I joked, "We need more anesthetic because we have no souls."

He smirked. "I don't believe it's true." He took two short steps toward the head of Chessa's bed, stopped, and looked at me expectantly.

Chet was also watching me.

Enough with the bedside small talk, I thought. *It's showtime.*

And showtime was what, exactly? I had to try direct communication with Chessa's spirit, which would be a new skill for me. Up until now, the spirits who'd visited me had simply turned up whenever it suited them. Once, my aunt had purposefully summoned the ghost of Winona Vander Zalm, with mixed results. It was a two-witch spell that she'd performed on her own, dangerously opening a hole to somewhere that terrified her. My safety-conscious aunt had screwed up royally. On a scale from one to ten, with ten being the freakin' apocalypse, she'd rated the danger as four and a half, then spent a whole day fretting about our imminent doom. And for all of that fuss and worry, we'd only gotten two cryptic words written in the mist of the bathroom mirror.

Surely, I could do better. In Chessa's office, I'd been getting warmer and warmer.

Attention, Spirits of the Deep, I thought to myself in an announcer's voice. Then I imagined what Frank would say if he'd been there in the coma ward, watching me do an impression of his uncle, and I got the giggles.

The doctor and Chet continued to watch me. I clamped my mouth shut and cut off the giggles.

Time for some magic. Time for me to charm a spirit.

In movies, people always take the hand of the coma patient and talk to them. I took a seat on the chair opposite from where Chet sat, and I did that.

Chessa's hand felt waxy, and warmer than I expected. Someone had buffed her fingernails to a shine. Under the green sheet, she wore a pink summer dress. She smelled of perfume. The wall-mounted computer screen on the wall at her feet showed a pastoral scene, with sun dappling through gently swaying trees. If she did wake up, she'd see something beautiful to counter the shock of seeing me. I turned and watched the TV screen for a peaceful moment before turning back toward the sleeping woman. Except for the tubes snaking in and out of the covers, she fit perfectly with the image on the screen. In the blink of an eye, she could be taking a nap on the grassy mound beneath a giant oak tree.

Her hand didn't move. When I wiggled my fingers, I felt elasticity in her fingers, but that was from her tendons.

I looked across her at Chet. The devoted, heartbroken fiancé. His eyes were now fixed on the TV's summer scene, or some distant point beyond. I guessed he was thinking about the past or the future, anywhere but here. His jugular pulsed visibly in his muscular neck, but that was the only sign he was still alive. If he was still breathing, it was shallowly.

I felt neither the Spirits of the Deep nor any sign of Chessa. I did feel hungry. My stomach growled. I cleared my throat. The spicy scent of Dr. Bob's cologne filled my nostrils. I'd almost forgotten he was there with us, patiently waiting.

I gave him a wan smile. Dr. Bob returned the smile, the thin scar on his upper lip turning white.

Go on, he seemed to say with his eyes. Show this scientist what your witch powers can do. I dare you to be better than all my medicine.

I flicked my gaze away from the beseeching doctor, up to the ceiling. It was just an ordinary ceiling, like you'd see in any hospital. I counted the tiles above the space comprising Chessa's area of the ward. Ten by twelve. If each tile measured a foot across, Chessa's space within the ward—her whole world for the last year—was one hundred and twenty square feet. The typical prison cell is six feet by eight, or forty-eight feet. Chessa had more space than a prisoner, but not much. And prisoners got to use the common areas throughout the day. All Chessa got was a few brief seconds inside my body, getting kissed by her fiancé. Or watching him kiss a redheaded witch.

My hand twitched. Had Chessa's fingers moved just now? I waited.

Once Dr. Bob's cologne cleared from my nostrils, I smelled the underlying scent of commercial, pine-scented floor cleaner. If I were Chessa, I'd never want to smell pine ever again, not even the real stuff, in a forest.

My butt was falling asleep. Why were the chairs down here so uncomfortable? I shifted. My skirt was noisy, the crinoline protesting even the smallest movements. My back was damp with sweat that had cooled. I tried to focus on Chessa, repeating her name in my head, but my stomach kept turning it from Chessa to cheesecake. Cherry cheesecake. It wasn't fair that her name sounded so delicious.

I wondered, how long had I been sitting next to cherry cheesecake? Uh, Chessa?

An hour already? Two hours?

I checked the time on the clock on the wall above Chessa's head.

Twelve minutes had passed.

Now what?

Another five minutes of obsessing over cherry cheesecake passed slowly.

Dr. Bob broke the silence. "I'll give you some privacy." He left the eight-by-ten area, and exited the ward on soundless footsteps. Once he was on the other side of the door, in the hallway, he sighed loudly enough for me to hear him inside the room.

I raised my eyebrows at Chet. Had he also heard the doctor sigh? Chet continued to stare at the TV screen, which was now showing frolicking sheep in a bucolic pasture.

My mind wandered back over my day, and my emotions felt clearer in review, as though I were writing in a journal and gaining perspective. I remembered the joy I felt for Frank, who was thrilled about being able to fly. My skin felt hot as I recalled Detective Bentley admiring my legs. A rush of anger flashed through me when I thought of Chet, sitting in the van watching the door nervously, then smiling like an idiot when he saw the redheaded librarian walk out of the library's front doors in her stupid poodle skirt.

Wait. That wasn't my memory.

Chessa?

No response.

I squeezed her hand.

Still nothing.

I crossed my legs, my crinoline making a ruckus yet again in the hushed room.

Had Chet really smiled in the van when he saw me exit the library? I couldn't have known, since I wasn't in the van with him, but Chessa's spirit had been. And she remembered. Maybe if I just relaxed into a dreamlike, hypnagogic state, more of her memories would come to me.

The clock on the wall was ticking softly. I focused on the tick-tock and dropped down, down, to the threshold of consciousness between waking and sleeping.

Down I went, sinking.

The tick-tock of the clock became bubbles.

My mind filled, not with a veil, but with cool blue water.

Chessa was just beneath the surface, below the membrane. If I let myself drop down, through the threshold, I could meet with her.

The water rose, filling me, and I kept sinking down within it. My breathing stayed calm and measured.

The tick-tock was only bubbles. Down here, there was no peace, no crinkly skirts, no ticking clocks, no time passing.

The water was murky. A shape emerged, striped. An eel. It swam past, flashing dark and light stripes.

I sunk down farther, to where platinum seaweed pulsed in the deep abyss.

My bare feet touched a surface. Sand.

My eyes were open, and I had landed facing an enormous stone statue of a face. The glinting platinum seaweed parted to reveal more. The face was Chessa's, and it was twenty feet high. Her stone eyes were closed.

I reached up and grazed the bottom rim of her eyelids with my fingertips. But my fingertips were razor-sharp, pointed, and they cut the granite surface, so that it bled. I jerked my hand back, but it was too late. The statue's eyelids bled. She appeared to be crying blood, which turned gray as it commingled with the surrounding water.

There was something in the sand, something buried. I fell to my knees and began digging with both hands. This was why my fingers were sharp. Not to hurt her, but to save her.

I dug and dug, expecting to find her body just below the surface, so I could set her free, but there was only more sand. As soon as I excavated an area, it filled from below with more sand that bubbled up like lava.

I knelt before the giant stone face and pressed my hands together. My fingertips were bleeding, and I was melting into the water.

And then I was praying. Speaking words I didn't know, in a language I'd never heard.

The water around me turned from cold to warm. *Warmer and warmer.* I hadn't noticed I was freezing, trembling from the chill, until the warmth set in. I hadn't known what I had until it was gone.

The words continued to pour from my mouth. My eyes were pinched closed now, and I didn't dare open them.

The warmth around me turned to light. Pure-white light.

My body hummed with light and purity, and it pierced my heart with a pain that bordered on divine.

I would open my eyes, and I would gaze upon her face, and she would look into my soul, and everything would be set right in the world.

I would open my eyes... any minute now.

Just one more minute in this light. Just a little longer.

Suddenly, there was pain.

I fell forward on my hands and knees. The ground beneath me was no longer soft sand, but broken shards of discarded pottery, broken shells, broken glass. My hands and knees bled, clouding the water.

The warmth was gone. The light was gone. Everything was dirty and broken and wrong. All was decay and destruction. Darkness.

The ground ripped open beneath me, and I was falling but not free. Sharp points were everywhere, piercing my skin, shredding me, tearing at my flesh until I all I could see was the rich, fiery red of my blood.

CHAPTER 18

TWO HOURS LATER

"YOU BROKE HER," Zoey said. "I loaned you my mother, and you broke her."

I was back in my house, sitting on the sofa, with only a dim recollection of how I'd gotten there.

"Give her some space," Chet was saying to my daughter. "Get her some water, or something to eat. What's her favorite kind of food?"

"Cherry cheesecake," I murmured.

Zoey clapped her hands. "She speaks! Mom, we don't have cheesecake, but would you settle for vanilla ice cream with maraschino cherries on top?"

I agreed, and she brought me a sundae with three kinds of cookies, a sliced banana, and ice cream covered in bright-red cherries. I forced it down like a champion.

The vision or dream state I'd entered at Chessa's bedside had been intense. I was still unraveling what all the imagery meant. The giant stone face had presumably

153

represented her. I'd sensed she wanted to communicate with me, but I wasn't able to get her stone eyelids open before a malevolent force had opened the ground beneath me.

Back in the coma ward, as soon as I came out of the vision, I'd described everything to Chet, in ragged sobs.

I'd been crying. Devastated. Because for a brief moment, I'd felt the radiant goodness of Chessa, and when the darkness had swallowed me, I'd been torn apart by her absence, by the loss of her. The world was a darker place without her.

Chet had helped me to my feet and dragged me away from her bedside. I clung to the footboard of her bed, despondent. I didn't want to go. I told him that I understood finally how much he loved her, and why men would die for her. But I was weak, and finally, I let him pry my fingers from the bed frame.

I'd been inconsolable on the drive back home. Even now, my pink blouse was soaked from the ocean of tears I'd shed. My eyes, however, were dry now, and the pain had been replaced by numbness.

"Another sundae, please," I said politely. Zoey was already bringing one from the kitchen. We'd run out of cherries, so this one was heaped with toasted nuts, butterscotch syrup, and those rubbery green and red squares—candied citrus rind—that we'd bought before Christmas with the intention of making fruitcake as a gag gift for friends. Doing magic ate up calories in the body, and the vision in the coma ward had been intense. These sundaes were medicinal.

"Mr. Moore, what did you do to her?" Zoey demanded.

Guiltily, Chet said, "Nothing."

"Her eyes don't look right."

"She's got normal eyes," Chet said.

"Thanks," I said flatly. "I've always dreamed of being told I have normal eyes."

They continued talking, as though I'd said nothing.

"They keep changing," Zoey said.

"That's what hazel eyes do," Chet said. "They look brown one minute, green the next, sometimes blue or gray."

"Her pupils are weird. They just shifted into keyholes, like goat eyes. You broke her!"

Chet said, "I don't see whatever it is you're seeing. But stop saying I broke your mother. I told you already, she volunteered willingly to come with me to the place where I work—"

"The DWM," Zoey interrupted. "I know everything, Mr. Moore, so you don't have to talk in code to me. She went there to channel the spirit of the fiancée you never told her about until yesterday, when she magicked it out of you."

I asked, "Are we using *magicked* as a verb now?"

They suddenly regained the ability to hear me talking. Both turned to stare at me.

Zoey asked, "What happened?"

I pointed my sticky spoon at Chet. "He kissed me in the elevator."

Zoey covered her ears with both hands and squeezed her eyes shut. "Grosssssssssss."

Chet gave me an amused look. "She's been spending a lot of time with Corvin, and he's rubbing off on her."

I kept pointing my spoon at him, swirling it like a wand. "I'm feeling more lucid now. Did you already tell my daughter everything?"

He got up from his seat on the coffee table in front of me and circled the room uncomfortably before settling in a chair. I took his silence to mean *no*. He hadn't told my daughter about the document Chessa had been decoding in her free time before her accident, or attack, or suicide —whatever it was. He leaned uneasily on the armrest of the chair. I'd never seen a person make a comfy chair look so uninviting. I wondered if he was more comfortable in wolf form, when he wasn't expected to talk.

Zoey took a seat next to me on the sofa. "What do you mean by *everything*?"

I licked my spoon clean. "The DWM has an ancient scroll with your name on it. Literally. It's some sort of prophecy, and next to your full name it says Soul Catcher. But wait, there's more." I waved the spoon in the air. "They opened the vessel containing the parchment before you became *you*, if you know what I mean. The prophecy might be responsible for your existence."

Zoey twitched her nose. "Mom, I thought a six-pack of Barberrian wine coolers was responsible for my existence."

I dropped the spoon in the empty bowl with a clatter. "I guess the prophecy *made me* drink the Barberrian wine coolers."

"Really?" She gave me a look that was pure Zinnia. "A prophecy made you drink a bunch of wine coolers?"

I turned to Chet. "You can go home now. We're about to have a mother-daughter discussion about life choices." I made a shooing gesture with both hands. "Get out while you can."

Zoey said, "I called Auntie Z, and she'll be here any minute now."

I widened my eyes at Chet. "Run for the hills!"

Chet shot up from the chair as though being ejected. "You know where to find me," he said.

"We have to talk to Chloe," I said. The vision at Chessa's bedside had been intense, but I hadn't forgotten about what happened in the elevator. Chessa had used my lips for more than kissing Chet. She'd told him to talk to her sister, and she'd claimed to have been attacked by a flying creature. I didn't know how to get a spirit back into a body, but learning more about the circumstances leading to her situation could help. If we could find the chunk of poisoned apple, so to speak, we could dislodge it from Snow White's mouth.

Chet paced the room again. "Chloe doesn't know anything. We've talked plenty."

"Fine. I'll talk to her myself. I can stop by the bakery before work tomorrow."

He growled disapproval.

"Chet, you heard her speak. She said Chloe knew something."

"Don't go by yourself," he warned.

"I'll bring protection. I could wear welding goggles to prevent myself from being gorgonified." I looked over at Zoey and raised my eyebrows at my new word. "Gorgonified," I repeated.

"Gorgonified," she said, nodding her approval. "Good idea about wearing eye protection, but due to neither of us being welders, we don't own any welding goggles."

Chet made an exasperated sound. "I'll go with you. Knock on my door in the morning when you're ready." He glanced down at the pink poodle on my skirt as he backed away.

"Don't worry," I said, smoothing my crinkly skirt. "I'll wear something appropriate."

"Yup," he said, or maybe it was just a gulp. He was safely out the door within seconds.

The living room itself seemed to relax in Chet's absence.

Zoey turned to me and asked, "What was that all about? Is it a wolf shifter thing? He ran out of here like a woolly dog who just got offered a B-A-T-H."

"Guilty conscience, I'm guessing. He really did kiss me in the elevator."

She wrinkled her nose. It was understandably gross for her to hear about her mother smooching someone.

"It was brief," I said. "No tongue."

She made a gagging face.

"And to be fair, it was right after I channeled his fiancée, who told him she'd been attacked by some flying creature. And I want to believe that, even though our feelings and memories were getting mixed together, and it's possible she was remembering what happened to *me* in the woods, thinking it was her."

"Getting possessed is more complicated than one would imagine."

"On the plus side, I'm gaining skills. Thanks to Winona, bless her heart, I could plan a six-course meal if I wanted to. And thanks to Perry Pressman, rest in peace, I've gained the ability to understand IRS tax forms. That will come in handy at the library in January."

"What skills does Chessa bring to the table?"

"She's a cryptanalyst. When I was in her office, I noticed she'd been doing crossword puzzles with a pen."

Zoey made an O with her mouth. "You might be able to beat me at Scrabble."

"At the very least, I'll make you work harder to defend your champion status."

Zoey's expression clouded over. "If Chessa wasn't attacked by a creature, what do you think happened to her?"

I weighed my words carefully. "She might have harmed herself. She was found washed up on shore, all cut to—" I stopped myself from saying cut to ribbons. "Cut up," I said.

"Suicide?"

I felt an echo of the pure-white light radiating from the underwater statue. My heart filled with hope and goodness.

"Absolutely not," I said. "Her heart was full of hope. She was excited about something that was going to happen."

Zoey looked at my wrist, at the bracelet.

We were both quiet. In the silence, I grew more certain of Chessa's state of mind before her accident. She'd been keeping a secret, but soon all would be revealed, and it would bring joy to everyone she loved. She'd been teeming with life.

"Mom?"

I smiled at my daughter. "I'm still me."

"Did the prophecy really have my name in it?" Zoey held her hand up to cover her mouth, but I could see by her eyes she was smiling.

"Chessa's translation to English did. The parchment was pretty much triangles and squiggles. Why are you grinning?" I blinked. "Oh. It's because you've been waiting for some sign you're a witch, and that your powers are coming."

"Uh, you think?"

"I'm happy for you, kid, but promise you'll be careful. And remember, you don't need a prophecy to tell you that you're special."

The doorbell rang.

Zoey yelled, "Doorbell!" She sprang up from the sofa, ran to the door, flung it open, and greeted Zinnia.

* * *

"I have one pressing question," Zinnia said after we'd caught her up on recent events. "What's a Barberrian wine cooler?"

"A local winery made it for a few years, but it never caught on nationally," I explained. "It's a sickly sweet beverage with three kinds of berries, and it was the leading cause of teen pregnancy in my hometown." I levitated the teapot to refill my aunt's teacup. "Please tell me that's not the only part of today's events that concerns you."

Zinnia smoothed one hand over her lush red hair, which was dashed with a handful of white streaks and tightly fastened in a bun. "Don't be so dramatic, Zara. I'm simply trying to understand the big picture of this situation you've gotten yourself into."

"Me?" I overfilled her teacup, flooding the saucer. "Chet Moore is the one who got me into this situation."

She tapped the tea-flooded saucer with one finger, and the excess moisture disappeared.

"Cool spell," I said.

Zoey also cooed in appreciation. She'd been quiet for most of the conversation, her nose in the old mythology book, where she'd been trying to locate a creature that matched Steve the Lawyer's description.

We were sitting in the formal dining room because it was the room Zoey and I rarely used, and therefore the most clean and tidy place to entertain my aunt. A Scrabble board lay on the table between us, but Zoey had suddenly become interested in reading a book. She swore it had nothing to do with her worry that I might take the crown of House Scrabble Champion from her.

Zinnia glanced at the unplaced letter tiles as she lifted her teacup with a delicate grip, pinkie stretched out. "And how are your novice studies coming along?"

"Good," I lied.

"Zara, without the appropriate effort, one cannot expect to acquire the skills necessary to make a difficult spell appear to be effortless." She gestured at the sugar cubes, which were forming a cheerleader pyramid formation with practiced ease.

I squirmed guiltily in my chair. "Uh, I've been a bit busy trying to not get gorgonified."

The sugar cubes spiraled through the air in a perfect circle before locking back into a block formation.

Once the cubes stopped moving, I tried to repeat the trick, but I was so tired and distracted that the cubes collapsed into a heap of loose sugar.

"Ta da," I said, as though that was what I'd meant to do.

By the shade she was throwing with her eyes, Zinnia wasn't buying it. She sipped the tea, set the cup down, and flung up both hands with an exasperated sigh. "All I know is that today's the second day in a row that *your daughter* called upon me for guidance. I would have thought, after the events of last week, that you'd take some time for quiet reflection, and stay out of—"

"Trouble?"

"Exactly," she said. "You should *not* have cast the bluffing spell on Chet Moore. His type have a particular distaste for spells, more so than others."

"What? His type? Do you mean wolf shifters?"

"Oh, all shifters." Zinnia blinked rapidly, as though it were the most obvious thing in the world and everyone knew, and why was I so stubbornly ignorant anyway? "They find spells to be vulgar, something to be performed in private only, and as infrequently as possible. Surely I told you that. You must not have been listening. Sometimes I look at your face when I'm speaking, and I can see by your expression that you're too busy formulating your next smart comment to even hear what's being said."

I'd had just about enough "motherly help" from my aunt, but I held my tongue.

"Mmm," I said, nodding. Frank was a shifter, and he'd squealed with delight over my powers, so if it was true that shifters found spells disgusting, it was a learned prejudice.

Zoey held up the mythology book, pages facing us. "Mom, did you say Steve the Lawyer had a forked tongue and a scaly iguana face, like this?" The page showed a woodcut illustration of a beast with a cat-like body.

"Close, but Steve was more regal, more refined."

"But only because of his law degree," Zoey said. "If this dude here had gone to a fancy college, he'd look refined."

Zinnia pushed her chair back and got to her feet. "Thank you so much for inviting me over," she said politely.

"Thank you for coming," I said. "Honestly, I'm so glad Zoey and I have you. I'm trying to be a good witch."

Her mouth tightened. "I know you're trying," she said.

"I'll try harder, and I'll take a break after I finish helping Chet."

"Good luck with that. Perhaps by the next time I see you, he will have gotten the closure he needs. Then he'll be able to move forward pursuing a romantic relationship with you, as you desire." She turned and exited the dining room. I had to jump up and chase her down the hallway to catch up.

"That's not too likely," I said. "If *his kind* thinks that *my kind* has magic witch cooties, how would that even work?"

She gathered her light summer coat from a hook next to the front door and pulled it on gracefully—possibly using magic, but I couldn't tell for sure.

"Some mixed couples find a way to overcome their differences," she said. "But if you ask me, their kind isn't worth the trouble. To be perfectly honest, I find the whole animal-shifter thing rather repugnant." She scrunched her nose.

"It's a moot point if his fiancée wakes up," I said.

"She's been in this coma for a year now, Zara. Life is not a fairy tale. People enjoy those heartwarming stories because in real life, Sleeping Beauty doesn't wake from her slumber."

CHAPTER 19

WEDNESDAY MORNING, I got up early and went next door to the Moore house so we could pay a visit to Chloe before I went to work.

To my surprise, Chet played the role of Mr. Chivalry. He was quick to open the passenger-side door for me, and then asked how I was feeling and if I'd slept well and did I want to stop somewhere for a coffee before we dropped in on Chloe at the bakery?

"They probably have decent coffee at the Gingerbread House," I said warily. "Why are you being so nice? It makes me suspicious that I'm walking into a trap, and I'm about to become someone's startled yet lifelike concrete lawn ornament."

He shrugged and started the engine. We were driving in his regular truck, not a Department van. As usual, Chet's vehicle interior was so spotless, you'd never guess he had a wild ten-year-old boy.

"Zara, I do appreciate your help," he said.

"You're welcome, I guess."

"I've been thinking about what you said to me on Monday—before you cast your spell. About how it's hard to be a single parent because you've got nobody to confide in, and you don't want to burden your kid. It's so true. And being what we are, it's an extra layer of complication."

"About that," I said, happy to bring up the matter. "Is it true that *your kind* finds *my kind* to be repulsive?"

"Do you mean librarians, or redheads?" He shot me a teasing grin, and for a second I caught a glimpse of the Chet I'd met when I first moved to Beacon Street. Gone was the prickly version of Chet, and here was the chatty single father who was so comfortable with himself, he'd made me feel at ease in my new home. With our Internet history, it had been a homecoming of sorts. I moved in next door to a ready-made friend.

I laughed at his joke, not because it was funny, but for him to keep using his sense of humor.

"You know darn well I meant witches," I teased back. "But last night, my aunt accidentally gave me useful information without me having to drag it out of her. She told me you shifters find our spells to be distasteful."

"Your aunt said that?"

"It does explain why Chloe was so quick to go all snake-hair, hissy-hissy-bitey-bitey mode on me."

He tensed his jaw, and the grin disappeared. "Not all shifters are the same, just like how not all witches are the same."

"I take it by your evasive conversational maneuvers that you *do* find my spells repugnant, except for when they might help you get what you want."

He cleared his throat but didn't comment.

"Coffee," I said with a sigh. "I promise I will be a more pleasant Watson to your Sherlock once I get some more coffee in me. I had one at home, but it didn't take, as evidenced by my current irascibility."

He shot me a confused look.

"Irascibility means you're short-tempered," I explained. "Growing up as a redhead, I acquired an extensive vocabulary in one particular area." I blinked innocently. "Not that it's true, what they say about my kind."

"Of course not," he said, a little too vehemently.

* * *

When we arrived at the bakery, Chloe wasn't at all surprised to see us. She was dressed in her baker's whites, though she hadn't tied her long hair back or even covered her ringlets with a hairnet. She did wear a white headband, which kept her hair off her face, but not necessarily out of the food. She'd always worn her hair down, but I hadn't noticed until now. Was it the snakes? Did they get hissy-hissy-bitey-bitey if she smothered them in a hairnet?

"I'll be with you two in a minute," Chloe said, as though we were regular customers.

Chet leaned over and told me, "I called ahead."

"Probably for the best," I whispered. "There are some scary creatures you don't want to startle."

Chet elbowed me. His dirty look warned that he was one of those scary creatures, and he didn't find my comment funny. Was a distinct lack of humor the reason for the divide between shifters and witches? That would explain why Frank was so easygoing. He could—and did—laugh at anything.

Chloe finished loading muffins into the display cabinet. A customer left with her box of croissants, and the front of the bakery was empty except for the three of us. Chloe waved for us to come around through the gap in the front counter. She ushered us back, through the delicious-smelling, flour-dusted prep area, and into a private office at the back of the bakery.

The office also served as storage, and was lined with metal shelves holding every kind of baking pan imaginable. A computer desk had been stuck in one corner, seemingly as an afterthought.

Chet and I both took seats on either side of a small pine table. The table was extremely familiar. Was I getting one of Chessa's memories?

I rubbed the yellowed surface until more of the memory came to me. The table was made by Ikea, and it was the same model of table I'd gotten as a hand-me-down when Zoey was a baby. I'd since given it away, so it hadn't made the move to Wisteria.

I hadn't thought about my first table in many years, but seeing this other version made me nostalgic. Why hadn't I at least taken a photo of the artwork Zoey had drawn on the underside? Back then, I thought I'd have all the time in the world to enjoy my daughter's drawings, but then she became so serious and book-oriented as soon as she learned to read. Her crayon artwork had ceased. Time was marching on, and we were both growing up, she with her independence at high school and me with my... *whatever this was*.

Chloe covered the small pine table with baked goods and mugs of coffee. She gave me a few cautious glances. We hadn't seen each other since our visit at her house two days earlier, when I'd insulted her by avoiding eye contact. But then yesterday, she'd sent the peace offering through Detective Bentley. How could I stay angry at someone who sent me donuts at work? Or anything edible, really.

"Chloe, thanks for the pastries yesterday. The other staff and I enjoyed them very much."

She flicked her pale eyes up to mine and locked on. "You're welcome."

I was careful not to blink. I kept looking straight at her. No way was I going to be the one to break eye contact first. Not even if my cheeks were streaming with tears.

Chloe broke eye contact to look at the table. "We need more savory options," she said. She left with a toss of her golden ringlets, and returned a few minutes later with mini quiches. She was about to dart out again when Chet barked at her to sit down.

"It's time for the three of us to talk," Chet said, his tone intimidating.

Jordan Taub, Chloe's husband, arrived at the office doorway. He stood blocking the exit, wiping flour from his hands onto his white apron. "Everything okay in here?"

Chloe waved him away. "I can handle this," she said.

Jordan shot me a look of friendly embarrassment. The last time we'd seen each other, our relationship had been strictly baker-customer. Now, two days later, everything was upside down. He knew I was a witch, and I knew his wife had hissy-hissy-bitey-bitey hair, but I still didn't know what Jordan was, other than a baker.

Jordan Taub looked about thirty. His skin was dark, but not as black as Chet's coworker, Knox. Jordan was muscular and tough looking, a former army soldier, but not quite as tough as Knox, who was a mountain. Knox had turned into an eagle. Was Jordan also an eagle shifter? Was it racist to ponder if skin color or ethnicity had anything to do with powers? People had been dropping comments about redheaded witches, and I couldn't help but wonder.

Jordan remained in the doorway, still human. Chloe shooed him away again. What if the man didn't have supernatural abilities? What if he didn't even know about me? Or his own wife, for that matter? If I were a gorgon, would I tell my future husband? What an interesting conversation that would be.

Jordan smiled at me. "Zara, thanks for helping us," he said.

Ah, so he did know. "I haven't helped much yet."

"But you'll be getting a discount from now on," he said.

"There's a discount for supernaturals?"

His expression screwed up into profound confusion. "There's a discount for friends and family," he said. "What do you mean by *supernaturals*?"

My mouth opened. No words came out.

In the silence that followed, you could have heard a silicone spatula drop onto a soft towel.

Jordan's face cracked into a grin. "C'mon, Zara. I'm joking. I thought you witches had a wicked sense of humor."

Across from me, Chet guffawed.

I pointed my finger at the tall, dark baker. "You got me, Jordan. I was speechless, thanks to you, and that's no small feat."

Jordan waved his big hands in the air. "Don't turn me into a frog. I swear I'll behave myself from now on."

I cackled theatrically and rubbed my hands together. What was it with people thinking I would turn them into frogs? The doctor at the DWM had said the same thing. Maybe it was just one of those clichéd things people said to witches.

Jordan checked to see that we had cream and sugar for our coffee, and left us to our meeting. The coffee was excellent. I usually picked up pastries only on my way in to work, then made a fresh pot at the library. The Gingerbread House blend had a pleasant touch of spice.

I relaxed and enjoyed my coffee and pastries while Chet relayed the details of the previous evening's visit to Chessa's bedside.

Chloe didn't ask any questions. Once Chet was out of details, we both waited for Chloe's response.

She fussed with her white headband and then twisted one golden ringlet in her hand while she stared into her coffee mug. Without looking up, she said, "Are you sure she didn't mean Charlize? Chessa was much closer to her than she ever was to me."

"That's not true," Chet said. "Why are you lying?"

I detected a faint hiss coming from Chloe's bouncy ringlets. I not so subtly shifted my pine chair a few inches away from her. Chloe looked up at me, her pale eyes nearly colorless. I clenched my jaw and held eye contact. If I backed down again, and fled the premises like I wanted to, she'd know she could intimidate me. Plus we'd never get our answer.

"Thanks again for the donuts yesterday," I said sweetly. "Detective Bentley makes a fine delivery boy."

"Bentley," Chloe said, her pretty forehead wrinkling. "Does he know about us?" Chloe nervously glanced from me to Chet and back again.

Chet said, "He's not a member of the inner circle, but he's no dummy. It won't be long."

"I hear he has some interesting talents," Chloe said. "The DWM should put the squeeze on him. See what he does." The corners of her mouth twitched up. "I could squeeze him for you. I can be very good at squeezing."

Chet pointed a cinnamon twist at her. "Stop changing the subject. What was going on with Chessa before her accident? She was very clear that you had answers about her emotional state. You remember how she was before the accident. Always sneaking off to be alone. Defensive. Moody."

Chloe squirmed in her chair. Three of her ringlets changed into a trio of undulating snakes.

I jumped up from my chair and put it between me and the gorgon.

She reached up and stroked the snakes, calming them. Watching me closely, she asked, "You can see them?"

"If by *them* you mean three snakes with golden scales and pointy fangs, yes. I can see them."

"They don't bite," she said. "Not even when Jordan Junior tugs on them. Zara, would you like to touch them?"

I pushed the chair out of the way without hesitation.

"Sure," I said. "When one is invited to touch magical hair snakes, one should not pass up the opportunity." I reached out and chucked one writhing snake under the chin. The gold-scaled snake seemed surprised, its dark eyes widening, but it didn't bite me. The other two snakes jostled for attention. Soon I had both hands in Chloe's den of hair snakes, which now numbered over a dozen.

Chloe giggled. "That tickles," she said.

I dropped my hands, suddenly embarrassed to have both of my hands in another woman's hair, even if her hair was magical snakes.

"Not that I mind the tickling," Chloe said quickly. "It's kind of relaxing to let my hair down, so to speak."

"I'm sorry we got off on the wrong foot the other day, over at your house," I said.

"Let me cook for you again sometime. We can have a girls' night. You could bring over this daughter of yours that I haven't met yet. Miss Zolanda Daizy Cazzaundra Riddle."

The hairs on the back of my neck raised. Hearing a gorgon refer to your daughter by her full name is not an everyday experience.

Chet interrupted with a gruff, "Let's stick to the topic at hand."

Chloe took a deep breath and gave me a bored look as she exhaled. "I told you guys, I don't know anything I haven't already shared, with the DWM, and with the regular cops. Chessa was emotional before the accident because that's how she was. The three of us are very passionate. And family oriented. Especially—" She choked on her words. Her eyes filled with tears. She reached for a napkin and dabbed at the corners of her eyes.

Her tears looked real enough, but something about her outburst struck me as theatrical. Perhaps it was the echo of memory in my mind, Chessa's memory of Chloe throwing tantrums over the years.

I took a seat in my chair again and turned to face Chloe. "How did you know my daughter's full name?"

She had dried her eyes. "From the scroll," she said plainly. "The one Chessa was working on." She dabbed her dry eyes rhythmically. "And then Chet and I worked so hard to bring Zoey here, to Wisteria. She was all I thought about for weeks on end, so of course I know her name."

I slowly turned my head to focus on Chet. "What?"

Chet growled at the blonde baker, "Stop talking, Chloe."

"Don't stop," I said. "What do you mean, you worked so hard to bring Zoey here?"

Chloe reached up with one flour-dusted hand and twirled a pair of coiling hair snakes. "You didn't tell her everything? Oh, Chet." She shook her head. "That's no way to treat a woman. Especially a witch. You're going to pay dearly for keeping Zara in the dark."

Yes, he is, I thought. *There's a price for keeping me in the dark.*

"Thanks for the help," Chet said coldly as he got to his feet. "We're going now. Don't say another word, Chloe. I think you've done enough harm for one day."

Her golden snakes hissed in unison at Chet as he prowled around the table toward the office's door.

I ran after him. He was wise to stay a few steps ahead of me.

I caught up to him outside, in the bright morning sunshine.

Breathlessly, I asked, "Is it true? You and Chloe had some scheme to get my daughter here to Wisteria?"

He glanced around furtively. The bakery was on a busy street, and plenty of people were within earshot. "We're not discussing this here," he said.

"Fine. Let's get in your truck and talk somewhere else."

We were standing next to his vehicle. He looked down, pulled his phone from his pocket, and frowned at it. "I've got to get to work."

I used my magic to grab his phone and toss it up, into a tree. I didn't care if he found magic distasteful. I didn't care if someone saw me practicing magic out in the open. He was going to explain himself.

"You can be a few minutes late," I said. "Is it true what Chloe said back there?"

He looked down at the sidewalk between us.

I put my hands on my hips. "I'll take your silence as an admission of guilt."

"I'm only guilty of trying everything within my powers to help my fiancée."

"So, the end justifies the means? My family is expendable, if it helps you get Chessa back?" There was a bitter tang in my mouth. "Wow. She must be a super-special shifter, or monster, or whatever. Is that her power, Chet? She makes people do terrible things for her?"

He hunched his shoulders and glanced down the sidewalk. "We shouldn't be discussing this here."

"Tell me what she is. What is this power she has?"

"She..." He shook his head. "It's not what you think."

"You're not in my head. You don't know anything about what I think. You only care about your own selfish needs. Your own selfish desires."

He winced and looked around us, at anything but me. "Zara, it was Chloe and Charlize. They were so sure your daughter was the Soul Catcher," he said. "Zoey was our only hope."

"You thought a sixteen-year-old girl was your only hope. But then—surprise, surprise—you got stuck with me instead."

"And I regret what I've done, Zara. I truly do."

I took a step back. "You regret meddling in other people's lives? Or do you specifically regret bringing me here?" I held up one hand. "Don't answer that. I don't even want to know what you meant. What am I to you?"

"A friend."

I snorted.

He lifted his chin and barely made eye contact before looking up at the tree overhead, searching for his phone. "It's really up there," he said. "I'll have to drive back later today."

He was worried about his phone? And not about apologizing to me for whatever scheming he, Charlize, and Chloe had been up to? Some friend he was. I'd meant to get the phone back down right away, once I'd gotten his attention, but now I wanted him to be inconvenienced. Actually, I wanted to punch him in his busted ribs, make him scream, but the decent part of me abhorred violence. And I had to hold onto my humanity, my decency.

What had Chloe said to Chet? "*That's no way to treat a woman. Especially a witch. You're going to pay dearly for keeping Zara in the dark.*"

A gorgon had her ways of making a man pay for disrespect, but I was a witch. My powers were subtler, and I still had my humanity, but Chet would pay.

I felt a sly smile twisting my lips.

"Good luck driving anywhere without your keys," I said.

"My what?"

I'd already drawn his keys from his pocket and into my hand. As Chet watched, stunned, I wound my arm back and pitched his keys into the tree. I used my magic at the last minute, safely out of sight of people passing by, and snagged the keys on a twig. The phone and the keys weren't coming back down without a fight.

Chet swore under his breath.

I started walking away.

"Don't worry about me," I called over my shoulder. "I can walk to work from here."

He muttered something that sounded like *broomstick*.

CHAPTER 20

AFTER I ARRIVED in Wisteria and discovered my aunt "coincidentally" lived there as well, I'd brewed up a few conspiracy theories. My aunt claimed innocence. She said that when the local library contacted her for a letter of reference, it was the first she'd heard about me moving there. She told me it was the work of magic itself—mystical forces beyond my comprehension. "Magic has a mind of its own," she was fond of saying.

And I'd believed her. Because once you find out magic is real, the world actually makes more sense. The inexplicable becomes... not mundane, exactly, but less mystifying.

But since I'd learned about Chessa and been visited by her spirit, it seemed she was the one behind my cross-country move.

No sooner had I warmed up to that idea, though, than the carpet was yanked out from underneath me.

And I'd learned the truth from the lips of an honest-to-goodness gorgon.

The invisible director of my life had been right under my nose. My neighbor, Chet Moore, had been the one tangling my string of fate, weaving it with his own.

While I walked to the library, I replayed my first day on Beacon Street, and my first face-to-face meeting with Chet. My emotions had been heightened that day, so the memory was crystal clear, thanks to my witch powers.

That fateful Saturday afternoon, I'd been standing at the back of the moving truck, grabbing a box jokingly labeled XL PMS Sweatpants. The box actually contained pots and pans, but Zoey and I had created joke labels to make packing more fun. The goofy labels had made unpacking less fun, but that's beside my point.

Chet, the helpful neighbor I hadn't met yet, walked up behind me. With his rich, deep voice, he'd said, "You're Zara the Camgirl?"

I turned around slowly. It had been over a dozen years since anyone had recognized me from my fifteen minutes of fame on the Internet.

"I'm just Zara now," I'd said. "My Camgirl days are over."

"Chet Twenty-one," the man said, introducing himself by his screen name.

At first, his screen name didn't ring any bells. But then I took a look at him, and my Hunk Detector set off a five-star alarm. He was so attractive, his face blanked out the center of my vision. I couldn't discern his actual features, other than that he had eyes, the greenest of green, with glints of silver and gold.

I complimented his eyes and asked who he was, besides his screen name.

He introduced himself as Chet Moore, and told me he lived next door, in the blue house with the goat on the roof. Then he did the cutest thing and bashfully said I probably wouldn't remember him specifically, since I'd had so many fans in those days.

Chet twenty-one. CHET21. While I tried to recall someone posting under that name, I bought myself time by introducing him to my daughter.

And then, as soon as he grinned at us, I felt a rush of familiarity. He had been studying engineering back in those days, and he'd confided to me, presumably under the anonymity of an Internet chat room, that he didn't know where his career would take him. His father had a plan all worked out, but he wasn't sure if he could follow in the older man's footsteps. I *did* know him. I knew this man's heart. He was kind and generous and brave. He took charge in an emergency. He was Chet, and he was one of the good guys.

All of that knowledge about Chet Moore hit me like a wave breaking, but I didn't mention it because I was so in awe of his eyes and then his teeth. The memories of him tucked themselves away, like folded clothes slipping into a drawer, right where they belonged. His smile made my whole body sing.

"You're staring at me," he'd said that sunny Saturday. "Is there something on my face?"

I'd wondered at the time if the memory of talking to CHET21 on the Internet was real, or wishful thinking. But did it matter? The guy lived next door to me now. Whether I really did remember his individual story or he was just a composite character formed from dozens of my young male fans, our past didn't matter as much as the present. And *those eyes!*

After a bit of my babbling about craft supplies and googly eyeballs, he said warmly, "You should fit right in here on Beacon Street. Welcome to the neighborhood. We should probably shake hands now."

I couldn't shake hands due to my armload. I jiggled the box, making the pots and pans clatter. "I'll be done moving in about an hour."

He took my box from me, shuffled it to one strong-looking arm, and shook my hand. At the touch of his hand on mine, I stopped questioning whether or not I remembered him from my Zara the Camgirl days. In my heart, I knew *his* heart, and knew it to be good and pure and loyal.

"It's official," he said. "I now pronounce us neighbors."

"Neighbors," I repeated. "Til death do us part."

He jerked his hand away from mine abruptly. His eyes were darker, the light gone out. The hollows in his cheeks caught shadows. His face became long and lean, his eyes hungry, like a wolf's.

What had I said? Just a joke about being neighbors *'til death do us part*.

I apologized quickly, assuming his reaction had something to do with Winona Vander Zalm, his elderly neighbor who'd passed away, and whose house I'd just purchased.

I could not have known that the man standing before me was grieving his fiancée, who was in a coma, lying in a top-secret hospital bed twenty-some stories below ground.

He'd quickly changed the subject, offering to give me a hand with the last few boxes. We'd parted on good terms, but later that day, I'd gone banging on his door because I suspected his little boy had snuck into my house and broken things. Later, Chet brought young Corvin over to our place, gripping him by the collar, and made him apologize.

Zoey and Corvin traded insults, calling each other *pestilence*. They had taken an instant dislike to each other, not knowing they would become good friends within weeks, surrogate siblings to each other.

As I considered their blossoming friendship, I had to admit positive things had come from Chet guiding me toward Wisteria. Many positive things.

That Saturday evening, before I knew I was a witch and Chet was a wolf shifter, he and I had bonded over the challenges of being single parents. The kids joined us for housewarming pizza and lime cordial in martini glasses.

I couldn't say much for Corvin's manners, but he was a smart kid. "Your son is a clever boy," I'd said to Chet.

"He doesn't get it from me."

"What does your wife do?"

"Nothing," he said.

"Lucky lady," I said with a laugh. I had no idea the man had a fiancée who did "nothing" due to being in a coma.

"She's dead," he said, and I immediately stopped laughing.

He quickly added, "No need to apologize. It was many years ago, before I moved in next door with my father. Don was supposed to help me raise Corvin to be a well-adjusted and perfectly normal boy. As you can see, that didn't exactly work out as planned."

I was still reeling from the dead-wife bombshell. I'd blathered about how difficult it was to raise kids, and how I'd lucked out with my daughter, whom people said had an old soul.

An *old soul*. The sort of old soul who'd have her name on some ancient prophecy?

But I didn't know about the magic running through Wisteria yet. I didn't even know I was a witch.

That night, Chet and I had bonded quickly. I immediately felt more at ease with him than I'd been around a man for many years.

That first night on Beacon Street, Chet had encouraged me to talk about myself, to share how I felt about Wisteria.

"This town is an undiscovered gem," I'd said, laughing over my booze-free lime cordial martini. "There must be some magical spell shrouding it from the rest of the world because I can't understand why everyone isn't beating a path to move here."

"A magical spell," he'd repeated with a sly smile. "You don't believe in that sort of thing, do you?"

I'd snorted. "I love a spooky campfire story as much as the next gal, but I'm not one of those woo-woo types who's always falling for nonsense." I reached for another slice of pizza. "My family's not very close. We've got some weird relatives who are into various scams. My mother kept me far away from those other wacky folks." I looked him right in the eyes. "I'm the normal one in my family."

He bit his lower lip, as though holding back a sarcastic comment. "So, you don't believe in anything paranormal. Not even when you see things you can't explain?"

"Nah. If there really were such things as ghosts or bloodsuckers or werewolves, there would be scientific proof by now."

"What makes you think you can trust the scientists?" Chet asked playfully. "Maybe all the top scientists in the world are bloodsuckers and werewolves themselves, and they're working hard to keep their kind secret."

I pointed my pizza crust at him. "I like you, Chet Moore. You've got a wicked sense of humor and a wild imagination."

"And I like you, too, Zara Riddle. I always have." Shyly, he added, "Just like all the other lonely young men who used to follow your every move online. How many marriage proposals did you get in those days, anyway?"

"Not a single one that had any appeal." I gave him a sidelong look. "Chet Moore, aka CHET21, did you ever propose to me?"

His cheeks reddened. "It was a long time ago."

"I've still got all the chat logs, archived on a hard drive somewhere." I waved at the stack of boxes at the edge of the half-unpacked living room. "It might be in the box labeled Teddy Bears and Taxidermy Tools. I've got half a mind to unpack my old computer, plug it in right now, and do a text search on your username. You said it was CHET21, no spaces or underscores?"

"Don't do that," he blurted. "Please, let's let the past lie in its musty grave."

I'd shivered and rubbed the goose bumps on my forearms. *Let the past lie in its musty grave.* Between the werewolf talk and the mention of graves, I was getting a spooky vibe from my handsome neighbor. But I still liked him.

Later, the conversation would turn to the history of the house I'd just bought, and its colorful former owner. I didn't know Winona Vander Zalm's ghost was about to make my first weeks in Wisteria very complicated.

But before all that, I'd asked Chet, "Why do you live here in Wisteria?"

His expression changed, and the room grew darker, the shadows larger. "There's an anchor keeping me here. A heavy one, buried deep, and try as I might, I can't get free." His eyes shone with sadness. "I can't leave, but some days I think I can't stay, either."

"Moving is horrible," I said.

He lifted his chin and forced a smile. "Not the way you do it. That's a clever idea you had, putting silly labels on your boxes." He looked over the stack of boxes and smiled. "How did your daughter feel about moving here?"

"There were some tears, but she said she had a good feeling about it."

"A good *feeling*, hmm?" He kept his gaze on the boxes and asked, evenly, "Does your daughter have any special abilities? Any special affinity for certain subjects or activities?"

It seemed like an oddly phrased question, but I'd answered honestly. "My Zoey is excellent at anything she puts her mind to."

"Good," he said, nodding. "That's very good. We could use someone like her around here." He looked down at the pizza box and took another piece, dusting off some of the roasted garlic onto the wax paper.

"You don't like garlic? Are you some sort of monster?"

He paused, the pizza slice just inches from his mouth. "Here in Wisteria, you just never know. I've seen a fair number of strange things."

"I'd *love* to see more strange things," I said. "Sounds fun to me."

"Careful what you wish for," he'd teased.

And then Corvin and Zoey had chased each other through the living room. The conversation turned back to our kids and the local schools.

Chet must have thought I was a sucker, falling easily for a few kind words.

Not anymore.

He was going to pay, just as soon as I figured out everything that he'd done. And I was going to start by using technology, which couldn't lie to me the way my memories did.

* * *

I put in a solid shift at the library, working hard and being pleasant, even though my mind was elsewhere. Frank wasn't working that day, so it was easier for me to stay in librarian mode.

As soon as I got through the day and punched my timecard, I went straight home on a fact-finding mission.

I pulled out the cardboard box containing my old computer and archival hard drives.

It took a few hours to untangle the many cords and cables, and get my system running, but the old gal finally booted up. The Pentium Pro had been state-of-the-art technology at the time, a donation from one of my website sponsors. The computer would have cost thousands of dollars at the time, yet it didn't have the computing power of today's entry-level smartphone.

I pulled up the stored text data from my old website's bulletin board system. It had been a huge amount of data at the time, but compared to the size of current-day streaming video, my "massive" chunk of data was downright teeny.

I transferred the raw chat logs to my laptop because I wasn't sure how long the old gal would keep running. On the laptop, I did a search for username CHET21.

To my absolute lack of surprise, there was nothing under that name. Nothing. No record of a man named Chet, not under any variation of numbers and symbols in combination with any version of his name. I did have one fan posting as RogerMoore65, but he was a retired long-haul trucker with a passion for a certain James Bond.

My research proved what I already knew, deep down.

Chet had not been a fan of mine, nor had we been friends "back in the day." The easy familiarity I felt toward my neighbor was either wishful thinking on my part, or a memory implant, courtesy of Chessa's spiritual residue.

And that was exactly what he'd wanted. For months now, I'd been living next door to a man who'd started our relationship on a bedrock of lies.

I'd trusted him. I'd saved his life. I'd let him have the last slice of pizza.

And he'd played me for a sucker, all because my daughter's name was on some musty old rotten scroll.

I pushed away the laptop, got to my feet, and went to Zoey's room.

I told her everything. She had a right to know.

As angry as I was, Zoey was even angrier. "That's just... so..." She struggled to find the right word. "Rude!"

"Zoey, he didn't cut in front of us at a concert, or kick our seat at the movie theater. I wouldn't characterize what he did as *rude*. More like treacherous, or heinous, or punishable by being rolled down a hill inside a barrel lined with knives."

Zoey wasn't even listening to me. She'd gone to her bedroom window, opened it, and lobbed something at Corvin's window.

The little ten-year-old boy with the huge eyes and floppy black hair pushed open his window.

"Hi, Zoey," he called over.

"Send over the line," she said. "I need to chat with someone in your family."

Corvin's huge eyes got even bigger, and he quickly got to work. He tossed over a big can of tomato sauce, attached to a metal cable.

Zoey set the can on her dresser, and hooked the end of the metal cable onto an eye hook embedded in her bedroom wall.

"Hey," I said, confused. "You told me that hook was for a hammock."

She was already out her window like a ninja, crossing the chasm between the houses. I ran to her window just in time to see her reach the blue house and gracefully swing up into Corvin's open window.

The little boy gave me a gap-toothed grin, waved, and closed the window on his side.

CHAPTER 21

IF MY DAUGHTER'S witch powers never got around to kicking in, at least she had potential as a ninja.

With Corvin's help, she'd stormed the Moore castle, and was off to interrogate Chet. Proud as I was, I couldn't let her do it alone—assuming he'd ever gotten his keys out of that tree and found his way back home. If he was in the house, I had to get over there and tag in with Zoey so we could work as a team.

I climbed up onto Zoey's windowsill.

Sure, I could have easily gone downstairs, used the sidewalk, and then knocked on the Moore family's front door like a normal person, but seeing as how I was a witch, I didn't have to.

With a flick of my wrist, I pushed Corvin's window open. I didn't need to move my body to manipulate objects, but small gestures seemed to boost the power of my efforts.

I checked that the metal cable was secure, wrapped an ankle and one arm around the line, and slid my way into the Moore house, head first.

Five minutes later, I located both Zoey and Chet, inside the small den he used as a home office. Corvin was, thankfully, not in the room. I found the kid interesting, but I preferred for him to be interesting in places where I wasn't.

Zoey had Chet backed into a corner and was pacing as she talked. "Mr. Moore, I think you'll agree that up until now I've shown you nothing but respect, but some troubling facts have recently come to light, and I don't know how nice I can be to you anymore. When I think about how you've lied and manipulated my mother, it makes me want to teach Corvin some really bad swear words—the likes of which you've never heard before. And I'm in high school, so you should be warned I have access to epithets that would make the wallpaper curl off the walls of this den." She paused and tilted her head as she looked at the wall. "Is that pattern supposed to be all the classics of literature on wooden shelves? That's cute." She waved her finger at him. "But don't think I'm going to be easily distracted by wallpaper. No, sir. I'm here to get the facts about what you did and how you got me and my mother here to Wisteria."

Behind her, I raised my hand politely. "Ditto," I said to Chet. "And you should be warned that I know a few swear words that aren't so current but still have bite."

Zoey wheeled around to face me. "Are you here to call me off, or tag in?"

"Officer Riddle, here to tag in." I puffed out my chest in my best cop impersonation. "I see you've cornered the perp."

Chet rubbed his temples. "You two win," he said wearily. "A wise man can see when he's outmatched. I'll tell you anything you want to know."

I jumped on the opportunity with the first question that popped into my mind. It was something that had been bothering me all day.

"What is Steve, other than a lawyer?"

Zoey put her hands on her hips. "Yeah, what is Steve? I've looked everywhere for the iguana-lion monster Mom described, and I can't find anything."

"He's not a monster. Steve is a rare chimera called an Iguammit, which is a sort of second cousin to the Egyptian Ammit. He was much smaller when he came to us, but our scientists have been working on a Shifter Growth Hormone." Chet squeezed past Zoey, out of the corner, and took a seat in his computer chair, which squeaked as he leaned back. "And Steve would be mortified if he knew we were talking about him this way. He's a very private person."

"How private is he?" I asked. "Does he post on internet message boards under a screen name?"

Chet frowned and answered carefully. "I wouldn't know."

I took a seat on Chet's desk. Zoey came over to join me. "Interesting," Zoey said, resting her chin on her elbow thoughtfully.

I pressed on. "Would your Iguammit lawyer, Steve, lie to a woman and tell her they were friends on the internet sixteen years ago, even though they were not acquainted at all, and a recent text search of the internet chat logs from her old computer confirms he's a liar and a manipulative phony?"

Chet looked from me to Zoey. He had evidently decoded my subtext to realize I wasn't talking about Steve the Iguammit Lawyer. He shrank in his office chair and gave my daughter a pleading look, his dark eyebrows forming a peaked roof.

Zoey sniffed and waved one hand in a sassy gesture. "If you think we're going to play Good Cop, Bad Cop, boy, are you in for a surprise. Spoiler alert: we're both the Bad Cop."

"It's true," I stage-whispered. "More like Bad Cop, Worse Cop."

Just then, Corvin appeared in the doorway. I hadn't noticed the door opening, but there he was, watching us.

Chet shifted forward in his chair. "Buddy, can you give us a few more minutes?"

Corvin didn't move. "What are you talking about?"

Zoey slid off the edge of the desk. "Boring grownup stuff," she said with a playful eyebrow waggle. "Let's go play Ninjas while these two talk boring grownup stuff." Corvin agreed happily. Before Zoey left, she leaned in and whispered, "Don't pull any punches."

The kids left, and I used my magic to close the door. "Oops," I said. "I keep using my distasteful magic."

"It's fine," Chet said. "I'm getting used to it."

His gaze was on the desk, to the side of where I was sitting. There was nothing on the desk, but as I looked at the smooth, dark-stained oak surface, I remembered something. Being on that same desk, with the door shut, my skirt pushed up while Chet kissed my neck, breathless. It wasn't a fantasy, though. I was far too annoyed at him to be thinking such things. I was reliving one of Chessa's memories. One of her precious moments with her lover. It had been hasty and furtive, a brief reconnection after something bad. A trip? No, an argument. A silly fight over nothing in particular. He could be so stubborn, so quick to walk away, so obstinate about hiding his feelings. But there were ways to draw him out of his shell. Removing his clothes was the first step. A few light scratches down his spine was the next.

Meanwhile, in the present, Chet seemed to sense something was going on inside my mind.

He said, "Anything you'd like to share?"

"No," I said, a little too quickly. Could he see my cheeks flushing, my pupils dilating? The small computer den was not brightly lit, and the book-themed wallpaper was dark. I leaned back, trying to hide what I was feeling.

"Your daughter must have used magic to get inside my house. The house was quiet, and then suddenly she was in here, threatening me, but in a very polite fashion."

"No magic," I said, snapping back to reality. Thinking about my daughter brought me out of Chessa's memories, and not a moment too soon.

He rubbed the plastic armrests of his chair, which brought back another of Chessa's memories, even more vividly. I shook my head and looked around for something non-sexy to focus on. There was a cactus sitting on the windowsill. Good. I stared at the cactus until the images left my mind.

"I got my keys and phone down using a stick," Chet said. "Took about ten minutes, tops."

"Next time, I'll have to put them higher."

He rested one elbow on the armrest and leaned to the side casually, his chin on his hand. "You should. I deserved it for messing around with your life. Zara, I want to make it up to you."

"Start by telling me what you did. I don't mean the part about pretending you were one of my Internet fanboys. That's pretty obvious. A quick search online would have been all the research you required, then you told me one lie, and I bought it. Like a fool." I took a deep breath. "Serves me right for being so gullible. What I want to know is, how did you get me to Wisteria?"

"You're not angry?"

"More curious than anything. You'll know when I'm angry." I made a twirling motion with my fingers. "Also, you'll find yourself transformed into a tiny tree frog. Now spill the beans." I didn't have a spell to turn him into a frog, but he didn't know that.

His chair squeaked as he swiveled slightly to the right, so his shoulders were no longer square to mine.

"The three of us did what we had to do," Chet said. "Chloe did most of the research, since she was on bed rest from the pregnancy." He gestured to indicate computer typing. "Charlize was able to hack your home computer network. It was easy to feed you the librarian job posting. We pulled some strings on this side, and we were monitoring your online activity in case we had to massage the deal"—he paused, his hands midair—"but then we didn't need to do much after all. You wanted the job, and you accepted with no problem. To me, it felt like maybe fate had always meant for you to move here, and I was simply one of fate's pawns."

"But why the subterfuge? Why didn't you come visit us, and ask? I've always tried to help people in need."

Chet let out a low laugh. "Because I'm not an idiot. I know how it would have gone if some guy showed up at your door, asking you to help him find a ghost. You would have called the cops, assuming you even gave me five minutes at your kitchen table to explain myself. How do you think it would have gone over?"

"That's a trick question," I said. "I wouldn't have buzzed a stranger up from the apartment entrance. My old neighborhood was pretty sketchy."

"And that's exactly my point, more or less," Chet said. "Your guard would have been up instantly. Plus it's difficult for me to leave town except on official DWM business, which this wasn't. They're paying for Chessa's ongoing treatment, but there's nothing in the budget for what they deem experimental treatments."

"You guys have the equivalent of an HMO?"

"It's complicated. They prioritize being battle-ready over anything else." He swayed his chair from side to side. "But you and I, we're both on the same team. We're the good guys."

"Good and bad are highly subjective. That's what Zoey always says."

"You're doing a good job raising a kid who questions everything."

I glanced at the closed door. "Speaking of my daughter, do you have any idea why she didn't get any powers on her sixteenth birthday? It seems like this Soul Catcher power went to me instead. Or maybe I didn't get her power. My aunt calls my situation being Spirit Charmed, which sounds much less active."

He looked genuinely perplexed, holding out both hands, palms up. "Honestly, I don't know. Chessa's the cryptanalyst. Once we get Chessa back, she can tell us both what's happening."

I looked from Chet's face to the wallpaper. Then at the closed door. Then the four walls of the tiny room. The cactus on the windowsill had spikes that looked as soft as a kitten's whiskers but weren't. Things were not always as they appeared.

Chet's words echoed in my head like a hypnotic suggestion. *Once we get Chessa back, she can tell us what's happening.*

Was it that simple? Catch the spirit and shove her back into her body, then I'd get all the answers I was looking for? Seemed awfully convenient. What else would reviving Chessa do for me?

"Enough," I said, sliding off the desk to stand, towering over Chet in his chair. "I don't like the way this is going. This feels too much like the job posting, all over again."

He held his hand to his chest and blinked repeatedly, his eyes wide in an affected expression of surprise. "Zara, I've told you everything now. It's all out in the open."

"Is it?" I backed up toward the small room's door. "I may not be a cryptanalyst, but I can spot patterns. I can see how neatly our interests are now aligned. You want your fiancée back so you can be with her, and— conveniently enough—she's the one person in the world who holds the key to my daughter's future."

"We should call Zoey back in here," he said calmly. "Corvin can entertain himself for a while. He did just fine before you two moved in next door."

"You're not speaking to my daughter," I said. "Not tonight, or ever. Not until I know who I can trust."

"Zara, you can trust me."

I shook my head slowly. No, I couldn't. And hearing him ask me to put my faith in him only set off my alarms louder.

"That scroll," I said, narrowing my eyes at him. "The only thing printed on it was a bunch of squiggles and triangles that didn't look anything like a name. That's why you needed a full day to prepare before you brought me in to see her body. You had to get into Chessa's files to set up the translation overlay. You set me up, showed me what you wanted me to see. And I don't know how you did it, but you fed me the perfect date to make me think the prophecy was real."

Chet got to his feet and moved toward me slowly. "Zara, slow down. You're being paranoid. Chessa was like this, right before her accident. She was moody and anxious, and she even said people were plotting against her."

I pressed my back against the wall next to the door, my hand on the door handle "Maybe people *were* plotting against her, Chet. Maybe one of those people was you."

He stopped, facing me. Through gritted teeth, his face mere inches from mine, he said, "You can't believe that. Why would I hurt her? I loved her."

"Consider the facts the way a good cop would see them. Two women in your life have been attacked by giant birds. First Chessa, and then me."

"But I was with you that day in the woods. And you know I'm not an avian shifter."

"You had an accomplice. Rob, or Knox, or both of them."

"They would never— I would never—"

I yanked open the office door and yelled, "Zoey! We're leaving! Right now!"

She came running. When she saw the look on my face, my daughter took me by the hand. "Mom, you're scaring me."

"You should be scared," I snapped. "This man lives next door to us, and we've given him unfettered access to our lives, and we don't even know who he is."

Chet crossed his arms. "Calm down and let's talk this through."

"Not here," I said. "And not now. I need fresh air."

I led the way out of the house, using the conventional front-door method. Zoey followed, tight on my heels, her hand still gripped in mine.

We reached the sidewalk, walked past our house, and kept going.

Zoey was talking, trying to communicate with me, but there was such a din of voices and noise in my head. She wanted to know what Chet had shared in his den, but I didn't want to discuss it yet. And I could barely hear anything she was saying. I needed to get clear of all the confusion, all the noise.

She yanked her hand from mine. "Where are you dragging me?"

I stopped and looked around the neighborhood's houses, confused. "Which way to the beach?"

"The opposite direction of where you're heading," she said. "Why?"

I looked up at the reddening sunset sky. "Because I need to go for a swim to clear my head."

"What kind of a swim? Underwater?"

I turned on my heel and began walking in the other direction. "We'll find out once we get there."

She made a squeaking noise, halfway between horror and excitement, and skipped to catch up with me.

CHAPTER 22

ONE HOUR LATER

"Do I LOOK any different?"

My daughter, who stood on the shoreline under the darkening sky, crossed her arms and shook her head. "You look cold," she called out over the water.

I adjusted the damp straps of my bra and forced myself to go deeper into the water. My legs were still pale and, well, legs. I hadn't changed or shifted. Against my human flesh, the water was chilly and unpleasant. Would it help if I went deeper? When I left Chet's house, I'd been dead-set on going for a swim. I thought for sure Chessa's spirit was with me, waiting to transform my body. I thought I'd become a mermaid, a sexy siren, but I was just a shivering witch. A shivering yet determined witch.

I took a dozen more steps, ever deeper, buckled my knees, and dropped my body all the way under the water line.

Change, I told myself.

Crouching underwater, I opened my eyes. The saltwater stung. I blinked and willed my eyes to be resilient, the way they'd been on Monday. The sting faded, but I couldn't see anything in the murky water, not even the shape of my own body when I looked down at myself. I had to pat my sides and legs to make sure I was still human.

Change into a mermaid, merlion, sea lion, or whatever you are, I told myself. *Go for it. Shifter powers activate!*

Still no changes, and my eyelids closed protectively.

I straightened my legs, emerged my head and shoulders from the water, and gasped for a refreshing breath of oxygen. I must have had gills before because I was no champion at holding my breath for ages.

On shore, Zoey shifted from foot to foot impatiently. "It's getting dark," she called out. "We can try again tomorrow."

I took one last look out over the calm, dark ocean. Why did I want so badly to swim away from the shore and dive down deep if my body wouldn't let me? It was cruel of Chessa to taunt me like this, to show me what I couldn't have. Like the memories of her joyful moments with Chet. Why wouldn't she show me helpful things, such as what happened to her, or how to get her back? Instead, her spirit was always showing me sexy stuff; she had a real one-track mind.

Zoey yelled, "Do I need to come out there and drag you in? I can see from here that you're shivering!"

"Coming!" I began trudging back toward her, stepping slowly. The loose rocks were quite sharp under my still-human feet. My previous visit to the ocean, only two days earlier, had been completely different. That night, the beach had felt as comfortable as my own house.

When I reached dry land, Zoey patted me dry with the hem of her T-shirt before helping me get my clothes back on over my salty, wet skin.

She said, "You must have done something different from how you did it on Monday. Auntie Z says some forms of magic are very particular about the details."

"Maybe I was more relaxed before because I didn't have any expectations."

"Like a coyote in a cartoon, before he realizes he's walking in midair."

"Exactly." I shook the sand out of my shirt and started pulling it on. "Maybe it was beginner's luck. Remember the time I went to a bingo game with all the ladies from the apartment building? I did so well, I had to sneak out the bathroom window with my winnings so they didn't shank me with sharpened bingo dabbers."

She twitched her nose. "How does one sharpen a bingo dabber?"

"I don't know, but the idea sure sends chills down your spine, doesn't it?"

She shook her head and used her sleeve to rub more saltwater off my lower back, where the hem of my shirt was sticking. "Those chills are because you're freezing. We need to get you home and warmed up."

I gazed out over the calm, dark ocean. "I wish I knew what I did on Monday, so I could recreate it." I touched my wrist. "I'm wearing her bracelet and everything."

Zoey made a thoughtful sound. "I know." She struck the air with one finger. "You were wearing black underwear that day, and it looked like a bikini, whereas today you're wearing a mismatched set of pink and blue underwear that's awfully transparent when wet. You look like an extra from one of those movies about girls gone wild."

I twisted my hair into a rope to squeeze out the seawater. "Just an extra? I don't get a starring role in this theoretical wild girls movie?"

"Starring roles are for girls with *matching* underwear that's awfully transparent when wet."

"Good to know," I said.

"You know, if you really want to go diving, there are options for this sort of thing. You could take scuba lessons."

"Or tuba lessons. Or underwater scuba tuba." I grinned. "See what I did there?"

She rolled her eyes.

I used my socks to wipe the sand off my feet, stuffed the socks in my pockets, and pulled my shoes on.

We began walking back toward our house. The sun had set, and everything was flat and gray, like an underexposed photo. We didn't talk for a while, and I could feel the disappointment hanging over us like a dark cloud. Zoey still didn't know what the so-called prophecy meant for her, and I didn't know how I was supposed to help Chessa, or even if I wanted to.

Chet had assumed I was angry with him, but I'd calmed down since the big bombshell that morning. I loved my new career and my new home. Sure, I'd never trust him any further than I could throw him, but I had to give the man a few points for making my life better.

"Long day," I said with a sigh, putting my arm around my daughter's shoulders.

"I'm sorry you didn't get to shift into anything," Zoey said. "It must be disappointing. But I'm also *not* sorry, because I genuinely prefer my mother to be human shaped, and not just because we can borrow each other's clothes."

I hugged her close to my side. "And I'm sorry that your name turned up on that scroll, whether it's been on there for hundreds of years or it's all part of some nefarious scheme to get me working for the DWM. I'm sorry you got dragged into this."

I felt her shrug. "It's been a slow news week for me."

"Got anything you want to talk about? I've missed having dinner with you every night this week so far."

"I'm fine," she said with an air of martyrdom.

We made our way along the narrow trail between the oceanfront mansions and back through the alley.

After a few minutes of easy silence, she stopped walking, looked up at the sky, and said, "Wow."

I gazed up at the sky as well. There weren't many streetlamps in this area, and the ones we had were shielded at the top to prevent light pollution. Above us, in the dark sky, were sparkling stars. So many stars. The longer I looked, the more appeared. I pointed out the major constellations.

Zoey knew the stars as well as I did—if not better—but she humored me and didn't interrupt.

Once we started walking again, she asked, "What if *this* is everything? As good as it gets? What if the whole point of us coming here to this town, and you getting the Spirit Charmed or Soul Catcher powers, was so that you and I could go to the beach and watch the sun set, then view the stars on the way home?"

"I take it you're not furious with Chet anymore."

"We had fun tonight. First, I got to use my ninja wire, and then, you should have seen the look on Mr. Moore's face when I found him in his den and told him to start talking." She laughed. "Then you came storming in, looking like you were about to shoot blue lightning! I almost felt sorry for the guy."

"That was pretty dramatic."

"The Riddle girls know how to party."

I took her hand in mine and squeezed it. "I had fun with you tonight, too. We make a great team."

CHAPTER 23

ON THURSDAY AT WORK, I rested my elbows on the counter for all of a few seconds, and my mind dashed off someplace else.

The calm, soothing ocean.

Oh, how I longed to swim in its murky depths. I dreamed of its secret waters.

When the sudden sound of a dropped book startled me out of my reverie, I wondered, was the ocean also dreaming of me?

It was a silly thought, but I'd felt something. The pull was mutual.

All morning, no matter how many cups of coffee I drank, my thoughts kept slipping away. My shift couldn't be over soon enough.

I was so distracted by the ocean's hold over me, my whole recommendation routine went haywire. I actually suggested a nihilistic dark comedy to a patron looking for a breezy summer beach read, and a kinky billionaire sex series to a book club of octogenarians.

"Bold choices," my boss, Kathy, said when she found me groaning to myself with my head in my hands.

"The sarcasm, it stings," I whimpered.

Kathy blinked behind her horn-rimmed glasses. "Zara, I meant what I said. You gave those two patrons what they really wanted."

"I did?"

"Both of them walked by our display tables marked Beach Reads and Book Club Winners, just to ask you for a personal recommendation. You're some kind of *librarian empath* who picks up on people's true desires. You have a gift, and this is your true calling."

I took my head out of my hands. "Either you're paying me a compliment, or your sarcasm is seriously next-level stuff."

She wrinkled her pointy nose and pushed up her glasses. "You're doing well here, Zara. It's not time yet for your official three-month review, but I wanted to give you some positive feedback. You clearly have found the right path in life. You're a woman who knows exactly who and what she is."

"Thanks," I said, stifling laughter. If Kathy knew I'd taken an extra-long shower that morning, trying to get enough water on me so I could change into a sea creature, she wouldn't be saying that. "Please let me know if there's any way I could be of more help to you."

She glanced around to make sure we were alone. We stood together by the New and Notable table, where I'd been making sure it was well stocked with high-demand titles.

She came closer and said softly, "What's the deal with Frank?"

"In what sense?"

"Not the obvious. We're all well aware of *that* because he's constantly telling us. I meant, why is he spewing random flamingo facts at everyone? This morning, he told me about how both the female and male flamingo produce crop milk for their young, from their necks. It's blood red and contains traces of blood. The man is obsessed."

"Oh, that's all my fault," I said.

"How so?"

"I, uh, came up with a great theme for the Children's Summer Reading Program. We're doing birds. Our theme for the kids this summer is birds."

She clasped her hands together and made a hooting sound. "We can wear costumes for special group events!" She looked up at the ceiling and scratched her head. "I'll have to start planning now, so I can think long and hard about what kind of bird I would be."

"Really?" Was Kathy's sarcasm truly next level, or did she genuinely have no idea how much she looked like an owl? Did she not have any mirrors? Surely she had glimpsed her owl-like features in other reflective surfaces. She had to be trolling me. Had to be. If I was a librarian empath, she was a librarian with sarcasm skills so next level, even she was unaware of them.

She hooted softly and looked up at my hair, smiling. "Zara, with your red hair, you should be the Northern Cardinal. In that species, even the females have red plumage on their feathers. Not that I object to you dressing in the manner of a male bird. We're a very progressive library. I'm just trying to save you from the ordeal of attracting the wrong sort of attention from the WBS."

I raised my eyebrows. I knew about the DWM, but the WBS sounded equally ominous. Something twinged in my mind. Call it witch's intuition.

Kathy excused herself and went back to her head librarian duties, leaving me wondering.

Later, I did a search on the computer. WBS stood for the Wisteria Bird-Watching Society. Officially, anyway. They had a website, but the text was suspiciously vague about their meetings and activities.

Just before closing, I brought the organization to Frank's attention. He was also intrigued.

"We could go undercover to a meeting," he said. "Find out if WBS secretly stands for Wisteria Bird Shifters." He bookmarked the website on his phone. "Or I could ask Rob and Knox when I see them tonight. We're driving up to a remote location to practice shifting and flying."

"Lucky you," I said.

"I know." He waggled his eyebrows. "Did you see them up close in their bird forms? They're majestic, and much larger than their natural bird counterparts. In their monster state, they're practically mythical."

"Monster state?" It didn't sound like a term you'd use to describe yourself or your friends—not unless you were a fan of that singer, Lady Gaga, whose legion calls themselves Little Monsters.

Frank waved a hand dismissively. "They call themselves monsters, so it's not offensive to use that term."

"How can people who call themselves the 'good guys' claim to be monsters?" I shook my head. "I don't know if you should be hanging out with those guys. Chessa might have been attacked by a giant bird, and she was paranoid that someone within the DWM was working against her."

Frank kept grinning at me. "Jealous much? You can come along if you like. There's a lake in the mountain, where you could go for a dip. I could keep an eye on you in case you grow fins or scales or"—he made a loose undulating gesture with both arms—"flappy snake tentacles."

"Thanks, but I'll keep trying with the ocean before I hit the freshwater." I twisted my sea-glass bracelet on my wrist. "I've got a good feeling about tonight."

"Don't get yourself drowned."

"I could pick up a pair of those inflatable arm things they put on kids. Water wings."

Frank smirked. "You, in water wings? Now you're tempting me to change my plans. Are you sure you don't want my help with this thing? Especially since your no-go beau has shown his true Machiavellian colors."

"What did you have in mind? Another summoning of the Spirits of the Deep?"

"I could paddle along in a dinghy while you flail around in your water wings." He looked past me, at the patrons using the rows of public computers.

"Have Rob and Knox told you much about Chessa? She had the power to make men fight over her." I pointed to my head, even though Frank was looking at the computer section and not me. "I've had flashes of visions, her memories. Mostly about how she drove one man in particular crazy."

Frank's attention snapped back to me. "As in...?"

"Yes. Unfortunately." I reached for one of the bottles of hand sanitizer we kept on the counter and put a glob on my palms. Since becoming a witch, my skin had been stronger in everyday life. Either the alcohol in the gel no longer stung my paper cuts, or my paper cuts healed immediately. I tried to focus on the antiseptic scent rather than wallow in the intimate memory that was now playing in the back of my mind—Chet, opening a bottle of champagne at the beach, on the evening of their engagement. It was springtime, just months before her accident. Her emotions were shooting high and low, off the charts. I could feel her excitement, fluttering in my own chest. Chessa wanted to tell him something, but she had to keep the secret just a little while longer. She had to make sure she had a secret to share.

And then, just when I wanted to stay inside the memory and learn more, the sunset scene on the beach dissipated.

Frank hadn't noticed me zoning out.

"All I know is Rob and Knox weren't in love with Chessa," Frank said. "According to them, she did have an effect on men, but knowing about it took away some of the power." He paused, looking thoughtful. "They did say something weird."

"How weird?"

"People keep using the word worship. Chet worshiped the ground she walked on, and the communications departments worshiped her cryptography skills. Plus Knox called her a goddess."

"Her sister Chloe did claim they were descended from the gods."

"That settles it, then." Frank took the bottle of hand sanitizer from me. "Now that you have all the details, go ahead and raise a goddess from the dead. Get right on that, Zara Riddle, and I'll go confiscate the bag of chips that was opened sixty seconds ago at computer number three." He sniffed the air. "Barbecue chips."

* * *

That Thursday evening, I went to the ocean for the third time that week.

This time, I was ready to raise a goddess from the dead. I was wearing my lucky underwear. Or at least the same black underwear I'd been wearing on Monday.

Once again, Zoey waited patiently on the shore as I waded into the water.

Once again, nothing happened.

I returned to shore with my head hung low.

"We're too early," Zoey said. "Maybe it only happens at sunset."

I slipped on a loose beach cover-up, and we laid out our picnic dinner. I was too nervous to eat much, but I pecked at the sesame noodle salad, buckwheat pancakes, sweet and sour meatballs, dill pickles, peanut butter cookies, and miniature wax-coated cheese balls.

Zoey looked over the empty takeout containers. "Not hungry at all, huh?"

"You shouldn't go swimming on a full stomach."

She offered me the last cookie, but I declined. She took a bite. "How does it work? Where does the food go when a shifter changes into an animal?"

"Beats me," I said. "Adult flamingos weight about six pounds. I don't know where the rest of Frank went, let alone his stomach contents. It's magic."

"The physics of magic," she said. "We're very lucky that we know the truth about the world."

"Very lucky," I agreed.

* * *

The sun was setting when I tried again to merge with the sea.

I walked deeper than before, until my toes didn't touch the ground and I had to tread water. I took a breath, held it, and stilled my legs, sinking under. I opened my eyes underwater. I released the air in my lungs as a slow, steady stream of bubbles.

Nothing was changing. I stayed submerged as long as I could before I burst up again, gasping for air.

A dog was barking.

I rotated around to see my neighbor, Arden, paddling in his yellow boat with his brown labradoodle standing at the bow. In shadowy profile, the dog resembled one of Neptune's wooden angels, a carved nautical figurehead. Sailors in Germany and Belgium believed in spirits or fairies called *Kaboutermannekes*, who dwelt in the figureheads to protect the ship from rocks and dangerous storms. If the ship sank, the water fairies would guide the sailors' souls to the Land of the Dead.

I wondered, was Chessa one of the Kaboutermannekes? Was she trapped between the land of the living and the dead with no spirit to guide her through?

The dog barked again.

"Hello, Doodles," I called out, waving.

Arden paddled the boat over to where I was treading water. "Are you caught up on something under there, Zara?" He chuckled. "Has a gigantic clam nibbled on your foot?"

"No, but that would be some giant pearl if it did!" I swam to meet him and reached a point where I could stand instead of treading, my toes on top of a boulder.

"That would be quite the pearl!" Arden laughed, and his fluffy eyebrows came together like two caterpillars meeting on the side of a bald, pink mountain. "How's the water tonight?"

"The water's n-n-n-nice," I said through chattering teeth.

Arden glanced around, then leaned over the side of his yellow boat as though concerned someone might overhear us. "Why are you out here? Is this some sort of therapy thing? If it is, then I should give you some privacy."

"I suppose you could call it therapy," I said lightly. "I'm certainly learning a lot about myself during these sea excursions."

"To each their own," he said.

I reached up and gave Doodles a chin rub, his brown curls sticking to my wet fingers. "So, what is it you two do out here? I don't see a fishing rod in your hands, or a tackle box in your colorful boat."

"We're monster hunters," Arden said proudly.

Something in my mind lurched, like a car braking for a red light. Maybe it was just my imagination, or seaweed, but it seemed like something swished against my legs. My body shook, more than just a shiver from the cold.

I stammered, "M-m-m-monster hunters?"

"Yes," he said. "We hunt sea monsters."

"Like the Kraken, or the Loch Ness Monster?"

He chuckled and answered in a cartoonishly thick Scottish accent. "I'd love to catch us a Nessie, but I'm afraid we're a long way from Scotland, lass."

"Is there a sea monster associated with this particular area?"

"Nothing that has a name. And I doubt we'll ever get to use this." Arden pointed to something in the bottom of his boat. I stood on my tiptoes in the water and peered over the edge. At his feet lay a long rod of metal, tipped with three barbed hooks. My body shook again.

Carefully, I said, "Looks like you've got a pointy trident there." My heart pounded in my chest while my senses screamed *danger!* Evenly, I said, "The traditional weapon of Poseidon, or Neptune, god of the sea."

"That's right. You know your sea gods!"

"In Hindu mythology, it's called the trishula, the weapon of Shiva, the creator, destroyer, and regenerator." I clenched my jaw to stop my nervous flow of facts.

"I'm afraid this is just a plain old trident from a camping and fishing outlet."

"Are you planning to do some spear fishing?"

He lifted the trident and struck a pose with it upright. "This is mainly for show," Arden said through a chuckle, his gray eyes crinkling with mirth. "If Doodles and I do find any monsters, we'll probably just take pictures." He gazed at the horizon. "I've seen things out here that can't be explained. Haven't caught one of the beasts in a picture yet, but some day."

"What does it look like?" I'd taken a few steps back from the boat. My senses tingled with danger. I could use a combination of telekinesis and spells to protect myself, but it was wise to put some distance between me and the pointy trident.

"I can't describe it." Arden patted Doodles on the head. The dog whined and rested his chin on his master's knee.

"Tentacles? A blowhole? Shiny scales?"

"No, I really *can't* describe it. The memory turns into a black hole. It's the absence of memory that alerted me to it. Spans of time I couldn't account for. The thing wipes your memory right after you see it. That's why people around here don't know."

"Maybe it's for the best. My aunt always says *secrets revealed are trouble unsealed*, which makes me think of Pandora's box. Some things are safer when they stay buried."

"Oh, I reckon one of these days I'll catch something," Arden said. "Then I'll be sure to come by your house and show you the proof." He looked right at me, his gray eyes in shadow. "Speaking of houses, how are you liking the Red Witch House?"

I let out a high-pitched laugh. "I'm thinking about painting it a different color, so people will stop calling it that." I splashed the water to give them a cheery wave, and I started moving toward the shore. I could have started swimming, but I felt more comfortable upright, where less of my body mass was visible on the water surface. "See you around."

"Be careful," Arden warned. "If you're just going to walk around like that, you should watch your step."

"I'm tougher than I look," I replied with grit in my voice.

"People think the seafloor is flat, like the beach, but there are pits and canyons you could fall into."

"I'll be very careful," I said.

I headed straight for the shore, keeping visual contact with my daughter and not looking back at the man in the yellow boat.

I'd always gotten a friendly, neighborly vibe from Arden, but that trident of his could do some serious damage to a person or creature. Could Chessa have mistaken the man, the trident, plus the dark-brown dog, for an attacking bird? She might have been shocked and confused if someone was stabbing her with a trident.

Back on shore, I was grateful for the warm, fluffy towel Zoey had brought along for this expedition. And I was glad to be on dry land again.

CHAPTER 24

"Penny for your thoughts."

I looked up from the antique wooden card catalog. Our library's database was computerized, and it had been decades since the library had used paper index cards, but the wooden unit with all its tiny drawers brought warmth and character to the center of the atrium. Plus it held a growing collection of tropical houseplants. I'd been tucking the plant fertilizer back into the drawer labeled F.

The man offering me a penny for my thoughts was Detective Bentley.

I gave him a polite smile. "Good morning, Detective. If you'd like the contents of my head, at one penny per thought, that'll be a buck fifty."

"How about a donut?"

I closed the F drawer and straightened up. "Is there something I can help you with today?"

He looked down at his shiny shoes and chuckled. He straightened his mouth and tried to get control of himself, but the smile kept emerging.

"Detective, if something's *that* funny, you should share it." I braced myself for another smart comment about my attire. That morning, I'd dressed in white from head to toe. It was a deliberate tactic to attract Chessa's spirit by dressing like her. Unfortunately, I didn't own a lot of white clothing. There's a reason bright-white trousers are associated with rich people on golf courses and at horse races. If you want to wear white, you need enough cash to make your clothes disposable, and I enjoyed food with vibrant sauces far too much to maintain a white wardrobe.

So, I was wearing the only white thing I had: a vintage wedding dress I'd picked up at a thrift store with the intention of dying it a fun color or harvesting the lace trim for something else. Ever since watching the old eighties movie *Pretty in Pink*, starring the patron saint of oddball redheads, Molly Ringwald, I'd been in love with the idea of combining multiple dresses into a funky new original.

I fully expected Bentley to comment on my outfit, perhaps calling me Bride of Chucky, as my daughter had that morning, but he didn't.

Still guffawing, he looked up at my face, not my dress. "Do you know Old Man Wheelie? He lives over on Spencer Crescent."

I leaned against the wooden card catalog casually. "I know his actual name is Wheelchuck, and they started calling him Wheelie after he got the wheelchair, which seems cruel, but I understand it was all his idea." *How did I know that?* Had someone at the library told me, or was it residue from Chessa? It felt like something I'd known for a long time, yet I'd only lived in Wisteria a few months.

Bentley didn't notice me spacing out, freaked by my uncanny recall. He kept talking, describing how he'd had to take an early-morning police call for a domestic disturbance because no uniformed officers were available at the time.

"So, I get to his house, and I can hear him yelling, just like the neighbors reported, but I can't find him," Bentley said. "The front door is unlocked, so I step in and look around. Still no sign of Old Man Wheelie. But I hear this thumping sound. I go out the back door, and I nearly trip over a pair of disembodied legs."

Now he had my full attention. "What?"

"Don't worry. They were just prosthetics. A few years back, Wheelie had them custom made, fitting right below the knee. Now, most days, he gets around in the wheelchair, but for special occasions and group photos, he'll use the legs and walk around. And, apparently, he also uses them to climb a ladder when he wants to go up on the roof and think." Bentley made the motion of tipping back a bottle. "And by *think*, I do mean drink."

"Up on top of his roof? Sure, I can see it. He probably wanted a better view of the stars."

"Plus there's something to be said for being on a different plane than other people." He moved his hands through the air as though petting the back of a tall horse. "By which I mean a different elevation. It helps your head to feel clearer to be on a different stratum. Like when you're on the top floor of a skyscraper, or at the peak of a mountain, high above everyone."

"Or flying," I said.

"Like a bird," we both said in unison.

"Like a bird," he repeated. "Or in an airplane."

"Okay," I said. "So, Old Man Wheelie was stuck up on his roof like Humpty Dumpty, drunk and yelling at people?"

"He'd been up there all night and had mostly sobered up. But he accidentally dropped his legs off the roof, so he couldn't get himself back down the ladder. He'd managed to call over a couple of kids who were walking by on the way to school, but when they saw the legs on the ground, the boys screamed and ran." Bentley laughed before regaining control over himself. "That's why I had to take the noise disturbance call. The kids' parents had phoned in a report of a strange homicide, but they weren't sure of the address, so all the on-duty uniforms were searching the surrounding neighborhood for body parts."

"What did you do? Climb the ladder and bring him his legs?"

Bentley blinked at me, dead serious. "No. I just left him there. Do you think I should go back?"

"Of course you should go back! Are you going to leave a legless man on a roof all day lo—" I stopped talking. "You're teasing me."

Bentley smiled. "Yes, I brought him his legs, and then made sure he got down safely. I called the other officers, and we brought the traumatized kids over for an explanation plus milk and cookies." He made a brushing-off gesture with both hands. "And the town of Wisteria is safe for another day."

I tossed my hair and leaned forward to press my hands girlishly against Bentley's broad chest. "Thank goodness we have the likes of you to protect us, Detective."

He looked down at my hands on his chest. "All's well that ends well."

I cleared my throat and gracefully withdrew my hands. "Is there anything I can do for you, as a librarian?"

"No. I was just returning that amnesia book." Now he stared at the lace on my bustier, seemingly noticing the vintage wedding dress for the first time. "You're a beautiful bride," he said, and then he quickly looked away, turning his back to me. "Oops," he said over his shoulder. "I don't need to accumulate any more bad luck."

"It's just a white dress," I said. "And that superstition only applies to the groom."

"I'd like to keep my options open," he said with a nod, and then he walked away with his head held high as he left the library.

Behind me, a creature made a hooting noise.

I turned around to find Kathy with a huge grin on her face. She sang, "Zara and Bentley, sitting in a tree. K-I-S-S-I-N-G."

"Not likely," I said. "Honestly, up until this week, I thought he hated me."

"It's a fine line between love and hate. And I should know." She paused dramatically. "Because I'm married."

"Oh, Kathy. I don't know if that's funny or sad."

"Me neither," she said, making a strange sound that could have been laughing or tearless crying.

For the rest of the day, I thought about what Bentley had said—about him marrying me, but also about Old Man Wheelie trying to find somewhere peaceful to think.

A library is a wonderful place to think, but I spend most of my days inside a library, so I was used to the quiet, accustomed to it. If I wanted to find somewhere even more peaceful, such as the bottom of the ocean, I'd have to get creative.

* * *

That Friday night, I visited the ocean for the fourth time that week.

This time, however, everything was different.

I'd had enough of Chessa's teasing, luring me to the ocean only to have me flail around like a mere mortal. I wanted to see the beautiful seafloor and swim with the fishes. And why not?

I was the captain of my own ship, the master of my destiny.

I was a witch who didn't let obstacles such as a constant need for oxygen stand in her way.

I was a novice scuba diver at her very first diving lesson.

"You look ridiculous in that getup," Zoey said, laughing. "You walk like a penguin."

I replied, "And you, young lady, walk like a duck who ate too much dinner."

"Quack, quack." Zoey took a bow, her neoprene suit squeaking from her movement.

Our scuba diving instructor, an endlessly patient and hunky man named Leo, continued loading up the boat with scuba diving supplies.

Zoey and I linked arms and attempted to square dance, comically encumbered by the enormous diving flippers on our feet.

CHAPTER 25

AFTER OUR FIRST dive, Zoey said breathing oxygen from a tank was "intriguing," but she preferred sticking to non-water places, where the oxygen was readily available. She asked if she could take the money I'd been willing to pay for her diving lessons and apply them to a future sport or activity of her choice. I'd agreed readily.

We went home exhausted after our first lesson, but she stayed up late quizzing me from the assigned reading for my diving education.

When I shared my new interest with Zinnia, she wasn't thrilled about my lack of devotion to my novice witch studies. But she reluctantly agreed that learning to dive could be a worthwhile pursuit.

"You ought to do what you can to help a lost spirit," Zinnia said. "Please, just promise me you won't put your life in danger."

I'd groaned and told her that was why I was getting trained in diving rather than just barging into it without a clue. Besides, I'd tried barging in a few times already, and it hadn't worked.

At work the next week, Frank applauded my efforts to acquire a new skill.

"This is what lifelong learning looks like," Frank said, proudly pointing to me while he told some library patrons about my new interest in scuba diving. "Zara is a true seeker of wisdom, a Renaissance woman."

Kathy agreed. Later that same day, she called me aside and asked if there were any attractive men participating in the local dives. I confessed to her that the vast majority of them were attractive men, and having all that eye candy around was a true test of my memorization of the diving safety protocols.

Kathy commented with an eyebrow waggle, "Who wouldn't love to be tested like that?"

"It's great fun, but I feel guilty for having so much fun with all those cute guys," I said. "I'm the only female there, surrounded by a half dozen of the handsomest bachelors in town. It's scandalous."

"Why? You're single, aren't you?"

"I'm—" I bit off the word *engaged.* I wasn't engaged. It was just Chessa's spirit that made me feel guilty whenever the instructor, Leo, leaned in close to help me with my tanks. It was Chessa who made me say no to an invitation to have drinks at the pub with the other male students.

Chessa was a real buzzkill for my dating life. How could I move on and get past my crush on her fiancé if she wouldn't let me?

Kathy wished me luck with my lessons, and we both got back to our jobs.

* * *

Between my job and the after-work scuba diving lessons, the week went by quickly. I focused on learning how to dive safely, but my mind was never free of thoughts about Chessa or fleeting emotions from her memories. Our connection was growing stronger, building to something. Each dive seemed to invigorate her life force, each visit to the sea acting like a puff of breath blown over hot coals.

She and I were on a journey together. Where was this metaphysical road trip taking me? I'd have to wait and find out once we got there.

I suspected it wasn't just the ocean bringing Chessa to me. At my diving sessions, I was the only female, surrounded by healthy, vigorous men. The attention they paid me was not at all diminished by being shared by two women: me, and the stylish blonde who dropped in from time to time. And her presence radiated out, affecting my reality. Not a single one of the men teased me about having red hair or being a librarian. It was a first.

Our diving instructor in particular, Leo, seemed to have a glint in his eye whenever he spoke to me.

On Thursday evening, when I looked at the man, while the setting sun turned our faces golden, I felt a buried memory surface, an emotion. Anger over someone's betrayal. The desire to hurt someone, to punish them. I quickly turned away from his face. *Don't start another fight,* I told myself with what sounded like Chloe's voice. Leo continued joking around with the other guys on the boat, and soon we were diving, down where we weren't men or women, single or otherwise, just black-and-blue things with goggles and flippers and bubbles.

Later that evening, when I got home, I found Chet sitting on my front step. I had been yawning, exhausted from the dive. The instant I saw him, I stopped, mid-yawn, and my tiredness disappeared.

Chet pointed a thumb at my front door. "Your daughter said you'd be home any minute from diving."

"So you decided to wait in ambush?"

He frowned and got to his feet. "You've been avoiding me, screening my calls. It's been over a week."

It was true. I hadn't felt like chatting since the previous Wednesday. "Eight days," I said. "It's been eight days, which is barely a week."

"Zara, I live right next door. You can't avoid me forever." He looked at the bracelet on my wrist. "We should take you to see her again, as soon as you're ready. Unless you've had some progress on your own?"

"That depends. Is it possible the cuts on Chessa could have come from a fishing spear?"

He looked surprised. "Did you see something in one of your visions?"

"Not exactly," I said, and I explained about my second watery meeting with our neighbor, Arden. I described the yellow boat, the sharp trident, and Arden's declaration that he was a "monster hunter."

Every word from my mouth seemed to cause Chet more pain. He backed away from me along the front walkway.

Hoarsely, he said, "That's something I can look into myself." He turned to look in the direction of Arden's house, up the street. "I know exactly who you mean."

An emotion flickered across his face, like a fire crackling to life behind his eyes.

"Don't hurt him," I said. "He's just a harmless old man."

"I'll do what I need to do," he growled.

I grabbed him by the arm. "Chet, without our humanity, we are lost."

His posture changed, his tension melting. The red fire in his eyes simmered down. His voice low yet soft, he said, "That's something Chessa used to say."

"And for good reason," I said. "She's right. Without our humanity, we are lost." I released his arm. "Keep a cool head."

"I will," he promised.

"Try to relax," I said. "That's something my scuba instructor, Leo, is teaching me. You've gotta stay loose so your muscles work the way they're designed to. If you're all stiff and tense, things bunch up."

He took a few steps away from me and stopped. "Leo?"

"My scuba instructor. He's nice. You'd like him."

"If you say so," Chet said darkly. He reached up and grabbed a leaf from one of my overgrown hedges. "What are you doing Saturday morning?"

"Sleeping. It's been a busy week, and tomorrow's a big day."

"Well, when you do crawl out of bed, come over to my place. You're right about me needing to relax. I'm going to throw a Grownups' Brunch."

"That sounds fun. What should I bring?"

He pointed both index fingers at me like imaginary guns. "Just bring your bad librarian self," he said. "Around ten o'clock. You can bring Leo if you want."

I snorted. Leo? Oh, no. I would never subject him to brunch with Chet.

CHAPTER 26

IT TOOK ME a full week to get my scuba diving certification, which is fast. I was disappointed to not break the local record of three days, but there are only so many hours in the day, and I did have to put in some shifts at the library.

The Saturday morning after completion of my scuba diving lessons, I woke up fuzzy headed.

My memory was working perfectly, though, and I knew I had to get up and go next door to the Moore house for Saturday brunch.

I tapped on my skull and groaned, "Begone, Spirits of the Deep, and take with you the residual of last night's margaritas."

The night before, my diving group had insisted on celebrating my certification. I could feel Chessa's spirit disapproving, but I threw caution to the wind and said yes. I was in the mood for fun.

The scuba instructor, Leo, took us to a cheesy sports bar that had a diving theme. The place was called The Dive Bar. They served fruity cocktails in miniature fishbowls, complete with floating frozen fruit chunks shaped to look like fish. I'd tried every flavor. And that was before the karaoke.

With a groan, I dragged myself into the shower, lathered my body and hair in every kind of product we had on hand, and emerged feeling fresh as a daisy. Ten points for having the recovery powers of a witch; hangovers weren't so bad.

I stood in front of my closet. Now, if only my witch powers could help me find the perfect outfit to wear to Chet's house for brunch.

Why not modify a spell to suit my needs?

I knew a spell to locate a place in a book, and a spell to pick out the ripest cantaloupe. What if I combined aspects of both of those spells, substituting a few words, and including a phrase about forecasting the weather, to make the spell pick out the perfect clothes for the day?

It took a few minutes for me to work through the grammar and the modifications. I was only a novice-level witch, but Zinnia wanted me to practice more, and I couldn't think of a better way than to find more instances in my everyday life to use magic.

I cast the modified spell, throwing in a clause about beauty and symmetry at the last minute.

The air sparkled with spell energy. The clothes in my closet began to shift left and right on the hanging rod. It was working! With a smooth swish, the sea of clothing parted neatly in two spots. The sparkles dissipated. I pulled out the highlighted items. My closet had suggested a sleek pairing of dark indigo jeans, boot cut, along with a bright-orange T-shirt the color of a traffic safety cone.

"Bold choice," I said to my closet.

My closet didn't answer back, which was probably for the best.

I pulled on the dark jeans and orange shirt then admired myself in the full-length mirror. I'd never worn the T-shirt before. It still had the tag on the label. I'd

224

grabbed it during a big sale to bring my total up to the dollar amount required to get a discount on the whole lot. I'd never thought of the shirt again, but only because I had no idea how amazing it would look with the ultra-dark jeans. The color brought out the glow in my hair, and made my hazel eyes sparkle with amber highlights.

I gave my closet the thumbs-up.

"Nicely done," I told the closet and myself.

As I headed over to Chet's house, I did wonder if the closet spell had done what I'd intended, or simply picked a shirt that was most similar to a ripe cantaloupe. Did it really matter? I looked so good, I could feel my happiness radiating out, making the world a prettier place.

I practically floated up the front steps to the Moore residence. The door was open, so I walked in. I hadn't been inside the house since entering it in ninja fashion, interrogating Chet, and then storming out. We'd bumped into each other a few times coming and going, though, and on Thursday he'd invited me to come by Saturday morning for what he described as a "Grownups' Brunch."

Zoey was already there, laughing. I followed the sound of her voice to the kitchen, which, unlike mine next door, had been fully renovated in the farmhouse-chic style, with polished concrete counters and a huge sink, deep enough to use for dismembering bodies.

I found Zoey at the industrial-grade chef's stove, making animal-shaped pancakes with Corvin, under the supervision of Chet's father. When I walked in, Grampa Don barely glanced up at me from his newspaper.

"Head on through to the back yard," Grampa Don told me. "That's where he's hoarding all the bacon and sausages."

"Thanks," I said, and I took a minute to say hello to my daughter and admire her pancakes.

As I was leaving the kitchen, Grampa Don whistled and beckoned for me to come closer to him. I smirked, remembering the sight of him in his underwear in that same kitchen, back when I'd been in spectral form two weeks earlier.

I leaned over and whispered, "What's up, Grampa Don?"

"Bring me some bacon, and I'll be your best friend forever," he said.

"Let me think about it," I said, and I left the kitchen.

I found Chet in the back corner of his yard, sitting at a wrought-iron patio table. Between the picturesque iron table, painted a bright aquamarine blue, and the lush landscaping, what I saw before me resembled a postcard from a fancy resort.

"You've created paradise back here," I said, admiring the greenery. He must have had the same size of yard as mine, but it was a different world. Whereas I had a jungle of unidentified vines, rotting wood that might have once been a picnic table, and stubby bushes, Chet had fragrant, blossoming trees, tidy perennials, and a burbling fountain with a pond. I knelt at the edge of the pond and dipped my fingers in, much to the excitement of a friendly trio of shimmering koi. "Aren't you guys adorable? What's that? *Blub blub blub?* Pleased to see you again, too! You're getting so big these days."

From his seat on the wrought-iron chair, Chet said, "Zara, you've never been back here before."

I stood up stiffly and joined him at the table. He was right. I'd peeked over the fence into his yard on occasion, but I hadn't met his trio of koi fish before. Chessa had. She'd bought him the fish, which had originally been a quartet, until a raccoon got one. I didn't share this insight with Chet. We were way beyond the cheap parlor tricks.

"Her spirit seems to come and go," I said. "I'm sorry I don't have better news for you, but our connection is weak."

"She's not going to ever wake up," he said glumly.

"I'm trying, Chet. If it's okay with you, I'd like to spend some time inside her house." I paused, reluctant to continue, but I did. "I'd like to sleep in her bed."

His eyes flicked up to mine. "Alone?"

My mind flooded with images of rumpled sheets and Chet, naked, rolling playfully and kissing my wrists, my shoulders, my neck. Him, over me, his breath ragged and urgent. The memory broke over me with a shockwave of bliss, and then it was gone.

I cleared my throat and reached for the pitcher of red-orange juice. "Yes, alone," I said.

"Zara, I would do *anything* to get her back."

I choked on the juice I was sipping. *Anything?*

His cheeks flushed pink. "I meant I could stay there with you, on the couch," he said. "You didn't think I meant—"

"Of course not."

I finished drinking the juice as I tried to banish thoughts of Chet's tanned skin, taut over rippling muscles, framed by crisp white sheets. I had to get Chessa's spirit back into her body. Being near her lover and unable to act upon her feelings was bittersweet, horrible torture. Why couldn't he have been a terrible, awkward lover? Why couldn't he be selfish and clumsy? Why did I have to know that he took his time, and within his patient arms, there was another whole world, in which time stood still?

I held up my empty goblet. "Is there champagne in here?" I hiccuped.

"We always have champagne at Grownups' Brunch," he said.

He refilled my glass, and I composed myself by looking over the food. There was a third garden chair pulled up to the table, and a third place setting.

"That's sweet," I said, nodding at the empty chair. *And creepy,* I added silently. Reserving a chair for the spirit of his fiancée was probably the right thing to do, yet it bothered me. Was he going to put pancakes on her plate?

I tore my gaze away and returned to admiring the landscaped back yard. If I played my cards right and got him his fiancée back, he could show his gratitude by doing a similar makeover on my jungle.

"We looked into the neighbor with the yellow boat," he said.

"Arden?" I leaned in and lowered my voice, just in case someone might be walking through the back alley. "Does he have an alibi?"

"Not exactly, but I wouldn't expect him to. It was a year ago, and the man lives alone," Chet said. "The DWM hasn't spoken to him directly, but he keeps his boat at a public marina. We had our best people examine the boat and the fishing spear for signs of blood."

"You have your own CSI crew?"

"Something like that." He looked up at the back of his house and stopped talking. Corvin had emerged from the back door with a platter of pancakes. He placed them proudly on the table. We both thanked the boy, and once we were alone again, Chet continued. "The trident was spotless. Completely clean of blood, human or animal. And when our psychic held it, she detected no trace residue of violence. To the best of our knowledge, that trident hasn't harmed so much as a minnow."

"Arden was sure he saw something out there, though." I picked up my butter knife and pointed it at Chet. "No more wiggling around, Mr. Moore, or I'll send Zoey after you with her ninja skills. You're going to tell me what manner of creature Chessa is, right now, or I'm off the case." It was a bluff, but he didn't need to know that.

He gave me a cagey look. "What makes you think she's not the same as her sisters?"

I used my magic to yank away the bite of pancake he was about to eat. I tossed the chunk to the grateful koi.

He glowered at me and set down his fork. "The truth is, Chessa was very secretive. I never saw her in her animal form, and neither did anyone else at the

Department." He looked down at the ground, his expression sad. "I thought once we got married, she'd trust me enough to let me see her, you know? But now, I'm afraid it's too late."

"She must be hideous," I said. "With swirling tentacles, and compound eyes, and three rows of sharp teeth."

Chet looked up just as the corner of his mouth twitched with a smile. "Just between us, I did have a few nightmares to that effect."

"But she was found in her human state, right? And if she couldn't shift while injured, that means she was attacked in human form."

"Not all creatures are incapable of changing while injured. The ones who aren't regular animals will always revert to human after death. It explains why museums don't have any manticores floating in jars."

"There should be a handbook for all this stuff," I said.

He didn't say anything.

"Let me guess," I said. "There is a handbook, but it's classified."

He glanced over at the jungle vines from my yard that were growing over the shared fence.

"That's my price," I said. "If I get Chessa back, I get a copy of the handbook."

His eyes widened.

"It's not up for negotiation," I said firmly.

He blinked and slowly nodded. "Deal," he said through gritted teeth.

I could hardly contain my excitement. Why hadn't I thought to demand a handbook before? Then I mentally kicked myself. Why had I made it conditional upon my success in retrieving Chessa? I should have demanded it in advance, as payment for my efforts regardless of the outcome, like a retainer.

Meanwhile, Chet had resumed his efforts to eat. He stabbed at his dog-shaped pancake before shoving a big chunk into his mouth.

"If only we knew more," I said. "Can you get me the accident report?"

He shook his head. "Stop focusing on her accident. I don't believe anyone was trying to kill her. With the way her arms were cut up, it's plausible she was drawn into a boat's propeller. Why look for malice when there's a perfectly logical explanation?"

Chet didn't want to imagine his fiancée being violently attacked by another creature. But being ignorant of reality wasn't going to get us anywhere.

"She said it was a bird."

Chet cut his pancake into tiny pieces. "That conversation was partly you and partly her. The bird thing must have come from your own mind. You were confusing your memories with hers. Remember, you thought Rob and Knox were a threat."

"But what *about* the flying creature who attacked us in the woods? That really happened."

"There haven't been any attacks or sightings since that day. I told you, Zara. Strange things happen in Wisteria, and for every mystery we solve, a dozen go unanswered."

"Do Rob and Knox have alibis for the day of Chessa's attack?"

"You mean her *accident*. Yes. They were up in the mountains, practicing aerial maneuvers, with Dr. Bob."

"And how well do you know this Dr. Bob? He kept hovering when we were visiting Chessa, like he was listening in."

Chet gave me a horrified look. He looked offended enough to storm out, except we were sitting in his yard. "Dr. Bob is the one who saved Chessa's life when we brought her in. He worked for hours and hours, sewing up her wounds and watching her vital signs. At one point, we ran low on blood for transfusions, and he donated some of his own. When he finally got her stabilized, the poor man fainted from exhaustion."

"Lucky he was already in a hospital," I said.

Chet watched me with narrowed eyes as I refilled my glass of mimosa.

I tilted my head to the side and asked, "What about Charlize?"

"What about her?"

"She seems possessive of you. There's more to your history than just being coworkers."

"We nearly dated," he said. "Then I met her sister, and I knew Chessa was the one for me."

"How did you know?"

He jerked his head back and blinked. "What do you mean?"

"Was it insta-love? Love at first sight? Did birds suddenly appear whenever she was near?"

He scratched his head. "You witches have the strangest ideas. Honestly, I don't know how you come up with some of the ideas you do, Zara. The things that come out of your mouth."

Before we could dig into more things that came from my mouth, another person emerged from the back of Chet's house. She was petite and blond, wearing a white summer dress. The summer sunshine made the dress glow. Chessa? Making a rare visual appearance?

One blonde ringlet twitched like a snake. Chloe? She wasn't carrying a baby, and she didn't move the way Chloe did.

"Charlize," I said, getting to my feet. Now I understood whom the third chair and place setting was for. We'd just been talking about her. *Speak of the devil, and she appears.*

CHAPTER 27

CHET JUMPED UP to greet the blonde.

"Hey, Charlie," he said, calling her by the boyish nickname he used for his coworker. "I see they let you out of your cage."

"Ha ha," she said. "You're such a juvenile boy, Chet, acting mean to a girl in front of your friend." To me, she said, "I'd never let them keep me in a cage. Cages are for domesticated creatures, and I'm wild."

I responded, "But are you housebroken?"

"Depends on who you ask."

I nodded at the bright aquamarine garden table. "That explains why Chet has us dining *al fresco*."

She tossed her head back in a silent laugh, her blonde ringlets bouncing. She reached where I stood and offered her hand. "It's nice to finally meet you in person, Zara."

I didn't shake her hand. I could play nice with people from the DWM as a favor to Chet, or even as smart self-preservation, but I didn't have to touch anyone I didn't want to. Charlize had been rubbing me the wrong way since the moment we met, or longer. The first time I'd heard her voice on Chet's phone, I'd taken an immediate disliking to her. Why? I wasn't usually so catty. Charlize brought out my kitty claws. Was I feeling her sister Chessa's emotions again? I'd liked their other sister, Chloe, instantly. Then again, on the day I met Chloe, she had been offering me a free pecan shortbread sample.

Charlize's hand hung empty in the air between us. The air hummed with suppressed supernatural powers, both hers and mine.

"We've met before," I said coolly.

She batted pale eyelashes. Her makeup was light and flattering, just a dusting of sparkling gray eye shadow paired with delicate pink lip gloss that smelled like bubble gum.

"I think I'd remember meeting someone like you," she said icily.

"I was horizontal then, being treated at your fancy underground hospital. You made your *hilarious* joke about flying cars."

Charlize looked at Chet. "She remembers that? She wasn't supposed to remember that."

"I never do what I'm supposed to," I said.

She took back her hand, unshaken, and walked around to take the third chair. She sat with a solid-sounding plop.

"No, you don't," she said to me without looking in my eyes. "You were supposed to bring back my sister, and now I hear you've been spending all your free time taking swimming lessons."

"Diving lessons," I said. "And I'm taking them to be closer to your sister's spirit. She keeps calling me to the..." I trailed off with a sigh. There was no winning with Charlize. I knew what she was like, from Chessa's emotions. Charlize could come around to logic eventually, but in her own sweet time. "Never mind."

Charlize stared at me with narrowed eyes the color of cold granite. There was a crackling sound, like ice breaking on a pond.

I looked away quickly. She wouldn't turn me to stone, would she? *Not in front of Chet.* No, she'd get me alone somewhere, and then she'd take me out of the picture. I'd become a lawn ornament, then she'd have Chet all to herself. Once the pesky redheaded witch was gone, and her sister's spirit couldn't talk through anyone, Charlize would pull the plug on her triplet sister.

Why was I so certain of this? Was it a warning from Chessa, or simply my own distaste for the woman?

I sensed her staring at me, and I resisted my curious urge to stare back.

"Zara, don't be shy," Charlize said. "You're far more powerful than I am, anyway. Even if I did turn you to marble, you'd change right back again."

"Let's not find out."

Chet, who'd been quiet through our interaction, said, "Help yourself to the food."

"Don't mind if I do," she said brightly, digging into the fruit salad. A pesky hornet was buzzing around the table, attracted by the bounty of food. Without warning, Charlize reached out and tapped the hornet midair. The insect crackled, turned to gray stone, and dropped to the table with a plunk.

Chet chuckled under his breath. "Showoff," he said.

Charlize plucked the stone hornet from the table and tossed it over her shoulder, over the fence, and into my back yard.

I stared after the stone hornet. Wait 'til Zoey heard about this! She'd always suspected the insect-shaped pebbles found in our back yard were more than they appeared to be.

Charlize reached over toward me. My ears started ringing with danger. She casually stroked the sleeve of my T-shirt. The cotton fabric didn't change the way the hornet had. Even so, I suppressed the urge to shoot blue fireballs at the gorgon.

"I love your colorful outfit," she said sweetly. "I could never pull off an orange that bright. It would be garish against my pale skin. But you have such *dramatic* coloring, with your flaming-red hair and your bright eyes, whatever you call that color."

"Hazel."

"Is that actually an eye color, or just something people make up to pretend they're too special to be categorized?"

"You got me," I said. "I made up the color hazel. I really like words with the letter Z."

She continued staring at my shirtsleeve, her face unchanging. "Whatever," she said vaguely. "This orange does suit you. I'll borrow it some time. I could soften it with a scarf."

As her words washed over me, I caught a mental image of slapping Charlize across the cheek, and the two of us wrestling each other while another blonde, Chloe at age ten, stood by screaming. This memory switched to a scene of us at thirteen, all three of us pulling each other's hair and then scratching and biting, retaliating for snake bites. I didn't have snakes in my hair, but I could hurt my sisters. I tasted Charlize's blood in my mouth, heard her pleading for my forgiveness. I'd bitten her. And for good reason. The story and memory shifted forward, wrapped up, and I knew.

I was back in Chet's sunny back yard, at the Grownups' Brunch, looking right at Charlize.

"You stole Chessa's boyfriend," I said coolly.

She feigned innocence. "Says who?" Her face was blank, but the snakes on her head were stirring, appearing in place of her tight ringlet curls.

I pointed to my temple and raised my eyebrows knowingly. "His name was Leo, and you made him kiss you, even though you knew Chessa liked him."

She rolled her eyes. "I didn't *make* Leo do anything."

The memory expanded. "Wait. I know this guy. It's the same Leo who teaches scuba diving now, isn't it? You kissed him, and Chessa bit you, but you totally had it coming. Then Chloe took Chessa's side, and you guys didn't speak for months."

"That was years ago." Charlize crossed her arms and tossed her writhing snake hair back over her shoulder. "And that was just kid stuff," she said. "But good for you." She clapped slowly. "Cute little magic trick."

Chet growled, "Charlie, play nice."

She shot him a wounded look, and the snakes on her head calmed into ringlet formation once more.

"Tell me more about scuba diving," she said to me. "Is Leo still sexy?"

"Not at all," I lied. "He's gross."

She narrowed her eyes. "Does scuba diving really help you feel closer to my sister's spirit?"

"Not as much as being around Chet," I said, partly because it was true and partly because I knew it would irritate her.

"Interesting," she said cryptically. "Tell me more about your methodology, Zara. You witches are so fascinating with your archaic, demonic ways."

I bit my tongue. The gorgon with the snake hair was calling *me* archaic and demonic? The nerve of her. I could understand why her sisters had been trying to slap some manners into her since the day they were born. Not that it had done any good.

I shot Chet a dirty look. He shot me back a surprisingly parental look. He had really honed the fatherly eyebrow lift.

Fair enough. He'd invited us to a Grownups' Brunch, so I could make an effort to behave like a grownup, even though Charlize's presence brought out residual sisterly rivalry.

Charlize adjusted the pale-blue shoulder strap of her breezy dress. She gave me a sweet, almost flirtatious look. "It's fine if you don't want to share your witchy secrets.

We all have our stories to keep. How do you like scuba diving?"

I liked Leo. But I didn't dare let her know, or she'd go put her lips all over him again.

"Diving is fun," I said lightly. "It took a while to get used to the sensation of breathing from a tank, but the view down there at the bottom of the sea is worth it."

She seemed genuinely interested, so I went on, telling both of them about how cute Zoey had been at the first lesson, even though it wasn't for her in the end, and about how the group of students had all bonded with each other.

"Fighting is a way of bonding," Charlize said.

"I remember," I said. "I mean, I can feel Chessa's memories." I closed my eyes to focus. "I can see you apologizing for kissing Leo. How you tried to make it up to your sister with countless small gestures, like making her tea when she got sick over the Christmas holidays. And by not going to that New Year's Eve party when he asked you out."

"She knew about that?" Charlize stared at me with wide eyes.

"Why do you think she finally forgave you?"

"Oh," she said, nodding. She reached out and grabbed my hand. "Zara, tell her that I'm sorry I wasn't a better sister."

My fingers were tingling, but I didn't yank my hand away. In my heart, I knew Charlize wouldn't hurt me. She'd never hurt her sister, either. Not on purpose.

I started to tell her the communication didn't work that way but stopped myself. Tears were shining in Charlize's pale eyes.

"She knows you love her," I said. "Both you and Chloe. She'd do anything for you two, and she knows you'd do the same."

Charlize let go of my hand. "It's true," she whispered.

I wanted to hug her, to show my sister how much I cared about her. She wasn't just a part of my family—she was a part of me.

But Charlize wasn't my sister. She belonged to Chessa. I looked across the brunch set out on the aquamarine table. I looked at Chet, ever watchful with those wild green eyes. All of this belonged to Chessa.

I reached for the pitcher and refilled my glass.

* * *

We ate pancakes and talked about food, the weather, and everything but the woman who lay lifeless on a hospital bed, twenty stories underground.

Chet got us a second pitcher of mimosa, and we had a playful debate over whether it was a pitcher of *mimosa*, singular, or *mimosas*, plural. We decided that it was mimosa while still in the pitcher then became mimosas when poured into the glasses. And the more mimosas we had, the more enjoyable our Grownups' Brunch became.

By the end of the second pitcher, when Charlize invited me to hang out with her "soon," I agreed without hesitation.

"Who knows," I said with a shrug. "It could help me get closer to your sister's spirit." I grinned. "Even if it's just to strangle you for making out with poor, sweet Leo, who had no idea what he was getting into."

Charlize tipped her head back and laughed. "You're almost as hilarious as me," she said.

I pushed my chair back and stood. It's always good to leave on a high note. "Thank you, folks, you've been a swell audience," I said.

"Don't go, Lady Traffic Cone," Charlize said.

I straightened my orange T-shirt and pretended to be offended. I wasn't.

"We need to plan our girls' night," she said.

"Uh..." I tried to remember what I'd unwittingly agreed to.

"You two can stay at Chessa's house tonight," Chet said. "Zara, you did say you wanted to spend some time there to connect with Chessa's energy."

I touched the bracelet on my wrist and shot him a wide-eyed look. Did he *want* me to get turned into stone? Was a marble statue of a fleeing librarian the final finishing touch he needed for his back yard?

"Great idea," Charlize said. "I'll go take care of some other business this afternoon, then I'll swing by and pick you up at your house." She pointed next door. "It's that red one with the moss on the roof, right?"

I put my hands on my hips and looked at my roof. Had it always been so mossy? I hadn't noticed before.

Charlize said, "I'll pick you up at eight."

"It's a date," I said with a forced smile.

CHAPTER 28

Zoey was horrified. "You're having a sleepover with a gorgon?"

We'd just gotten back home from Chet's brunch, and were hanging out in my bedroom. Zoey sat cross-legged on my bed with her laptop while I played around casting spells on my closet.

"Two gorgons," I said. "Charlize is going to invite Chloe. It would be rude not to, since she only lives a few steps away from Chessa's cottage."

Zoey looked down at her laptop and muttered, "My mother's having a sleepover with two gorgons. This is our life now."

"Cheer up," I said with enthusiasm. "Maybe they know some gorgons who are your age, and can make introductions."

"Gross." My daughter stuck her tongue out at me. "Don't get me wrong. I think it's great that you're making new friends here, but does it have to be ladies with hissy-hissy-bitey-bitey snake hair? They have the ability to turn living things into statues. You can't blame me for being a little alarmed."

"I'll keep my wits about me. Plus I have Chessa's memories, and even the worst bits are just kid stuff, sibling rivalry." I chuckled as I got a flash of memory involving the triplets putting baby clothes on the family's pet dog. The dog was a Chihuahua. No, a beagle. Or was it a golden retriever? More memories flashed by like photographs. A sour taste came to my mouth. It was all of those breeds of dogs. The family had gone through a lot of pets.

"That must have been weird, growing up," Zoey said.

"It was. I mean, yes, I imagine it was."

"But nice to have sisters." She stared at my closet, her eyes unfocused and her little rosebud mouth in a pout.

"Zoey, I tried to get you a brother or sister, but the company who made Barberrian wine coolers went out of business."

She rolled her eyes. "Careful they don't do weird sleepover stuff to you after you fall asleep. Like soak your bra in water and stick it in the freezer."

"It's not going to be a huge slumber party. Chloe has her own bedroom in the big house at the front. I'm sure she'll return to her own house and her baby."

"All the better for Charlize to get you alone and petrify you with no witnesses."

"Petrify!" I snapped my fingers. "Petrify: A verb, meaning to frighten someone so that they are unable to think or move, or to change organic matter into a stony concretion. That's the word I've been trying to think of all morning. Thanks, Zoey."

She set her laptop aside and leaned forward to grab the stony wasp from my bedside table. "Poor little dude," she said, stroking it with one finger. Then, in an abrupt change of mood, "Can I keep it?"

"You have been lobbying for a pet, so... sure."

She cradled the concrete wasp lovingly. "I shall hug him, and kiss him, and call him Fuzzy."

I was happy for her. She'd been looking to adopt a dog or a cat to expand our Riddle family, but her last few visits to the pet adoption center hadn't panned out. The cages had been empty, which was probably a good thing. According to the kind people who ran the pet shelter, the people of Wisteria took excellent care of their cats and dogs, so animals had to be shipped in from other cities.

I sat on the bed next to her. "I feel bad leaving you alone here tonight." I clapped my hands together. "You should invite some friends over from school and have a slumber party of your own."

She juggled the concrete wasp from one hand to the other. "Fuzzy will keep me company. Plus I can catch up on my reading."

I glanced guiltily at the to-be-read pile on my own bedside table. "Tell me about it. Between the ghost drama and the scuba diving, my reading pile is getting seriously neglected. If I don't finish a few more books in the next week, I may need to turn in my cardigans, my corkscrew, and my librarian status."

"You'll catch up, once you bring back Chet's fiancée. Then he'll be busy with her, and he won't be dragging you into DWM business."

"That would be nice," I lied.

"I'd sure like to talk to Chessa about my name being on that scroll. Allegedly."

"No matter what happens, you'll always be my Chosen One."

She groaned and gave her concrete wasp a look of wide-eyed annoyance.

I draped my arm around her shoulders. "Come with me tonight! We'll cancel the male strippers and make the night G-rated and family friendly. Of course, I'll have to forfeit my deposit for the Bunny Boys, and suffer through a lap-dance-free weekend, but being a good parent is about making personal sacrifices."

"Nice," she said sarcastically. "Is there really a male stripper group called the Bunny Boys, or did you make that up?"

I squeezed her around the shoulders. "You'll find out on your eighteenth birthday."

She groaned.

I whispered ominously, "Two more years."

CHAPTER 29

CHARLIZE ARRIVED AT my house to pick me up a half hour late, with no explanation for her tardiness.

Such a Charlize move, I thought, courtesy of Chessa's emotional residue.

I wasn't surprised to see her vehicle, a bright-yellow Volkswagen Beetle. Nor was I surprised to find the vehicle interior crammed with loose clothes and half-eaten bags of candy. At sixteen, Charlize had been the one who filled the triplets' shared car with forgotten homework and empty bottles of Diet Coke.

I brushed loose jelly beans off the passenger seat so I could settle in.

"Now, this is a vehicle you can ride out a natural disaster in," I said. "Forget tanks and Hummers. This little bug's got a three-day supply of Hot Tamales."

Charlize gave me a sidelong look as she started the engine. "That sounds exactly like something Chessa would say."

"She and I have been getting closer," I said. "Sometimes her words come out of my mouth."

"How does that work?"

"Beats me. I don't have a handbook. Do you have a handbook?"

She looked over her shoulder into the Beetle's tiny backseat. "I have a few books. Oops. I shouldn't have told you that. Most of them are overdue."

"But do you have a DWM handbook? Sort of an operations manual?"

She gave me a guilty look and turned her attention to the road ahead. "That's classified," she said crisply. "Chet warned me you might pump me for information."

"Of course he did. What a guy."

* * *

Chloe was already waiting for us inside Chessa's cottage. The house seemed smaller that Saturday evening, the way most places seem smaller the second time you visit. I tried not to take the claustrophobic feeling as a bad omen.

Chloe had Jordan Junior with her. It was well past his bedtime, but he'd been fussy and wouldn't go to sleep when his parents tried.

She handed the three-month-old baby boy to me. "He wanted to stay up and see Auntie Zara!"

"Is it true?" I cuddled the little cutie. "Did you know I was coming to visit?"

He blew bubbles at me. If Jordan Junior was psychic, he'd have to learn better communication skills if he wanted to impress anyone with his powers of prognostication. He did, however, give me a sweet look that melted my heart. Plus he smelled amazing.

"He likes his auntie," Chloe said. "He knows you're family."

"But I'm not really his aunt," I said.

"You are," Chloe said firmly. "Look at the way he's gazing up at you. Don't fight it, Zara. We are officially making you one of Jordan Junior's aunties."

Charlize interjected, "That includes one equal share of diaper duty."

"I would be honored," I said, and I meant it. With no siblings of my own, and no spouse with siblings, this was my first—and possibly my only—opportunity to be an aunt. I rocked the baby and spoke to him softly. "Zara is a good aunt! Well, she tries to be a good aunt. Zara is the best aunt she can be."

We played with the baby for a while, taking turns holding him and hearing Chloe's stories about the new things he'd done in the last week. His mother described it as "hatching out of his shell," the way he'd been interacting with the world, enjoying music, and making social smiles.

After an hour, Jordan Senior came to check on us and take the baby.

"You could stay a while," Chloe said to her dark-haired, muscular husband. "You're welcome to hang out here with us girls for a while."

Jordan looked at the open bottles of wine on the coffee table. "Looks like you're doing just fine without me." He took a closer look at our wineglasses and made a tsk-tsk sound. "Red wine? You're drinking red wine on Chessa's white sofa? She's going to murder you."

"We're being careful," Charlize said.

Chloe waved her husband away. "Go back to the big house if you're going to be a tattletale. I spent nine months without a drop of wine, or even a sip of coffee, and I'm making up for lost time now."

"That's right," I said, getting into the rhythm with the others. "After this bottle, we're doing espresso shots. And then..."

I looked at the blondes.

In unison, we said to Jordan, "Tequila shots!"

He gave us one last tsk-tsk and left with the baby.

Once he was gone, I asked Chloe, "How's Jordan been sleeping lately? Has the sleepwalking issue gotten any better?"

The sisters glanced at each other and then stared at me, eyes wide.

"It's like Chessa's right here with us," Chloe said.

"I can stop letting her speak through me if you want," I said. "If it's getting too weird."

Chloe clutched my arm, nearly sloshing my red wine on the white sofa. "Nothing's too weird for us," she said.

Charlize had gone quiet. She was staring at my face. "Zara, maybe it's the wine, but you're actually starting to look like Chessa."

"We need a mirror!" Chloe exclaimed as she suddenly leapt up from the sofa. She flung my arm and sent my wine sloshing. Without thinking, I telekinetically caught the globules of wine midair, before they could land on the furniture. Charlize and Chloe watched with open mouths and stunned expressions as I magically gathered the red wine from the air and then pooled it in my wine glass.

I raised my glass, "To magic."

Charlize toasted my glass with hers while Chloe ran off in search of a mirror.

She returned with a piece of broken mirror from the top of Chessa's dresser. It was the perfect size and shape for reflecting our three faces together; Chet's bad luck was our good fortune.

We put our faces together, cheeks almost touching, me in the center, and examined ourselves in the mirror. Our bone structure was similar, and I resembled the triplets more when I tilted up my chin, shortening my face.

Charlize fussed with my hair. "Zara, if you change this wacky red color, and if you blot out some of those nasty freckles, you'd be a dead ringer for our sister."

Chloe swatted her sister's hands from my hair. "She's got *cute* freckles. Don't be mean to Zara. She doesn't understand that's how we show affection for each other."

Charlize replied, "I'm just teasing. You both know how much I love to joke around. You can't take anything I say seriously."

Chloe looked me in the eyes through the mirror. "It's true. Charlize was always causing trouble growing up, and she got away with it by making up something even more outlandish. She could have gotten away with murder. Our poor parents were outmatched and outnumbered."

At the mention of their parents, Charlize's smoky gray eyes lit up. She struck one finger in the air and gasped. "I know! Chessa has a blonde wig here, from when Mom was getting her chemo treatments. I'll get the wig, plus some makeup, and we can give Zara a triplets makeover." And with that declaration, she left me alone with Chloe in the living room.

"Sure, I'll let you guys give me a makeover," I said to the empty air where Charlize had been sitting.

Chloe laughed. "You're a good egg, Zara."

I gave her a sweet smile. "I'm trying. How about you? Have you thought of what Chessa might have meant, about you knowing something about why she was behaving strangely before her accident."

"What?" Chloe blinked rapidly. "How should I know what she meant? People attempt suicide all the time. It's not anybody's fault."

"You don't think it was an accident?"

Chloe emptied the bottle into her glass. "I don't know what to think. Out of the three of us, Chessa was always the most emotional. She could be moody, always yelling at us to leave her alone and let her think. Charlize and I never liked it when she was too quiet, though. It seemed like she was up to something."

"She was the odd one out. Different powers." I paused. "Similar but different."

Chloe sipped the wine. "I can't tell you what she was," she said meekly. "Chessa made us swear to never tell. I swore on my life. I've hurt her before, but I can't let her down again."

"Again?"

Chloe's expression twitched to fear before she masked it. "Just sister stuff, over the years," she said breezily. "There was always one thing or another going on with the three of us." She looked into my eyes. "But I loved my sister, and I never meant to hurt her. If I'd known how much she was suffering, I would have put a stop to it."

"A stop to what?" There was a roar in my ears, like a storm on the ocean.

Chloe sipped her wine. "I don't know," she said, gazing across the cozy room at the photographs on the fireplace mantel. "Chessa hasn't been the same since our mother passed away. It was very difficult for her."

I followed her gaze to a framed photo of the triplets' mother.

Chessa's memories rushed in, of her mother smiling sweetly from the hospital bed. The frail woman had told her daughters they had to be even braver now that they were on their own. I saw her gaunt face, brightened by the application of lipstick and a vibrant orange scarf around her head. The triplets' father had already been gone for five years, killed in a highway accident. They hadn't said good-bye to him, but they'd exchanged final farewells with their beloved mother every night for twenty-seven days.

My jaw ached, and my eyes stung. "Twenty-seven days," I murmured.

"Chessa shared that with you," Chloe said, blinking rapidly.

I held my hands over my heart. "I feel what she feels. That you're my sister, and Charlize is my sister, too."

Chloe rubbed at the corner of her eye and looked down. "Lucky us," she said with a chuckle.

Her sister could be heard rummaging in the bedroom for the wig, while narrating her findings in a singsong voice.

"Charlize can be annoying," Chloe said. "But sisters are a chunk of your childhood that can never be lost."

I nodded. "And when sisters stand shoulder to shoulder, nobody else stands a chance."

Chloe gazed at me, her expression soft yet strong. "Chessa used to say that as our rallying cry. And then Charlize would say if one of us ever faltered, she'd be there to pick us up, just as soon as she stopped laughing."

"That's Charlize for you," I said.

Charlize returned to the living room with a blonde wig and a tackle box full of makeup.

I playfully tried to escape the makeover, but Charlize caught me around the waist. She was strong, with a grip like a vise.

She waved the wig in the air with her free hand. "Don't fight us, Zara. This is happening! We're turning you into one of us."

"Snakes," I said. "We're going to need a lot more snakes."

Chloe laughed so hard, she snorted like a pig, and soon all three of us were pig-snorting like maniacs.

* * *

Sunday morning, I woke up feeling overdressed. I was in a bed, wearing a strapless pink gown with matching satin pump shoes.

I was in Chessa's pure-white beach-themed bedroom, and I wasn't alone. On one side of me lay Chloe, snoring away in a white wedding dress. On the other side was Charlize, wearing a half-unzipped strapless gown identical to mine.

The last thing I remembered, after the tequila shots, was the three of us trying to recreate one of Chloe and Jordan's wedding photos.

I shuffled down to the bottom of the bed without disturbing the girls, kicked off my pink shoes, and padded silently to the bathroom.

Looking in the mirror was a shock. The wig had stayed on through the night, along with a liberal application of makeup. The mirror reflected back a blonde stranger, possibly a prom queen who'd just fought off a horde of zombies.

Coolness washed over me, and my face changed.

Now I was staring at Chessa in the mirror, her ghostly face overlaying my own.

She looked down at the pink dress with a confused expression.

"Chessa, I know it's strange, but I'm only wearing your bridesmaid dress so I can help you."

The mouth in the mirror didn't move. She stood before me in stony silence. This was the closest we'd come so far to a face-to-face conversation. As much as one part of me wanted to scream *ghost* and run from the bathroom, I was going to stay and make the most of this opportunity.

"Your sisters are incredible women," I said, gushing. "Things have been rocky with me and Chloe, and I can't say it was much better with Charlize, but they've both grown on me. As you might know, I grew up an only child. I try not to get hung up on feeling bitter about the things I didn't have, but deep down, I've always longed for a sister. And you have two. Two hilarious, daffy, loving sisters." I moved my hand to my heart. The reflection hesitated, then moved her hand there as well. I saw a positive response in her eyes. She loved her sisters. She would have done anything for them, given them anything, given them pieces of her if they asked, and sometimes they did.

"I feel what you feel," I told her. "I'm trying to get you back into your body and awake, but in the meantime..." This part was hard to put into words, but I'd been thinking about it, mentally rehearsing a speech I'd give the woman if I could.

She waited patiently, not moving, but rippling slightly, as though underwater.

"In the meantime, I propose we share everything," I said. "You can be in my body and speak through me when you wish, and I can enjoy the company of the sisters I've always wanted. I don't know the best way to work things out with Chet, but I'm willing to try. Maybe there's a spell I can cast, so that I can disappear and leave you two some privacy." I shook my head and looked down at the tile floor, ashamed by my eagerness. How had this speech sounded reasonable to me the night before? The woman had one foot in the grave, and here I was offering to take over her life, all while acting like I was doing her a favor.

"Never mind," I said. "Forget I said anything. Do you have any ideas for how to get yourself awake again?" I looked up at her stony face, so cool it was nearly blue. "You do know you're not dead, right? That your body is in a coma?"

She nodded.

"And do you want to come back to the land of the living?"

She nodded again.

I crossed my arms, and she did the same. Her pink bridesmaid dress was pristine and unwrinkled, unlike mine.

"Then you've got to work with me," I said, exasperated. "I'm willing to do anything, if you'll just give me a hint."

The reflection uncrossed her arms and pointed.

I whirled around. There was nothing behind me except for the shower curtain, drawn across the opening of the shower.

My sense of hearing assured me I was alone in the bathroom, but my body thought otherwise. My chest pounded as adrenaline coursed through my veins. I reached out toward the crisp white shower curtain, and very slowly drew it aside.

Monsters!

No.

Nothing but tiles.

Nobody was standing or sitting inside the tub. I saw only bottles of shampoo, conditioner, body wash, a natural sea sponge loofah, and a notepad affixed to the tiled wall. I stepped inside the shower and sniffed the loofah. It hadn't been used in a year, and was dusty. Other than that, the loofah looked completely ordinary. I examined the notepad next. It was designed for use in the shower, made with waterproof paper. There was a magnet, presumably to hold the matching pen, but the pen was gone.

I looked over at the mirror to see if Chessa was there to give me a hint. Was I getting any warmer?

All I saw reflected back was me, wearing a wig, with enough layers of makeup to hide my freckles and give me an eerily unnatural tan.

"What am I missing?"

She was gone, back to the watery depths in which she spent her time when she wasn't delivering daydreams or cryptic messages.

I held up the notepad to the light. It reminded me of all those old detective movies, where the clever private investigator would use a pencil to lightly shade over a notepad, revealing what had been written on the previous sheet.

I heard noises. Outside of the bathroom, Chloe and Charlize were stirring from bed and grumbling over which one was going to make the first pot of coffee.

I tucked the waterproof notepad into a drawer in the bathroom vanity. I slipped out of the wig and the pink bridesmaid dress, turned on the shower, and climbed in. I was close. So close. I needed water.

Sometimes, when a breakthrough is just beyond your understanding, all it takes is a hot shower. The mind works best under suds and steam, with the white noise of splashing water drowning out distractions. In the shower, under the water, I could finally think.

And, as I squeezed the viscous body wash onto the loofah, the answer came to me.

I knew what to do next. And, if it didn't kill me, maybe it would bring back Chessa.

CHAPTER 30

TWELVE HOURS LATER

As THE SUN was setting on Sunday evening, I walked up to Chloe and Jordan Taub's front door. The summer-evening air was fragrant with lilac, jasmine, and charcoal smoke from family barbecues. Somewhere down the quaint residential street, a lawnmower ceased cutting, its sharp blades dormant while the operator pushed it, wheels squeaking, back into a shed. All was quiet. A screen door banged, and a mother called her children in for bed.

On the Taubs' front porch, I patted the book in the pocket of my cardigan. My book was ready for battle. And so was I.

I rang the doorbell. Chessa's spirit wasn't with me. I was on my own.

Chloe answered the door and smiled at me sweetly. "Zara! Did you forget something when you left the cottage this morning? You rushed out of there so fast, I didn't get a chance to say good-bye."

"I had something important to do."

She looked at my damp, limp hair. After my dive, I'd pulled on my clothes and rushed straight over. The seawater from my hair was now seeping into my shirt.

She exclaimed, "Zara, you're soaking wet!"

"I've been drier, and less prune-like."

She leaned over to look behind me. I was alone.

By the tightness of her lips, she knew something was up. "What's going on?" She gave me a fake smile. "Should I open another bottle of wine?"

I set my chin. "Contrary to how damp I am, I'm not here for a girly gabfest and wet T-shirt contest."

She shifted from foot to foot, glancing over her shoulder into the house. "This isn't a good time."

I took a step forward. "Convenient or not, it's time for the two of us to have a discussion. Alone."

She didn't move.

"For Chessa," I said.

Chloe stepped back from the door and invited me in, her voice quivering. Her golden ringlets shifted into snakes—feisty ones that were asking to be taken down a notch or two. I snarled my upper lip back and hissed at them. The gold snakes snapped their mouths shut and wriggled to the far side of Chloe's head, more frightened of me than I was of them.

Her husband called out, "Chloe, who's at the door?"

She answered, "It's just my sister. Go back to your game."

I raised an eyebrow at being called her sister but didn't comment.

She led me into the house, to the kitchen. The room was tidy and rumbling with the sound of the dishwasher running. I could hear the TV in the den, as well as her husband, Jordan, talking back to the sports announcer. The baby monitor on the counter emitted the soft sound of breathing. It was the picture of domestic bliss here in the Taub residence. The neighbors probably thought they were a normal young family, not a gorgon and heaven knows what else.

We passed through the kitchen. Chloe didn't offer me so much as a glass of water. She led me down a hallway and into a pantry, with walls lined in shelves of baking ingredients and jars of jellies and jams. She closed the door behind her.

She hissed. "What is it you want? Money? What's left of our cash is tied up in the business."

"I don't want hush money, Chloe. I just want the truth."

Her mouth pinched shut, but the hissing continued, thanks to the snake chorus. They were wary of me now, hissing from the safety of the hidden side of Chloe's head. A snake would peek at me quickly before disappearing, then another would do the same.

"The truth?" Chloe was feigning ignorance, but only halfheartedly. She knew that I knew. I could see it in her eyes, hear it in her hissing. Guilt. She was consumed by guilt.

I asked her a question I already knew the answer to. "Whom does Jordan Junior belong to?"

She blinked rapidly. "My son? He's Jordan's. I've never been unfaithful. Never."

I looked her straight in the eyes and squared my shoulders. "Who's the mother?"

She stepped back, pressing the back of her head against the door, which did nothing to calm down her snakes.

"I gave birth to him," she said, rubbing her hands over her belly as she spoke. "Jordan was there with me, at the hospital. Chet was in the waiting room."

"Did you know your sister kept a diary?"

"Where?" Her eyes widened. "Did you find it? We looked everywhere."

"I'll tell you where I found the diary if you tell me what kind of creature your sister is. I know that you know."

Her eyes flicked down, then up, then back at me. "You don't know," she said. The snakes hissed louder.

"Take the deal," I said. "I came to you first. Don't make me regret my choice."

"Fine," she spat. "You first."

I crossed my arms and strolled over to the far side of the room. The pantry was also a laundry room. My legs were numb from the diving. I tried not to let my fatigue show on my face as I casually took a seat on top of the washing machine.

"No. You first," I said. "Tell me what she is."

Chloe began walking toward me, her eyes like mercury. "My sister is like no beast who has ever walked the earth or swum the sea," she whispered. "To catch a glimpse of my sister in her mythical form is to turn your mind inside out. To look upon her fully for even a moment is to invite madness into your soul. You will die trying to break your head open, trying to get her out."

I sucked in air between my teeth. "So, she's not a mermaid."

Chloe stopped in front of me and grinned as she whispered, "She's not a mermaid. Not a selkie. And not a melusine, though she would have loved to have been one of those, half serpent and still half human. She longed to keep some of her humanity in her changed form." Chloe shook her head, snakes twirling dizzily. "My sister, the monster." She let out a bitter laugh. "And to think, everyone says Charlize is the worst."

I tilted my head and bit my tongue.

"Now, give it to me," she hissed. "Give me the journal." She grabbed for the pockets of my cardigan.

Her fingers grazed my forearms, stinging my skin. I looked down in horror as patches of my flesh turned as gray and stony as Fuzzy the Unlucky Hornet. Terror crept up my spine, and then calm. I pushed out, and my stony flesh sizzled as it turned back to flesh.

"Back off," I growled.

Chloe kept grabbing for my pocket, so I hit her with a taste of blue lightning. Just a small fireball. It was *my* fire, my power, and I had more control over it now.

She lurched backward, windmilling clumsily. The blast had been more than just a taste, after all.

I jumped off the washing machine and caught her before she fell.

She went limp in my arms. She began sobbing, burying her face in my chest. "I didn't mean to hurt her," she cried. "I didn't know the fertility treatments would make her suicidal."

"They didn't," I said.

She sniffed and looked up at me. "You mean, you didn't find her suicide note?"

"Just her journal," I said.

"That's all?"

Now it was my turn to laugh ruefully. "That's all? Let me tell you, it was no picnic to retrieve."

She pulled away from me, wiped her face with the sleeve of her shirt, and gestured for me to explain.

And I did. I told her how I'd been feeling a pull toward the ocean, ever since visiting Chessa's home. Every time I talked about her, walked in her footsteps, we'd grown closer. I'd gotten a small taste of her powers during my first swim in the ocean, but then I hadn't been able to access her powers to shift again.

"It must have been because her body was growing progressively weaker," I said. "Her mortal body kept deteriorating."

"She's gotten so frail," Chloe whispered.

"But she's a fighter," I said. "And so am I. That's why I learned how to scuba dive. I didn't know what she had planned for me, but I wanted to respond to her calls for me to dive, without the inconvenience of drowning."

Chloe wrinkled her nose. "Charlize and I both hate swimming. We tried, but we could never keep up with her." She wiped her cheeks dry. "Why did she want you to go diving?"

"To retrieve her journal," I said. "Did you know she went down to the bottom of the ocean, to where it was quiet, to think and write about her thoughts?"

"How? Wouldn't the paper fall apart?"

"She had a waterproof journal. The kind scuba divers use. I got the idea when I saw the memo pad in her bathtub, and I connected it to something my diving instructor used."

"How did you find it?" She cast a suspicious look at the square lump in my cardigan pocket. "You don't have anything," she hissed. "You're bluffing."

"Am I? It's true that the ocean floor is a very large place," I said. "Even after I knew she'd been keeping a journal down there, I still didn't know where. After I left the cottage this morning, I had a diving buddy go out to the ocean with me, and I let my intuition guide me. After three hours and no journal, I figured out how to use my witch powers. I cast a spell on the local diving reference guides, and one of them unfolded to photos of an underwater cave. When viewed from an angle, the opening of the cave looks like a woman's face."

Chloe gave me a skeptical look. I reached into my sweater pocket and pulled out the item I'd been hiding— the diving book. I showed Chloe the photo of the cave.

She nodded, and her snakes calmed down. "That's not much of a face."

"But it matches my vision," I said, and I described to her the imagery I'd seen during my commune with Chessa at her bedside. "At the time, I figured the statue was a metaphor for Chet's fiancée being larger than life, a monolith." I snorted. "But then I saw this picture, and I knew. I dove down, dug around in the sand, and there was the journal." I looked her straight in the eyes. "I have the journal, and it's currently in a safe place."

"So, you know about the eggs," Chloe said.

I nodded. "She felt terrible about your fertility problems. She blamed herself, thinking it was something she must have done to you during your development in the womb. That her powers took away from yours."

"What? But that's crazy. It wasn't her fault. It was just nature, just bad luck."

"However it happened, she wanted to donate her eggs to you because that's the kind of sister she was. She loved you so much, she was willing to give you a piece of herself." I paused to let it sink in. "And when we get her back again, I think she will agree that this whole thing was worth it. Especially when she holds Jordan Junior."

Chloe clenched her jaw. "That's never going to happen."

"Don't be so sure of that," I said. "We can get her back. But we need Charlize to help."

Chloe's hands fluttered up to her mouth. "I'll have to tell Charlize everything. Tell her what I did, and how I kept Chessa's gift a secret." She sniffed and looked down. She'd only kept the egg donation a secret because of her guilt; she was certain she'd driven her sister to suicide, and couldn't bear to tell the rest of her family.

"You're not to blame," I said.

Chloe sniffed. "She really did have a difficult time with the hormone treatments and the mood swings."

"Yeah," I said, nodding. "I know. I kinda read her diary, remember?"

She sniffed again, and I sensed she was about to crumble. We didn't have time for crumbling. Chessa was getting weaker by the minute. I hadn't gotten a memory or message from her all day, not since her appearance in the mirror.

I took Chloe by the hands and squeezed them, despite the stinging of her powers. "Chloe, you've got to stay strong, for your sister. What we are about to do is dangerous."

She lifted her chin bravely. "Dangerous?"

"I know who's trying to kill your sister," I said. "It's time for us to fight back."

CHAPTER 31

IT WAS MIDNIGHT, approximately, when I heard him enter the room. I didn't dare look up from where I sat, next to Chessa's hospital bed, and check the clock on the wall.

I heard his soft-soled shoes lightly scuffing the floor as he walked over to the bed. In a sudden flash of movement, he whipped back the curtain and exposed the two of us women.

Beautiful, radiant Chessa lay motionless in her bed. Her skin glowed, still coursing with life, even after everything that had been done to her. Despite the horror.

Then there was me, seated next to her. I wore Charlize's DWM access cards on a lanyard around my neck, along with a plastic bag holding a rather disgusting object. I shifted my body and watched the doctor's eyes as they went to my plastic bag, and the bloody eyeball it held. His nostrils flared. He'd seen what I wanted him to see, thought what I wanted him to think.

I was seated next to Chessa's bed, but I wasn't wearing a goofy costume this time. I'd come dressed in leather. Black leather. And lots of it.

I slowly raised my head and squared my shoulders to face him. I didn't stand. Not yet.

His gaze went to my head, to the wire-and-sea-glass coronet I wore.

The crown was hurting me. It had been fashioned hastily, and had rough points digging in at my temples hard enough to make me bleed, but I used the pain to stay focused. Over on Chessa's head was a matching crown. We were a matched set. Linked. Two souls for the price of one.

Dr. Bhamidipati, also known as Dr. Bob, took a leisurely stroll around the foot of Chessa's bed. He hadn't spoken yet.

"Hello, Dr. Bob," I said, cold as Arctic ice.

"And a very good evening to you, Ms. Riddle," he said with his friendly lilting accent. "I see that you are attempting some type of witch magic to help our sleepy girl." He looked at the video monitor showing the patient's vital signs. "Fair enough. I suppose whatever you are doing shouldn't do any harm." He reached up to tap a button on the controls for her IV drip.

"Wait a moment." I used my magic to push the wheeled machine holding the controls out of his reach. "Chessa is communicating with me right now, and she has a question for you, Dr. Bob."

He turned slowly and locked his eyes on mine. "Oh, I doubt that very much."

"She wants to know who you're building the army for." I faked a confused look. "What army?"

His hands fluttered up before he shoved them into the pockets of his white coat. "She must be speaking about our training program. You see, it's my job to help all of our DWM agents be the very best they can be."

I turned my head to the side, all the better to show him the stream of blood running from the crown's pointed metal tip, down my cheek. I pushed the blood from my vein, and feathered it wider, like a warrior making herself bloody to show her opponent she fears no pain.

"Let's talk about the other army," I said. "The one you're breeding with the use of Chessa's eggs. It wasn't enough for you to take the extras from her donation to her sister, was it? No, you wanted them all." My blood pooled under my chin and fell to the floor with a smack. "You're a monster."

"Eggs?" He let out a high-pitched, crazy laugh. "My goodness gracious, Ms. Riddle. You witches and your paranoia. Your type never got over those witch hunts, did you?"

"This isn't about me."

He bared his teeth like a cornered dog. "Ms. Riddle, my dear woman, if you've been suffering from unwanted thoughts, we do have some types of medication here at the DWM specifically for our agents. Technically, we're not permitted to prescribe them to civilians, but for someone such as yourself, I could make an exception."

"You're a monster, and you're greedy," I said. "You realized something once you got the extra eggs from her sister's round of in vitro. The pregnancy took. And you told Chessa the extras would be destroyed, but you kept them. And when you thought about what you could have, if you got more of her precious gift, you took control. You attacked her and left her bleeding on that cold shoreline. Isn't that right?"

"This is preposterous," he said. "I saved her."

"That's what you wanted everyone to think. When they found her limp body on the shore, they brought her right to you. And you were so brave, weren't you? You worked for hours to stitch her up and keep her heart beating, but not out of the goodness of your heart. No. You wanted her body, here with you, completely under your control."

He cleared his throat. "Ms. Riddle, I'm very sorry, but I must ask you to leave this ward. I'm afraid you are delusional." He licked his thin lips. "In fact, I'm afraid that given your heightened state of paranoia, you may be a danger to yourself."

I stood from the chair and raised my voice. "Doctor, you kept her here, in a chemically induced coma, and you kept dosing her with hormones so you could dig into her, again and again, removing her fertile eggs, again and again. That's why Chet noticed she looked tanned. It was the cocktail of drugs and vitamins you were feeding her, all so you could steal her most precious gift." I lifted both of my hands, palms out. "Tell me who the army was for, right now, or I'll blast you so hard, there'll be nothing left of you but a smoky stain on that back wall."

"You wouldn't," he said. "You don't have control over your powers."

"Don't I?" I pulled my left hand into a fist, summoned my blue fire, and sent a warning flare out. The fireball hit the doctor squarely in the chest.

I beamed, victorious. "Now tell me who the army is for. Where are the eggs now?"

"Let me show you." He reached around inside his lab coat, to the small of his back, and produced a gun. It wasn't a wacky DWM prototype, either. It was a solid-looking black handgun, the kind a police officer carries. As he brought the handgun around to bear on me, electricity shot through my arms with ease.

I gave him another blast of blue lightning, this time with both hands.

He didn't even flinch.

What was happening? I'd seen the blue fireballs leave my hands and strike him. I hadn't missed.

Dr. Bob chuckled. "Ah, the pyrotechnics of your attack powers are much more beautiful when they aren't frying my internal organs."

"These are defensive powers, not attack powers," I growled. "And why aren't you on your knees?"

He shrugged and waved the gun casually. "Ever since that day in the forest, when you tried to electrocute me to death, I've been preparing myself."

"You attacked me? Why?"

"This town didn't need another one of your kind. You witches are always meddling, getting into places you don't belong."

"Too bad, because now this town is stuck with me," I said, and I fired a blue ball of pain directly at his chest.

He winced, but he didn't go down. "It's no use, Ms. Riddle. I've been inoculating myself against such attacks."

"You're bluffing," I said.

"Am I?" He aimed the gun directly at my center of mass. "Ms. Riddle, you could try hitting me with your most powerful blast, but I must warn you, the safety's off, and my finger's on the trigger." He sneered. Something was different about his mouth. The scar I'd seen on his upper lip had healed completely. He continued speaking with a mocking tone, as though lecturing a child. "You do understand how the human body responds to an electrical shock, don't you?"

"Your hands would contract, and you'd pull your trigger as soon as I hit you. If I don't dodge out of the way in time, I'll be shot." I tilted my head back and stared at him through narrowed eyes. "But I do heal quickly, and after learning about what you did to Chessa, I'd gladly take a bullet if it means stopping you."

He twitched the gun, switching it to point at Chessa instead of me. "She heals quickly, too, but she won't come back from a bullet to the brain."

I sucked in air between my teeth. "Leave her out of this."

"In a minute," he said. "First, remove those two crowns and stop whatever it is you're doing. I don't like how she's filling your head with all these crazy delusions."

"Too late," I said. "The transfer is complete. She's waking up now."

"She is?" He looked frightened. And if he knew what kind of monster she was, he was right to be terrified.

"Look at her hand," I said.

Without shifting his aim of the gun away from her temple, he turned his head slowly.

There, on top of the green sheet, Chessa's fingers were moving. The fingers moved independently, jerkily, and then they moved with each other. She made a fist, then rolled it open.

Dr. Bob had been prepared for my blue lightning, but he'd forgotten about my levitation powers. Making a sleeping woman's hand move was easy for me.

While he was distracted, I jerked the gun in his hand straight up.

He had a strong grip on it, and he didn't let go. He cried out as he pulled the trigger.

With a deafening blast, the gun fired. I heard the zinging, and the impacts, as the bullet ricocheted in the concrete-walled underground room. One of the flat-screens on the walls exploded. Glass struck me from behind in a hailstorm.

I continued trying to wrestle the gun from the doctor's hand, this time prying at his individual fingers, but he pulled the trigger and shot it again.

After the second boom, my ears recovered quickly from the ringing. In the quiet, I heard someone groaning in pain. It wasn't the doctor. He stood before me, unharmed, both hands high over his head as he wrestled with me for control of the gun.

Then the moaning stopped. There was silence.

I screamed out, "Chet!"

Something banged on the door. It was locked. A bullet hole marred the center of the panel.

The doctor turned toward the door, releasing his gun suddenly. I was pulling it with such force that it flew over Chessa's body and struck me in the shoulder, sending me reeling.

As I struggled to catch my balance, the door to the ward blasted open in a hailstorm of splinters. Shadowy figures moved into the room, closing in on the doctor. But he'd seen them, and now that his gun was gone, he was changing tactics.

He was changing. Into a bird. Giant. Glossy sharp beak. Flashing talons. It was the creature who'd attacked me in the woods. The one who'd attacked Chessa.

The bird leapt into the air, its enormous wings creating a windstorm inside the room. He smacked noisily against the ceiling, but he remained airborne, and coming at me.

I had a gun now, so I used it. I pulled the trigger and willed the bullet's path to be straight and true. I fired twice at the attacking bird.

He kept coming, his sharp talons clawing away the sheet covering Chessa as he descended on me.

I aimed for a third shot, when a streak of darkness shot over my shoulder, straight at the bird.

It was a wolf. Chet. His sharp teeth snapping at the great bird.

Two monsters tangled, fur and feathers, teeth and talons, their struggles drawing blood from each other, as well as from the bare, unprotected legs of the sleeping woman they fought on top of.

I used what magical strength I had to push the snarling mass, the pair of them, off the bed, away from Chessa.

Out of sight, on the other side of the bed, there was growling, and then a snap. Bones breaking.

I didn't dare look.

And then I did.

Knox and Rob, still in human form, surrounded the two shifters, weapons raised. Blood was seeping from a wound on Rob's shoulder. Knox looked up at me, and in his eyes, I caught a glimpse of a rage so terrible, I stiffened and dropped the gun. It struck my ankle and clattered to the floor.

All was quiet. The bird had stopped shrieking, and the wolf was no longer snarling.

Someone took my hand. The fingers were soft, as gentle as seaweed brushing against me. The fingers tightened, taking form, taking back life.

I looked down into the face of the woman on the bed as she stirred.

Chessa's eyes fluttered open. She stared up at me blankly, as innocent and unknowing as a newborn baby.

I'd already removed the feeding tube from her mouth when I'd unhooked her from the IV and the drugs the doctor was giving her.

Her voice gravelly, she said, "Zoey."

I squeezed her hand. "I'm actually her mother, Zara. Zara Riddle."

Her eyes closed, and I thought we'd lost her again, but she opened them and came back stronger. Already, she was struggling to sit upright, removing the crown from her head and shaking out her long platinum waves. The cuts on her legs from the battling shifters were healing.

Rob let out a low groan as he put his weapon back into its holster. "What are the odds a stray bullet coming through the door hits the little scrawny guy and not the big tower of muscles?"

Knox chuckled, his big voice a deep rumble that changed the charge in the underground room. "It's fair, Rob. I took the last one. It's just probability."

"That's not how probability works," Rob said.

Knox shrugged.

Rob knelt down, so he was eye to eye with the panting wolf standing over the pile of feathers and dead bird. "Don't worry, Moore. We can take it from here. We've got your back."

The wolf continued panting.

Rob asked, "How'd you do that, anyway? You moved so fast, it looked like there were two of you."

The wolf blinked slowly.

"He's strong," Knox said, answering for him.

On the bed, Chessa had gotten herself up into a sitting position. She breathed heavily from the exertion. She looked down at the silver-wire crown in her hands, and then the one on my head. "What are these?" She gave me a dazed, questioning look. "You used metal and glass to transfer my soul?"

I reached up with an arm that felt like a bag of rocks, and removed the crown from my head. "This is just showmanship," I said. "Dr. Bob wouldn't have believed I was a powerful Soul Catcher if I'd revealed to him my entire plan, which was basically just unplugging your IV."

She blinked at me. "Zara Riddle. So, you're the Soul Catcher. Not your daughter."

I shivered. If she was saying that, it meant the scroll was real. Chet hadn't fudged it to get my cooperation. And if the scroll was real, that meant the prophecy was real, too.

Her attention went to the wolf standing at her bedside.

"Chet," she whispered.

He pressed his pointed wolf nose into the side of her hip. His breathing was ragged.

"I'm okay," she said, reaching up to stroke the top of the wolf's head. "I'm back, and everything's going to be okay now."

CHAPTER 32

ONE WEEK LATER

"JUST DO YOUR new closet spell," Zoey said. "It works great, and I love watching your closet magically reveal the perfect outfit for the day."

"Not yet." I cinched up my bathrobe and continued to manually dig through the sea of garments in my closet.

Zoey stood in my doorway, watching me with amusement.

"How about paisley?" I asked. "Nobody pulls it off quite like Frank, but I could get away with paisley." I waved the shirt at my daughter.

"That's not paisley. It's plaid, with bleach stains. Remember, we had a laundry accident, but you kept it as a crafts-and-hobbies smock. It was during that phase you were obsessed with gluing googly eyes onto things."

"That was a weird phase," I said, putting the shirt back.

"You're going to be late for your meeting with the triplets," Zoey said, leaning against my doorframe. "And if you show up late, they'll turn you to stone." She cradled her stone hornet in the palm of her hand and spoke to it. "Isn't that right, Fuzzy?"

"Then I'll risk being late," I said. "Aunt Zinnia always says we shouldn't become reliant on spells. Even after you master something like blue fireballs, you never know when someone's going to whip out a regular gun. We have to be prepared for anything, with or without magic."

Zoey came all the way into my bedroom and flopped back on my bed with a weary moan. "Who is this *we* you speak of?" She raised one arm and waved her hand limply. "Hello, I'm the one who was supposed to be a Soul Catcher before something went haywire and you stole my witch powers. I only *wish* I had powers that I could abuse."

"Be patient, and you'll get your wish," I said for the umpteenth time.

Without sitting up, she said, "Your emerald-green shirt dress. That's the right thing to wear to this baby shower. And if you're worried about showing too much leg, you can pair it with leggings."

I pulled out the shirt dress. It would be perfect, and she was right about the leggings. "Who needs magic when I have such a brilliant daughter? Now, about jewelry—"

"Grandma's pearls," she said. "Because pearls are *always* appropriate for afternoon tea parties with ladies, plus they're treasures from the sea."

She was right. Again. I pulled on the leggings, green shirt dress, and vintage pearls. I tucked Chessa's sea-glass bracelet into my chest pocket, then I twisted my damp hair up into a loose chignon and fastened it with a silver clip decorated with mother-of-pearl.

"Are you sure you won't come with me?"

She waved her hand for me to go. "I love having the house to myself so I can catch up on my weekend reading. Get out of here, Mom. And try not to get petrified."

I grabbed the wrapped baby-shower gift from my bedside table, blew a kiss to my daughter, and left for the baby shower with the triplets.

* * *

The party was at Chessa's. She'd gotten out of the DWM hospital within hours of regaining consciousness. After a year lying dormant in bed, she wasn't going to let a little thing like being barely able to walk keep her there another minute.

Her brother-in-law, along with Knox and Rob, had tackled the cottage behind the larger Taub residence. They removed two interior doorframes so that Chessa could get herself around in a wheelchair. She would regain her strength quickly and be able to walk on her own soon, but the changes would allow her to recover in the comfort and security of her own home.

Today's afternoon party wasn't the typical baby shower. The baby we were celebrating, Jordan Junior, had been honored once before, but Chessa had missed it due to her coma. The sisters had tried to organize a Welcome Home party, but Chessa refused that, saying it rubbed her the wrong way to be the focus of attention. She was, however, willing to host a second baby shower.

The baby had been conceived using Chessa's egg, with Chloe's husband as the father. Chloe had carried the baby and birthed it. Jordan had been kept in the dark, as had all of their family and friends. It was a complicated, sticky situation. He'd believed the egg was from an anonymous donor. The laboratory at the DWM rushed a test on the baby's DNA, and confirmed that Jordan was, indeed, the father. The parents loved and accepted their child no matter what, but had been relieved to find that Dr. Bhamidipati's dark plans had their limits. Jordan was still shocked about having been lied to, but the Taubs were working on restoring their trust.

That sunny afternoon, I walked past the concrete statues in Chessa's yard with the knowledge that they were exactly what I'd suspected them to be—wild animals petrified by Charlize. I didn't feel great knowing she'd turned living creatures to stone to practice her control over her powers, but on the plus side, at least she had some control. Also, I had eaten bacon at breakfast, and I did own a leather jacket. I wasn't vegan, so I couldn't dwell on my feelings of judgment too much.

Chloe opened the cottage door for me. Her blonde curls were tight and bouncy. Festivities had already begun, as I could see by the silly paper-plate hat she wore on her head.

Before we joined the others, I whispered, "How are things with Jordan Senior?"

She was slow to answer. "He's gotten over being angry that I kept it a secret. Now I think he's glad the baby might have inherited some of Chessa's powers."

"We all want what's best for our children."

"How's your daughter doing?"

I held up my hand and wavered it to mean *so-so*.

"Still no powers?"

I shook my head no.

Chloe gave me a sympathetic look and twirled one of her golden ringlets. "I was hoping she'd come with you today."

"She's only sixteen," I said. "I tend to think of her as a little grownup because of how mature she is for her age, not to mention how she lectures me about forgetting to use the plastic lid thingie in the microwave, but the truth is she's still just a kid. She does want to meet all three of you, but not just yet."

"In time," Chloe said. Brightly, she added, "She can babysit Jordan Junior, or help out at the bakery, or both!"

"I will certainly float the idea by her," I said.

Chloe's gaze went to my vintage pearl necklace. "Those are real," she breathed. "And they're breathtaking."

I thanked her, and was about to explain their origin when we were interrupted by Charlize, demanding we join them in the cottage's living room for the next baby shower game.

We joined them, and I took a seat on the edge of a pure-white ottoman. Who has a pure-white ottoman, anyway? They're literally for putting your feet on.

The baby shower was a small party, with just the triplets, me, and the baby. Supernaturals only.

Chessa was seated on her white sofa, her wheelchair folded to save space and leaning against the arm of the sofa. The scratches on her face had healed completely. She gave me a warm smile, moving her mouth in a silent hello. I waved back. We'd not spoken much since her return to consciousness, which was fine by me.

What do you say to a woman whose most intimate memories you've been reliving for the past few weeks? I didn't trust myself to open my mouth long enough to let out a joke about having sex on the beach with Chet on the evening of their engagement, getting sand in unmentionable places.

No, it was better that we communicated in polite smiles only.

Charlize handed out miniature chalkboards and explained the rules of the next baby-themed game. Jordan Junior was present, watching amiably from Chessa's lap. The two had evidently wasted no time bonding. Both split their time between watching the action in the living room and interacting with each other. Seeing them together like this, the mother-son resemblance was striking. Jordan Junior was a different skin tone—gingerbread to her sugar cookie—but he had Chessa's grace, and the same catlike eye shape. The boy's maternity was our little secret. To the rest of the world, Chessa would remain his aunt.

Chessa took the miniature chalkboard from her sister, gripping it easily. She was already stronger than she'd been just two days earlier, when we'd met at the DWM for a second debriefing and she'd barely been able to hold a pencil. She'd gained a few pounds, thanks to her sister and brother-in-law's delectable cooking. Unlike her sisters, with their corkscrew curls, Chessa wore her hair in the soft, undulating waves of a mermaid. Was she some type of mermaid? I still didn't know if it was true, what Chloe told me the previous week, about Chessa being so terrifying a creature my mind would melt if I laid eyes upon her.

Chessa noticed me staring at her. "Zara, you look stunning today. That green brings out your eyes."

"This old thing? Thanks. I don't know about stunning. More like stunned, maybe?" I laughed self-consciously. There's nothing quite like being in a room with a trio of gorgeous blondes to make a redhead feel weird.

Chessa waved her free hand. "You're beautiful, because no beauty shines brighter than that of a good heart."

I thanked her and took the compliment with grace. Where had I heard that expression before? Ah. From my own lips. I'd said it to Chet when he was driving me home right after Frank shifted for the first time. How many times had I quoted Chessa without knowing it for the past few weeks? Or months? Her spirit had been floating around for a year. Where did she end and I begin?

I leaned forward to get a soft pretzel. The bracelet in my shirt-dress pocket fell out. I scooped it from my lap and handed the piece to Chessa.

"Here's your bracelet back," I said apologetically. "I borrowed it to strengthen our connection. It's a lovely piece."

Instead of taking the silver-and-sea-glass bracelet, she closed my fingers around it.

"You should keep it," she said. "Don't stop strengthening our connection just because I'm awake again."

"Okay," I said hesitantly.

"Put it on. I'd love to see it on you."

I tried to unhook the fiddly clasp. Chessa chuckled as she leaned around Jordan Junior and pointed to my feet. "Zara, it's meant to be an anklet. It's awfully chunky for your wrist, don't you think?"

It was an anklet. And Chet never told me.

"If you say so." I leaned down and put the silver-and-sea-glass piece around my ankle. It did fit perfectly, and I was able to work the clasp easily with two hands. I pulled up my black leggings and admired my ankle. "That does look neat."

Charlize snorted in her bratty manner. "Don't let Chet see that, Zara. He has a weird thing for ankles."

Chloe chimed in. "He's so weird."

Charlize scrunched her face at Chessa. "What's with your fiancé and the ankles?"

Chessa didn't respond, except to smile.

"Probably a wolf thing," Chloe said with a shudder. "Blech."

I pulled the hem of my leggings back down over the anklet. "Don't worry. I won't be showing Chet my ankle."

"You'd better not," Chessa said with a laugh.

"I would *never*," I said, a bit too vehemently. "He's a dirty wolf boy. Blech."

The girls stopped laughing and glanced at each other the way only triplets could.

I shoved the soft pretzel in my mouth and chewed quickly. "This is good," I said around the mouthful. "Are we expecting more people? You've got enough food here for a dozen hungry lumberjacks. Not that I'm complaining."

Chloe beamed. "You like the soft pretzel? It's a new recipe. We're going to fire up the old wood oven at the bakery so we can do pretzels and bagels."

"Consider me sold," I said, reaching for a second one. I dipped it in hot mustard and let the spicy heat fill my sinuses.

"Not bagels," Charlize groaned. "You're trying to make me gain a million pounds, Chloe."

Chloe rolled her eyes. "Oh, please. A bagel isn't going to ruin your figure. Try running a bakery and having a baby."

"As if!" Charlize glared at her sister in mock outrage. "Your waist is already smaller than mine. You always had the skinniest middle, and your complaints are just requests for compliments."

I looked at Chessa, who gave me a weary look while her sisters argued over who had the better hip-to-waist ratio. "Some things never change," she said. "Can you believe these two are almost thirty years old?"

I smiled. "When do you all turn thirty?"

Chessa kissed Jordan Junior on the top of his head. "Those two turn thirty in a month, but I'll be turning twenty-nine again. Since I was in a coma for a year, that whole year doesn't count." She winked at me.

The other two were still bickering and didn't hear what their sister said. Once they heard about Chessa's plan to become a year younger than them, they'd have something new to argue about.

Eventually, the bickering settled down and we got back to the baby-shower games.

We played the classics, as well as a few that were new to me. We dabbed a selection of bright-hued baby foods onto sheets of paper, folded them, and created abstract art that doubled as Rorschach inkblot tests.

When asked what the pictures resembled, Chloe named off types of baked goods, Charlize saw clowns or squirrels, and Chessa named sea creatures.

I tried to play along, but everything looked like splattered food to me.

"That looks like the inside of the plastic thingie we use in the microwave," I answered when it was my turn.

Charlize said, "Not fair. You said that the last three times. Tell us what you really see, Zara. Is it something dirty and sexy?"

I made a gagging face. "Dirty, but not sexy. Not really." I tilted my head and looked again. "Okay, maybe a bit sexy."

Chessa looked at the unfolded waterproof paper, with its smears of vanilla and chocolate pudding that resembled naked flesh, if you squinted.

"Yes, I see what Zara sees," Chessa said smugly.

"No, I don't think you do," I said, giggling.

Chloe and Charlize demanded I tell them what I saw, but I demurely refused. "Get Chessa to tell you," I said.

From there, the conversation devolved, moving to a very strange place. All four of us were talking and saying the most outrageous things about the splotchy image, trying to one-up each other. I laughed so hard, I nearly cried.

And then we opened up some sparkling wine and loosened up even more.

At one point, I said something silly, and Charlize pretended to be offended. She prodded me on the shoulder, her touch stinging. My skin under the green shirt dress crackled into stone, and then back to flesh with a dull ache.

I cried out, "Ouch!"

Everyone stopped talking and stared at me.

I pointed at Charlize, who was covering her mouth and snickering. I grumbled to the other sisters, "Charlize keeps poking me and turning me to stone because she thinks it's funny." I rubbed my shoulder. "I know my powers turn it back again, but it still hurts."

Charlize stuck out her tongue and sassed me. "Oh yeah? Whatcha gonna do?"

I lifted both hands and sent her a little petrification of my own—two blue fireballs.

She froze, turning the color and texture of carved marble, from top to bottom.

And then, after a heart-stopping moment for me, she slowly melted back into her human appearance.

"Intense," Charlize said with admiration, rubbing the center of her chest where I'd struck her.

I turned to look at the other sisters. Chloe's hair snakes had shot straight up in the air, her golden snakes doing their best impression of blasting rockets.

We all started giggling.

Then, when I looked over at Chessa, I saw nothing.

Nothing.

Now, I don't mean I saw nothing *unusual*. I mean I saw *nothing*.

Where Chessa had been sitting on the white sofa, there was an abyss, malignant and unnatural. Reality ripped apart. It was as though all the world were being sucked into a void, and I sat at the torn, raw edge of it, the precipice of something impossible yet theoretical, like the square root of a negative integer. My breath whooshed out of me, swallowed by the gaping maw of the black hole.

As I stared into the yawning void, it stared back at me.

With eyes.

They were Chessa's pale-blue eyes, yet they were impossibly large and inhuman. As I gazed in horror and reverence upon her face, it brought to mind an octopus, then a dragon, and then a head with no body, and at the same time, a body with no head. Impossible wings sprung from its back, a sharp beak from where it might have had a mouth. This monstrosity, this deity, clung to the seams of the world, at the edge of the void, with long tentacles that hissed like snakes and flashed teeth like razor blades, the silver metal glinting despite the absence of light or goodness or anything else.

My shoulder stung. Words resonated somewhere within my frozen body: *Spirits of the Deep.*

I whipped my head to the right, a reflex reaction to the pain of my flesh becoming molten lava and then stone.

As I turned, my eyes would not obey, and stayed fixed upon the writhing, soul-destroying vision before me, but then the pain intensified. The monster in the void crawled inside me, through my optic nerves, and into my mind, where it gnawed on my last shreds of hope and humanity.

I heard someone's voice, far away. "Get her some water."

Another voice, "What did you do?"

"You were the one poking her!"

A baby was wailing.

I could see nothing now. I was, mercifully, blind. My mind turned in on itself, folded, and went black.

* * *

When I became conscious again, my head was throbbing.

Three blondes sat across the living room from me, watching nervously. In tableau, they looked exactly like Mizaru, Kikazaru, and Iwazaru, the Three Monkeys.

Chloe, as the monkey who sees no evil, covered her eyes with her hands. Charlize had her hands over her ears. And Chessa, whom my brain told me not to look at but I did anyway, covered her mouth. *Her mouth.* Her terrible abyss mouth with the razors for teeth and the nothingness...

The baby wasn't there, and by the change in the angle of the light coming in the window—not to mention the clock on the river-stone fireplace mantel—hours had passed since my arrival at the party.

Charlize dropped her hands first. "Oh, good. There you are. We were so worried that we'd already broken our new toy." She elbowed her sisters.

Chloe gazed at me with pouting lips. "Was it Charlize poking you? I told her not to play so rough. Unfortunately, moderation is not my sister's strong suit."

Chessa folded her hands on her lap gracefully. "I'm afraid it was me. My glamour powers haven't returned to normal yet. The coma weakened my ability to hide myself, and Zara has the perception of a witch." She looked down at the wood floor between us and whispered, "I could have killed Zara."

Charlize said, "But you didn't. Don't sweat it. Zara's a tough witch."

Chessa shook her head. "I could have driven her insane."

There was a long, silent pause.

Finally, I shrugged and said lightly, "It's not like anyone would have noticed."

CHAPTER 33

ON TUESDAY, TWO days after the baby shower, I was surprised to see Chet at the grocery store. He stood in front of a display of cantaloupes, looking overwhelmed.

I'd been avoiding him lately, and not just because his fiancée could turn my brain inside out in a flash if she wanted to.

The truth was, he'd been so nice to me ever since we'd gotten Chessa back, and it made me uncomfortable. He was nice in the manner of a stranger at an airport, as though we didn't know each other. But I knew him. Between the monsters we'd battled over the past few months, and the memories I'd held onto from Chessa's spiritual residue, I knew him deeply and completely. And I'd seen him tear apart Dr. Bhamidipati. Even though it had been self-defense, I'd seen him kill a man.

How could we have any sort of normal neighborly over-the-fence small talk now? What could we possibly talk about with any degree of sincerity? How could I look into his eyes and not see the wolf in him, remember the blood dripping from his fangs?

Lately, I'd been leaving my house by the back door and slipping down the side street rather than walk by the front of his house. I'd even been shopping at the grocery store that was two stores away from our neighborhood. The store was inconvenient and had a sub-par produce selection. Chet Moore should not have been there. But there he was, frozen with indecision by the pyramid of cantaloupes. Was he in that store to purposefully avoid me? The nerve.

I might have turned around and left before he noticed me, but he was standing by the cantaloupes. I happened to know the specific spell for selecting a perfectly ripe melon. It was as though I'd been preparing for weeks just for this moment. Was this really a coincidence? My aunt had a psychic sense, and she'd been the one to assign me the cantaloupe spell. If magic had a mind of its own, it certainly had a sense of humor as well.

I approached Chet from the rear. "Not that one," I said.

Chet fumbled the melon and dropped it. I steadied my instinct to use magic to grab the fruit before it hit the ground. You'd think it would be easy to prevent yourself from performing levitation magic in public, but it's not. That same instinct you have to lunge for something as it falls is still there, in magical form.

The cantaloupe struck the store's tile floor and split open, spilling orange guts.

Guts.

I recalled the wreckage inside the underground coma ward. Dr. Bhamidipati's entrails, spraying the concrete-walled room as a snarling wolf shook the giant bird's body in its jaws. Guts everywhere.

"What a shame," Chet said, looking down at the smashed melon. "That was a nice ripe one." He grabbed a plastic bag from the nearby roll and scooped the remains. "I don't know if this store has a you-break-you-buy policy, but I'll bring this up to the checkout."

"Because you're one of the good guys," I said.

He didn't reply. What could he say? I'd seen him turn into a snarling wolf and rip another creature limb from limb. Had it truly been self-defense? The doctor had been attacking me at the time, so Chet's actions were deemed, by the DWM, necessary force. But there wasn't going to be a trial. The DWM took care of its own business, buried its own bodies.

Chet tucked the busted melon into his cart, and turned back toward the display. "You look well," he said without looking directly at me.

"I wasn't hurt physically during the... accident." I rubbed my temples where the fake soul-transfer crown had dug into my flesh. All that remained was a memory, as my head wound had healed up within hours. "How's Rob?" The poor guy had taken a stray bullet to the shoulder.

"Back to normal." Chet's mouth twitched into the smallest of smiles. "Normal for Rob, that is. He complains a lot."

"And Knox?"

"Like a rock. I'll send them both your regards."

"Maybe I'll drop by your office sometime. I'd like to try that famous cherry cheesecake you have in your cafeteria."

Chet's smile disappeared. "Zara, you can't—"

"I know." I glanced around the produce section. The selection wasn't half as nice as the one at the store in our neighborhood.

Two swinging doors banged as a man in a dark-green apron emerged from the back with a rolling cart of bananas. One of the wheels squeaked.

The man gave us a curious look and asked, "You folks finding everything okay?"

I answered, "Yes. Fine. Just bumped into a friend."

Chet gave the man a friendly wave, and then said to me, louder than we'd been talking before, "I've been keeping busy."

"With work?"

"Furniture shopping," he said. "I had to buy Chessa a new dresser to replace... the other one."

I nodded. "The mirrored dresser that you smashed with your fist, during your temper tantrum."

Chet winced. "Oh, and I've got that manual you wanted. It's at my house. The, uh, one you asked for."

"You mean the one I negotiated for and earned, fair and square." We were talking about the DWM's operations manual, which promised a wealth of information about magic. Even if it wasn't a treasure trove, there had to be some juicy tidbits in there.

Chet nodded and watched the produce manager, who was pretending not to overhear us while he unloaded bananas. Right about now would have been the perfect time for me to use my sound-bubble spell to give us some privacy, but I didn't want privacy. Not like this.

I reached across Chet and grabbed a cantaloupe. "Did you know there are other ways to choose the perfect cantaloupe, besides smashing them open on the grocery store's floor? You can smell this little indented spot."

The produce manager cleared his throat and rolled his cart away. Now two, or three, or perhaps all four wheels squeaked without the weight of the bananas.

Chet leaned over the cantaloupe I held. "What am I smelling for?"

"Sweetness." I glanced around to make sure nobody was within hearing range. "But since we both just *happen to be* at the same grocery store that's an inconvenient distance from where we live, I might as well pick the perfect cantaloupe for you." I cast my cantaloupe-ripeness-detecting spell with minimal hand motions. The perfect melon lit up magically, glowing brightly for my eyes only. I plucked it from the display and handed it to Chet. "This one. Eat it within five hours for optimal taste and texture."

He gave me a suspicious look. "Did you do something to it?"

"No," I said vehemently, though I couldn't be certain if the spell *detected* ripeness or *facilitated* ripeness. I was still learning the language of magic, and some of the syntax was tricky. For every rule, there were dozens of exceptions. In the movies, they often use rhyming verse or Latin for spells. I *wished* magic were as easy as Latin.

He cupped the chosen cantaloupe gently with both hands. "What are you doing for dinner tonight?"

"This." I nodded at my shopping cart, which was empty except for a bag of multicolored marshmallows, a jar of peanut butter, and a bunch of celery.

"Let me guess," Chet said. "Ants on a log with pastel ants?"

"We call them elephants," I said. "And we pick out the pink marshmallows only, so it's pink elephants on a log."

"That sounds..." He grimaced. "Why don't you come over to my house for dinner? You can supply the, uh, dessert."

"That would be fun," I said.

"Chessa would love to see you again."

I snapped my fingers. "Oh. I just remembered. I have a big stack of homework. If I don't memorize a bunch of stuff, my aunt will reverse the function of my microwave and make it freeze food instead of heating it up. And I'm not just making that up as an imaginary punishment. She has actually threatened to do that specific thing."

"I understand," Chet said.

Did he? Did he understand that when I looked at him, I still felt a combination of Chessa's residual love and longing for him, mixed with my own natural crush on my handsome and mysterious neighbor? Did he know my dreams had only gotten more vivid since Chessa's return, and that when I woke each morning, in that nearly lucid state, I could smell him on me, feel the heat of his skin, taste his kiss on my lips?

Did he know that earlier that day at the library, I'd taken a casual look at the real estate listings and calculated the costs of selling my house and moving to a different street, just so I wouldn't be living next to him, continuously aware of his presence, his comings and goings whenever I heard his vehicle on the street?

He looked me in the eyes and repeated it. "I understand."

And then, I saw something inside him. The way I was able to see the snakes on Chloe and Charlize. I saw the tenderness he felt toward me, the daydream he was having right then and there, of reaching out and grabbing a handful of my red hair, pulling me close to him, and kissing me passionately as we bumped into the fruit display and cantaloupes rained down around us.

Then he blinked, and it was gone. "I should be going," he said, taking a step back. "Before we accidentally smash up all these melons."

"Yes," I said. "Have a nice dinner tonight with your family." I swallowed down the lump in my throat. "Send Chessa my regards."

Chet made a direct line for the cashiers without glancing back at me.

I took my time lingering over the assortment of cheese and dips to avoid bumping into him a second time in the parking lot. If he had his vehicle with him, he was likely to offer me a ride home, extending the awkwardness to excruciating levels.

The downside to my plan was that I found a dozen types of cheese that begged to come home with me, some of them on the pricey side. I was deliberating over the spicy goat cheese versus the mild flavor when my phone started ringing. I answered it without checking the call display, because I had a feeling it was my daughter, wondering where her dinner was.

"You caught me fondling various types of cheese," I said into the phone.

Instead of my daughter's sweet-yet-hungry voice, it was a male voice who answered with a mirthful chuckle. "That's pretty much what I expected you to say."

I knew who it was instantly. I squeezed the soft cheese in my hand so hard, it squished free of its plastic wrap. I tossed the mangled cheese into my basket and looked around me wildly. I didn't see him, but that didn't mean he wasn't there.

"Zara, are you still there? Don't hang up."

I clutched the phone tightly to my ear and demanded, "How did you get this number?"

"Now, now. Is that any way to greet a beloved family member?"

To be continued...
in Wisteria Witches book 4
Watchful Wisteria

For a full list of books in this
series, and other titles by
Angela Pepper, visit

www.angelapepper.com

Thank you for reading!
Angela

Made in the USA
Monee, IL
13 April 2021